Under The Maidenhair

Kit! Hope you enjoy this book!

Billie Milholland

Billie (Bug)

POISE AND PEN PUBLISHING

EDMONTON, ALBERTA

Billie Milholland/BHATOG Press

Publisher's Note: This is a work of fiction. Names, characters, places, and incidents are a product of the author's imagination. Locales and public names are sometimes used for atmospheric purposes. Any resemblance to actual people, living or dead, or to businesses, companies, events, institutions, or locales is completely coincidental.

Book Layout based on one by © 2014 BookDesignTemplates.com

Under the Maidenhair/ Billie Milholland. -- 1st ed.
ISBN 978-1-988233-56-7 (Physical)
ISBN 978-1-988233-57-4 (Electronia)

Under The Maidenhair

Most of the men in my family died in the wars before I was born, so I know a lot of dead people. When I sit beside the tall stones in Nana's garden, I talk to the Dead Uncles. A stone for each of her sons, except papa. When I sit up in the attic, in his eagle's nest, I talk to Granddad Smythe. He died because of the first Great War. The Dead Uncles died because of the last one - papa's war. In my family, except for Nana, I can't count on the living to help me puzzle out the truth about things. Nana says it's important to discover the truth, but it's not easy.

When I complained about it, she said, "Nothing worth doing is easy, Chickadee."

That's Nana for you. She doesn't hold with taking the easy way.

I tell Granddad what I hear when I sit under the maidenhair fern table in Nana's sun porch. Under that table, behind the long, crocheted table cloth (mostly pineapple stitch), I sit on a sofa cushion, and I listen to the goings-on.

April 23, 1953

Dear Diary,

The Move got everybody into a temper. Especially Mother. She pitched a conniption and took the train to Aunt Edie's in Red Deer when papa told her he was ready to move the family to the new house on the farm. Mother wants to stay in town. She won't believe papa changed his mind about becoming the mayor.

Nana says being far away at the war for so long, and ending up living while his brothers died, changed papa.

Before the war, papa was keen to be mayor. Mother says if we stay in town he'll come to his senses and be keen again. She says papa has had plenty of time to get over the stupid war and she's going to make sure he gets to be mayor when the elections happen next spring.

Papa won't live at the farm without Mother, so everything is in a muddle. Papa sold our house in town, and our furniture is moved to the farm, so that's why we've come to live at Nana's, in her big house on the hill.

After two weeks, Mother's finally returned from Aunt Edie's. She came out of her room to eat breakfast with us today and spoke civil to Nana. I don't know when she'll speak civil to papa. She's not speaking to him at all.

Papa is not a talker. Mother says he's a delicate man who got the shell-shock because he wasn't up to the rigours of war. Loud noises startle him. When an airplane flies over town he goes to his room. Nana says there's nothing delicate about papa. She says the shell shock can come upon the strongest and bravest of men.

April 23, 1953 after breakfast

Dear Diary,

Papa and Nana are coming into the sun porch to take tea and I'm ready, under the fern table, to copy their conversation. Please excuse me if it's messy writing. I'm going to have to write fast.

Papa carried in the teapot. Nana carried the teacups, her favourite eight-sided cup and the tall tea cup that was Granddad Smythe's. Papa says he doesn't have a favourite. During most of the war he drank his tea from dinted tin cups, so for him, any cup is a good cup now.

"Don't be hard on yourself, George, I don't mind having all of you here until everything is sorted out."

Papa put both elbows on Nana's table and made a steeple with his hands. "What if things don't sort out? I thought if I moved everybody to the farm, into the new house where there's peace and quiet… I thought if I made sure we couldn't move back… Oh, I don't know. If she would just give it a try. I want her to be happy, Marge. I do."

"I know you do. I'd like her to be happy, too, George, but the truth is, at the end of the day she's in charge of her own happiness, not you or I or anyone else."

"So you keep telling me. I want to believe you, but life has been so disappointing for her."

"Disappointing for her? George. Listen to yourself. All of us endured that war. Every one of us still deals with the aftermath of it. We each find our way. Lillian has to find hers."

Oh, Dear Diary, after that, there was a long silence. Nana drinking her tea, papa drinking his. I guess they were puzzling about Mother. I puzzle about Mother too. I know she's not happy. I know some of her unhappy is because of me and I don't like it one bit. Mostly I try not to think about it because that thinking is hard work. It makes me sleepy. It was cozy under the fern table; I dozed off. When I woke up, they were gone.

Copying conversation is the training I need to become a writer like Pearl S. Buck. When I'm grown, I'm going to live in a foreign country and write books like *Peony* and *The Good Earth*. I going to be a lady writer, but I need a lot more practice to get ready for it.

April 28, 1953

I'm glad I have you to talk to, Dearest Diary, my only constant friend. I do have Beanie. He lives next door. He's as good a friend as any, but he's not constant. I don't mind telling you, he's unpredictable. Sometimes I like that because with Beanie there's always an adventure, but he's not a good listener and I have a lot to say.

Mary's my friend, but she doesn't go to school anymore, so I don't see her every day. And she's timid. I have to be careful what I say to her.

My Dead Granddad is a good listener. The room at the top of the house where I sleep used to be his. He called it his eagle's nest.

Once up in his eagle's nest, he didn't come back down until he died. Nana said Granddad hated being an invalid from the mustard gas he got in the first Great War. He said if he had to be stuck somewhere, he wanted it to be high above everything, where he could see the sunset and the stars come out. Where he could look down on the town and keep track of goings-on.

Granddad died before I was born, but his invisible part is still here. He's glad for the company when I tell him about what I see and hear. I'm glad too, because the living people in my life get tired of my chatter.

Nana says we would have been great chums, Granddad and I. She's right. He rocks in his chair, nodding his head when I tell him what I see through his spyglass. He called it his long eye, good for keeping track of things in town.

Usually, at night I read, but on Monday I was stomach sick. Jeannie tattled that she heard me grunting and groaning in the bathroom. My sisters sleep below me on the second floor, in bedrooms that belonged to the Dead Uncles. Jeannie's room used to belong to Uncle Pete. It's closest to the bathroom, that's why she heard me. I should have gone all the way up to my own bathroom, but I didn't think I could make it in time.

In Uncle Pete's room, Jeannie has new chenille curtains, a chenille bedspread, and a throw rug that covers up where Uncle Pete carved words into the linoleum. He started carving into his floor when he got a Cooey .22, single shot, Model 75 rifle for his birthday the year he turned eleven. After that, he carved a list of his presents from birthdays and Christmas, every year until he turned sixteen. Nana said he had a part-time job by then and probably got out of the habit of keeping track of presents. Jeannie wants Nana to take up the old linoleum and put in new. Nana won't do it because she takes comfort from having Uncle Joe's carvings on that floor.

Laura has Uncle Wilton's room and his roll top desk for homework. Uncle Wilton didn't carve anything into his room, but he did make pencil marks on his door jam. Every year on their birthdays, he drew a line to show how much each of his brothers had grown: Uncle Joe, Uncle Pete, and papa. He didn't make a line for his own height. Nana says it's because he was the oldest and already tall at sixteen when he started measuring his brothers. Laura likes them there. She taped a valentine heart on the last of papa's marks.

When we lived in our own house, Mother sent me to Nana's when I got sick. Now Mother has no place to send me. She called Grandma Walters, but Grandma Walters doesn't tolerate the sick. I'm glad. Her house is stuffy because all her windows are nailed shut. It's bad for sleeping, and she's busy after washing everything. My hair, my face, my clothes. It doesn't matter if they're fresh and clean when I get there. She makes me sleep on a rubber sheet in case I wet at night. I never wet at night. I tell you, if I was a person who wet, I'd stay awake all night to stop it. Soiling anything at Grandma Walters' is serious business.

Mother made a ruckus about me being sick, complaining so much that Nana bundled me off to her own rooms next to the sun porch.

That Jeannie. I told her not to tell Mother about my stomach cramps. They weren't serious. I ate too many canned saskatoon berries, and I was a little loose. That's all.

The problem for Mother is germs. She hates that germs are invisible and forever lurking. Of all the germs in the world, the Infantile Paralysis germs worry Mother most. You can't scrub the Polio germs away with bleach because those germs hide deep down inside weak people. They lurk, waiting to leap out to ruin perfect people like Mother.

She can't help being scared. She doesn't want to lose her youth and beauty like her friend Katherine. Mother says, Katherine started with stomach pains and then ended up scrawny and pathetic in an iron lung.

Mother thinks I'm a weak invalid. She thinks I'm somebody who could harbour a polio germ. She's wrong. I'm only unhealthy in my foot. That's nothing. Mother doesn't believe it, and now, because I've been stomach sick twice this month I have to stay away from school for the rest of the school year. Mother doesn't want to be blamed for allowing her child to spread germs. I begged Nana not to protest for me. It's not good to rile Mother.

I don't mind staying home. I'm tired of all eyes in the class-room on me every time I clump up to the blackboard. I didn't care so much when I was younger, but being a Gimp wears a person down over time. There aren't many real school days left anyway; just May. June doesn't count. It's full of track and field, baseball and sports days.

I do schoolwork with Nana every morning. She put a new map of the world on her wall to help with my social studies. There are more countries in Europe now than there were before the last Great War and I know the names of all of them. I'm ahead of everyone in my grade, so I have time to look down on the town with the spyglass. I have time to write to you, Dear Diary.

Because Mother is stuck in the same house with me when I'm sick, she ordered medicine from the doctor, but Nana won't let me take it. Nana uses doctor medicine as a last resort. Mother uses doctor medicine as the *only* resort.

Mother ordered the medicine from young Dr. Masters. She insisted he deliver it himself. She wanted him to see how uncivilized Nana is, pouring boiled weed juice down my throat like I'm a funnel. Mother thinks people tolerate Nana because they don't know how strange she is. She always hopes for a way to show Nana up, but so far she hasn't had much luck.

Old Doc Rawson is young Dr. Masters' boss. He's happy to drink Nana's weed juice, so Mother gets no help there.

When Dr. Masters came up the hill with the medicine, Nana invited him into the sun porch for tea. She told him funny stories about my greediness for fruit. I don't mind Nana telling stories about me. She makes them nicely funny. She never calls me a brat.

Dr. Masters is handsome. He has a deep voice. I could listen to him for days. He looks like Gregory Peck, only not as serious.

"So, you make your own tinctures, Mrs. Smythe. Interesting. Time-consuming I would imagine."

"Not at all. Fresh plant matter packed into a jar. Covered with a good strong brandy and strained after several weeks. Fast, efficient, and it guarantees a high quality."

Nana passed him the plate of ginger cookies. Before he went home, he ate a good half dozen.

"This is extraordinarily good tea, Mrs. Smythe. I haven't met its equal, even in England."

"England at war isn't the best time to judge their tea."

It was warm under the maidenhair fern table and I must have dozed off. Again. That's a bad habit. Mother yelling woke me up. She stood in the doorway with only her toes over the sill.

"Marjorie, I won't have you turning people against me."

Nana poured another cup of tea. "Lillian. You sent for him. Would you have me rude?"

"You *were* rude. You refused the medicine he brought. You didn't treat him like a doctor."

"A doctor?"

"Sitting him down to tea like he's the next door neighbour. You made me out the perfect fool."

"How did I do that?"

"Like you always do." Mother made a high voice, trying to copy Nana. "Lillian misunderstood the symptoms. Lillian wasn't thinking straight." Mother flipped her hair with the tips of her elegant fingers. Everything about Mother is elegant. "Lillian doesn't ever think straight, does she?"

Nana sipped her tea, then set the cup down carefully in the saucer. "I don't remember a conversation like that."

"I know what you think. I know what you say to people. I know how you twist things." Mother swung around, her skirts swirling. She slammed the door hard.

Mother and Nana are magnificent when they row. Nana wins because she's older and has had practice thinking things through.

In Pearl S. Buck stories, young women start off willful and spiteful. They end up wise and kind because they learn how to think things through. Compared to Nana, Mother's a young woman. She needs more practice.

I stayed in Nana's room all day, sipping strawberry leaf tea and nibbling cheese. When Mother looked in after supper, I was playing crokinole with Nana. Mother sent me upstairs to my own room before Nana spoiled me beyond tolerance. Mother doesn't usually notice where I am or what I'm doing, but she worries about how much Nana spoils me when I'm sick.

April 29, 1953

Dear Diary,

I have a new project. Recording daily life for Historians of the Future. Nana says historians rely heavily on private diaries for information. There are not many private diaries to be had, so historians never have enough everyday details to make them happy. That's what I'm good at. Details. I'm a person perfectly suited to recording daily life. After Mother chased me out of Nana's room on Monday, I climbed up to my new bedroom with a copy of an old Saturday Evening Post Nana gave me. It has interesting information about daily life in 1942. On the cover it says – An Illustrated Weekly founded AD 1728 by Benj. Franklin. Five cents a copy, seven cents in Canada. I'll copy down the most interesting bits about daily life into this scribbler.

The first thing I see in this magazine is an advertisement for *Listerine* gargle to reduce germs. Can you picture it, Historians? Families over all the land, gargling with *Listerine* in 1942, spitting into basins and sinks and off the end of the porch? We have *Listerine* in 1953, but Nana won't use it. She says it's wasteful to spend money on a foul tasting fluid when everything needed to fight germs is in the pantry. Nana fights germs with salt, vinegar, baking soda, and lye.

Mother disagrees. She says *Listerine* has a tolerable taste, and people must use it to kill mouth germs. Nana and I gargle with salt water. That kills enough germs to suit us.

Oh Dear Diary, I'm still bothered by something I haven't told anybody. I wasn't going to write it in here, but it's weighing heavy on me, so I have to put it somewhere. I can't think straight about daily life until I do.

I have a secret. I didn't mean to get it and I don't know what to do with it. Nana believes in finding the truth about things, but she can't abide secrets, so I'll have to tell her sooner or later. It won't be easy to tell her what I saw. I tried to tell the Dead Uncles, but my mouth wouldn't spit the words out.

It's not the kind of thing you can tell a granddad either, no matter how dead he is. I could tell Beanie, but he's such a tattle-tale, he can never keep a secret. I tell you straight, Dear Diary – I didn't mean to see it. It just happened.

On Monday, it was still early when I got sleepy, so I dragged the feather quilt from the closet and made a nest in Granddad's big chair by the window. When I woke up it was the darkest night. Street lights were on all over town, winking and begging me for attention.

Looking down on the town with the spyglass at night is different than doing it during the day. You know what you'll see in the day, because people do what you expect, and you can't see into windows. Looking into windows is snooping. Nana's not in favour of snooping, but Granddad spied on the town when he was alive and I don't think Nana called it snooping. I don't know how he could have stayed away from windows.

At first, looking through the spyglass at night was spooky. Right off you can't see anything but black. If you move the glass along slowly, the black crawls up the tube into your eye like it will suck it dry. Just as you want to yank the spyglass away from your face, to save your eye from becoming a raisin, you get close to a light. The black turns to burnt sugar, then to taffy. Suddenly it's somebody's window.

I saw Mr. Chamberlain in the drug store, up on a stool, putting bottles on a high shelf. That's where he hides his whiskey, behind a big jug of gentian violet. I saw him drink whiskey from the bottle. No glass.

Nana's hired girl, Mrs. O'Kane, says he hides whiskey everywhere. I saw it for myself. Two bottles. One full and one nearly empty.

I saw Mrs. Hillman upstairs sewing long curtains. Mint green. For her daughter Susan's room, I guess. She's made new curtains for Susan's room every year since Susan was in grade one. Susan died when she was in grade four. From the polio. That's three years ago, but Mrs. Hillman doesn't stop making curtains. It's pathetic, Mother says, to go on like that after a child dies. I think it's nice. I'd like somebody to remember me if I died.

After Mrs. Hillman's window, the glass wandered over to Fat Freddy's house, because it's next door. Fat Freddy is the Mayor of Deep Creek. Mother says he's an embarrassment and now I agree with her, but I can't tell anybody why.

I saw Freddy's wife, framed like a picture in the kitchen window, washing dishes in the sink. I saw the hired girl behind her, hair tied up in a scarf, punching bread in a blue bread-basin on the table.

There was a light on in Freddy's garage making it the next stop for the spyglass. I know it's wicked to see a man like that, but my first looking was an accident. He didn't take all his clothes off. Just his pants and his underpants. I didn't have time to feel wicked when I saw it. I was mostly surprised. I didn't think to look away. You can understand why I couldn't tell Granddad.

I've seen Freddy do it twice, standing in the same place, throwing his pants over the hood of his station wagon the same way, like a man beating a fire with a gunny sack. Grabbing his poor little willie. Yanking for all he's worth. What a thing to do! I knew it hurt by the way he scrunched his eyes shut.

I'm not supposed to call him Fat Freddy. I'm supposed to call him Mr. Bugle because he's the mayor. Everybody I know, except Nana, and maybe papa, calls him Fat Freddy. I don't know if you could say he's really fat, but he's at least chubby, and soft, and pasty white like a poached egg.

I'm not sure if what Freddy does is a part of daily life that will be interesting to you people in the future. I suppose it might be. By the time you historians up there in the future read this, we'll all be dead and gone in Deep Creek. Nobody will be left to care about our secrets.

Finally, the last day of April, 1953

Dear Diary,

I have a problem with recording daily life. I want to start from when I was a baby, but I don't know much about the beginning of my life. Nobody tells baby stories about me. I can't find any baby pictures of me in Mother's photo album. Pictures of me start in Nana's photo album from when I was six, when papa came home from the war.

I asked Nana about daily life when I was a baby. She looked out her window into the garden where the four, river rocks stand up like soldiers by the fence. She made a sad smile, "It was war, Chicka-dee. Life was difficult."

Usually, Nana speaks plain and true when I ask questions, but she doesn't like talking about the war. I mean the last Great War. Pa-pa's war. Nana doesn't mind talking about the first Great War, even though Granddad Smythe died because he breathed in the mustard while he was in it, while he was caring for all the horses in France. Maybe she doesn't mind about that war because it's so far back in the past.

Uncle Pete, Uncle Joe and Uncle Wilton died in the last Great War. That's what the river rocks are for. One for each of Nana's dead men.

Granddad's rock is the biggest. When he could still walk around, he found it on the river flats and hired the dray wagon to bring it up to Nana's garden. She says it took four men to lift it down. It's a handsome rock. Wide as a kitchen table at the bottom, then slanted back up as high as my waist. That's what started the row of rocks. Granddad didn't mean to be dead when he put it there.

Uncle Wilton brought his rock to the garden before he disappeared into the army only to end up dead in Hong Kong. It's petrified wood. He didn't mean to be dead either. He put it there to remind Nana that wherever he was, he would be thinking of home.

Nobody imagined Uncle Wilton would become a soldier. He was at the university teaching philosophy, the most useless of all subjects. That's what Mother says. One day, out of the blue, he joined up. Then he was gone. Nobody knew he'd sailed over the ocean to Hong Kong. Nobody knew Uncle Wilton was killed in a hospital on Christmas day until long after Christmas was over.

That was my first Christmas. I searched in Mother's photo album for pictures of my first Christmas. I found pictures of Laura's and Jeannie's first Christmases, but none of mine. I know I was only seven months old when Uncle Wilton died, so there's nothing for me to remember, but you'd think somebody would have wanted to take a Christmas picture of me.

I guess everybody wanted to forget that Christmas. There was so much declaring war that year. The Japanese dropped bombs on Pearl Harbour. The United States and Britain declared war on Japan. Germany declared war on the United States. It was a bad year.

Uncle Pete got killed on the Atlantic Ocean before my first birthday. I was too little to feel sad. Nana and Crazy Marion found the tall, thin rock for Uncle Pete. Just like him, they said. Tall, hard and noble.

Papa found Uncle Joe's rock. Everybody says Uncle Joe was the most handsome of all Nana's boys, so you'll be surprised to discover how plain his rock is. A giant lump of gray with a deep punched in place at the top. In the summer, Nana fills the punched in place with water for the birds. The lovely part of Uncle Joe's rock is the front where papa used a hammer to crack a chip out of it. When water dribbles down over it, shiny flecks glitter in the sun.

May 1, 1953

Dear Diary,

After breakfast, when I asked Mother to tell me about when I was a baby, she lit another cigarette. She forgot she had one burning up in the ashtray. She flipped her new pageboy hairdo with her long fingers and looked up at the smoke she'd blown straight over her head. She clicked her fingernails on the top of her salmon pink, chrome dinette table, and went back to flipping pages in her movie magazine.

"A person doesn't want to remember things like that, little girl. It was war, more war, and everything standing still. You were a baby like any other. What's to remember?"

She doesn't call me Tally anymore, or even Natalie, just 'little girl' like I'm a stranger come in from the street.

Mother fought hard to get her Arborite dinette table moved into Nana's house. She sits at it every chance she gets. It has tube steel legs with plastic tipped feet. Nana says it's the silliest piece of furniture she's ever seen. Nana allowed it in the breakfast room because she got tired of arguing over nothing. Mother sits there every morning after breakfast, smoking her long cigarettes, and reading her movie magazines. She and Jeannie paint their fingernails there. I'm not allowed to paint my nails. I have to be at least fifteen before I can join in. Laura's seventeen, but she's not interested in nail polish or permanent waves or plucking eyebrows. Studying is what she likes.

Asking about my early life reminded Mother about when my foot got ruined. I'm sorry I brought it up. The accident that wrecked my foot happened during the worst wartime. It weighs heavy on her. I wish Mother could remember my baby life, but she can't. I brought her gin from the china cabinet to put in orange juice. It's her medicine. She feels better about things when she takes it.

I carried all the photo albums up here this morning. It took two trips. Nobody saw me do it, and I can tell you plain, Dear Diary, I didn't tell anybody either. I want to examine all the pictures without interruption.

After my foot got ruined, I lived with Nana until I was nearly five, because Mother was in and out of the hospital with her nervous breakdowns. When papa visited, he used up his time in Edmonton walking with her in the hospital gardens. He didn't come to visit us.

Nana has a few photos of me on her wall from that time. Sitting in a highchair, eating pumpkin pie with my hands; standing in her garden picking peas into a little pail; playing in the sand at Whitney Lake. None of those pictures are in Mother's photo albums.

Mother says my oldest sister, Jeannie, was a perfect baby. She never cried. She looked like an angel child from the first day she was born. I found pages and pages of photographs in Mother's album of baby Jeannie. In every picture, she's a wrapped up bundle with a crocheted bonnet sticking out. Jeannie brags that she had a different crocheted bonnet for every day of the week.

The baby bundles are in the middle of Mother's sateen bedspread. Mother is in every picture, like a movie star with her fingers making a tent for her chin to rest on. I think she had to kneel on the floor beside the bed to fit into the picture that way. Her movie star hair is in beautiful waves, her eyebrows plucked into perfect arches. She looks straight into the camera with movie star lips open in not quite a smile.

Mother said she had an easy birth with Laura, but she had a nervous breakdown anyway because Laura was a cranky baby, not an angel like Jeannie. A hired girl kept Laura at Grandma Walters' through the first year of her babyness. Jeannie is the only baby Mother kept to herself for the first baby year.

I found photographs showing Laura in a baby carriage with papa pushing her on a sidewalk downtown. It's beside a photo of papa grinning, standing beside a pile of leaves, his curling sweater buttoned up, and his fingers touching the brim of his tweed hat.

Before the war, papa practically lived at the curling rink, Nana says. Now, he won't go there. He says he got out of the habit of curling while he was at the war. Nana says the sound of curling rocks crashing against each other is more than he can endure.

In another photograph, papa kneels beside the carriage looking in at Laura's round, sleeping face. Her sweet little hand is against her cheek and her curly hair is like poplar fluff around her head. There's not one photograph of papa with me when I was a baby because, of course, he was away at the war then. I try not to mind about it. But sometimes I do mind.

Still May 1, 1953

I got interrupted by lunch, Dear Diary. I had to go downstairs because my sisters are at school, papa's at the farm, and Mother's at Grandma Walter's. It would have been rude to let Nana eat alone. I asked Nana about Laura's curly hair and mine. Mother doesn't have it. Neither does Jeannie. Nana laughed. She said, unruly hair comes from her side of the family and she doesn't regret it one bit. Mother doesn't like it. Curly hair misbehaves.

Mother keeps my curly hair trapped in braids to tame it. Mother and Jeannie have obedient hair that allows them to have any style that's fashionable.

Grandma Walters says my hair is stubborn, just like me. She told me I was stubborn right from the start. I refused to be born on time, and I didn't come out easy. I wish she wouldn't bring it up all the time. Last weekend, when she came to have tea with Nana, she had to complain about me again.

"My poor Lillian had enough worries with the war starting, and everything uncertain. She didn't need another baby."

Grandma Walters sniffed like she was going to cry. Instead of crying, she touched her fingers to the side of her face and tilted her head a little, and looked way up at Nana's hanging spider plants.

"I would have helped more with that stubborn child, Marjorie, but you know I've never been that strong."

Through the crocheted pineapple pattern, I could see that Nana didn't feel sorry for Grandma Walters. When she poured another cup of tea, it splashed on Grandma Walters' dress. Nana rushed to the kitchen for a cloth, saying she was terribly sorry. Grandma Walters had to go home to change her dress. I held my hand over my mouth to keep from giggling. I think Nana splashed the tea on purpose. She's way too careful to do it accidental. But, I tell you straight, Dear Diary, I'm not going to ask her.

May 2, 1953

Dear Diary and Historians of the Future, you're going to get plenty of daily life information from me. My friend Mary came over today. After breakfast. She's Granny Barclay's hired girl. Granny Barclay isn't my granny. In fact, I don't think she's anybody's granny because her son is a priest, her youngest daughter is a nun, her oldest daughter is the friend of Mother's who got wrecked by polio, and her middle daughter is a spinster lady who lives in Edmonton with another spinster lady.

That's what happens to tomboys, Mother says. No men will have them. They become spinsters in cities and live together with other spinsters to save on rent.

Nana invites Granny Barclay and Mary over once a week when Nana's hired girl goes home for the weekend. Granny thinks Mary is needed for heavy cleaning. She isn't. Nana does it to give Mary a chance to read with me. Nana can't tolerate education being interrupted, especially the education of a girl as smart as Mary. Fooling Granny doesn't worry Nana, but Mary feels bad. Nana says Granny Barclay underpays and overworks her hired girls. Mary's only fourteen, so she's too young to stand up for herself.

Nana's annoyed with Mary's family. They could keep her in school if they wanted to. Uncle Metro (he's Mary's father, and he isn't my real uncle) wants Mary ready for getting married by the time she's sixteen. He says going to school doesn't help a girl get ready for marriage.

Nana told him that smart girls like Mary need an education before getting married. Baba (she's Mary's grandma) and Auntie Olga (Mary's mother) agree with Nana, but it isn't their way to interfere in men's business. I don't know why Mary's education is men's business. Education in our family isn't men's business; it's Nana's business.

Mary was nervous at first. Every time the stairs creaked, she bobbed up and down like a cork in the creek. I told her nobody comes up to the third floor except me and Mother doesn't notice what gets cleaned and what doesn't.

The other thing that worries Mary is the money. Nana says it's important to pay Mary. It has to be done in front of Granny Barclay, so she won't suspect that cleaning isn't getting done. The money's an investment in Mary's education. Mary's supposed to buy books with it. Nana puts the money in a cellophane envelope, so Granny Barclay can't see how much it is.

Mary says she'll save the money and someday give it back to Nana. I told her Nana will never take it, but Mary insists. Mary is stubborn that way.

We're reading Pearl S. Buck's *Peony*, Mary and I. Pearl S. Buck's books are about women in Old China. The public library has books by Mrs. Buck, but children aren't allowed to read them because Mrs. Buck is sympathetic to the ways of the heathen. Also because she writes about concubines. Mrs. Webb is strict about who can borrow from the adult section. It's lucky for us Nana buys her own books in Edmonton.

Peony is about a Chinese girl who's a servant to Jewish people in China in the olden days. I think she's a slave because she was bought when she was little, and can't ever leave. Mary likes the Chinese story, but she thinks it's a fairy story, not one bit real because she can't imagine people living strange like that. In Pearl S. Buck's books, the only things not real are the actual people's names and such. Nana says people did so live like that in Old China, before modern times. Mary didn't grow up reading National Geographic magazine like I did, so she doesn't know how many ways there are for people to live.

Mary looks at Nana's National Geographics with me, but she gets flustered about the naked people. I tell her it's not shameful for them to be naked. It's hot where they live. Hot in winter, too. It would be uncomfortable to wear clothes, maybe unhealthy. Also, it would be a big nuisance to get clothes because there are no stores close by and no Simpson's or Eaton's catalogs to order from.

I hid the spyglass when Mary came over. I want to show it to her, but not yet. If I did, the next minute I'd blurt about Fat Freddy. That would be hard on Mary.

We take turns reading out loud. I love the sound of Mary's voice. She has a careful way of reading. Her words have a beautiful, round, Ukrainian sound to them because she didn't start school until she was eight. She didn't know any English before that. Her voice embarrasses her, so she can't understand why I love it. My voice is ordinary. I wish I had an accent. Any accent.

Still the 2nd of May 1953

After lunch, Nana took Beanie & me to Crazy Marion's ranch to pick stinging nettle. It has to be picked when it's just come up and still tender.

Crazy Marion isn't really crazy. After her husband died and she took to wearing his clothes, people in town called her crazy to make fun of her. I guess, Historians, you might think I'm rude to call her crazy, except you need to know she thinks it's funny and is not one bit put out about it.

Beanie, of course, wouldn't wear the gloves Nana brought for us, so his hands and wrists got all stung. I saw he was trying not to cry. I wanted to tell Nana, but he got so riled.

"Don't you say a word, Natalie Smythe, or I'll never let you play in my submarine ever again."

That Beanie. He makes me so mad sometimes. I don't even care about his dumb submarine. It's just a rusted old car in a lean-to beside his Aunt's garage.

He's lucky the Kokum came to his rescue. She took him to the creek and made him put his hands and arms into the cold water up to his elbows. Then, with thread, she tied dock-weed leaves against the stings. By tea-time, he was back to himself.

The Kokum doesn't talk. She lost her voice long before I was born, when a house fire burnt up her husband and her children. She's lived with Crazy Marion ever since. It was Crazy Marion who saved her from the fire, and stopped her from jumping into the river from despair. The Kokum used up her voice from crying for weeks and weeks, and when she finally stopped crying, she never talked again.

She sings, but she never talks. It's a sad story, Historians. I don't want to tell it, but I guess since I brought it up I better. Nana says it's rude to get people's hopes up and then leave them dangling.

The Kokum is an Indian lady. When she was young like Mary she married white and because of that the government says she's not an Indian anymore. I don't understand how that can be. I guess the government can turn anybody into anything they like.

Fat Freddy was a boy when the Kokum's house burned down. Some people think he and his friends set the fire. When the Kokum lived in town, his crowd came around at night, all likkered up, throwing stones at the Kokum's windows, putting cow poop on the porch. That's why Marion moved the Kokum and her family to the house on her farm. She wanted to get them away from the meanness of Fat Freddy.

Marion's house was big, built for the large family her and her Sidney would have had if he hadn't died. People in town thought she was a lunatic to move into the little granary shack and give her good house to the Half-Breeds. That's what some people call Indians who mix with white – Half-Breeds. It's a bad thing to call someone. It's like saying Bohunk or Gimp. Nobody proved Fat Freddy burned down the Kokum's house with her family in it, but Nana and Crazy Marion believe it was him.

The Kokum's brothers and sisters and other relatives come and see her because she knows about wild medicine, but she's not an Indian anymore, so she can't live with her family.

The Kokum cooked up nettles with onions and mushrooms. We had it on her fry-bread at tea-time. Beanie's never had nettle before and even though I told him it was delicious, he didn't believe me. Crazy Marion noticed him looking at his plate like it was full of spiders.

"It's a marvel, isn't it my boy? A humble plant like that with so much power in it. I bet your father is eating it right now, to build up his strength. There's iron in nettle. Makes strong muscles."

Crazy Marion must have known that Beanie would do anything to be like his father, who is still stuck in a hospital in England getting better from all the wounds he got in the war.

Beanie ate every leaf and asked for more. After tea, while Nana and Crazy Marion sorted nettle leaves for drying, the Kokum drizzled *Lyle's Golden Syrup* over more fry-bread, and I tell you, I was so stuffed I couldn't eat supper after we got home. Nana uses *Roger's Golden Syrup* at her house, but Crazy Marion's family in England sends her tins of *Lyle's* every year.

May 2, 1953, long after supper

Dear Diary,

I took a break from writing tonight and went down to listen to the radio with Nana, but she's got a program on about the Korean War and how everybody hopes it will be over soon. I couldn't sit still. So, I filled a bowl with raisins and I'm back up here.

I'm lucky to have my recording to get to. I want to finish with this *Saturday Evening Post,* so I can read the rest of Nana's old magazines. She has a closet full of them.

I'm skipping pages. One thing I think you Historians will be interested in is, *Campbell's Black Bean Soup.* In case you don't have it in the future, it's soup in a can that you buy at the store. I didn't know the Campbell people put any soup but chicken noodle in a can. We had chicken noodle soup from a can twice a week at our house in town on George Simpson Road.

Nana doesn't allow canned soup in her kitchen. She teaches her hired girls, including Mrs. O'Kane, how to make real chicken noodle. When they do it, the good smell fills up the kitchen and leaks into the rest of the house.

On the first day of chicken soup making, two or three old hens go into the canning kettle. They get covered up with water from the well. We have water from the tap too, but Nana says you can't count on tap water to be wholesome. Even the chicken's feet go in. That's the part that makes Mother wild. But if she thought it through, she wouldn't worry. The feet are removed first and I take them next door for Beanie's dog, Stella.

When the feet are gone, in goes onions; then carrots, bottoms and tops; bay leaves; little, black pepper seeds; rusty red clove flowers; allspice berries; and crumbles of thyme and rosemary dried up from Nana's garden. Lovage too, and maybe dill seed. As soon as a good boil starts, Nana pushes the canning kettle to the back of the stove so it can settle into a simmer. That's when she throws in pickling salt.

For the rest of the afternoon, wherever I am, the cooking smell follows me, making me hungry. You don't get that from canned soup.

After supper, the chicken juice gets strained and put in the cold room till the next day when Nana scoops off the yellow fat for frying eggs and potato cakes. The last time Nana made chicken soup she put in garlic from the farm. Mother got in such a temper over the garlic, she had to take the train to Edmonton for one of her overnights. She thinks garlic is only fit for peasants.

After chicken juice making day comes noodle making day. Mrs. O'Kane, Nana's hired girl, is an expert noodle maker. She dumps a bowl of egg yolks into a washbasin of flour. In the flour is salt, and ground up thyme and rosemary. Nana adds thyme and rosemary to everything, even her evening tea.

Crushing the herbs is my job. I use Nana's stone bowl and stone bulb to grind them into dust. I'm good at it. I can make a smooth powder with no big flakes left over.

On noodle making day there are noodles drying over broomsticks, over the clotheshorse, and on tea towels on the breakfast room table. When the noodles are dry and stiff we break them up. I put them into the battery jars in the pantry.

Each noodle soup gets a different ingredient at the end for a surprise. The first part of the soup making is always the same. In goes chicken cut up into small squares; and the chicken juice; onions; carrots and potatoes, chopped; and celery, diced. Sometimes mushrooms are the surprise. Other times it's corn or string beans. The noodles go in last.

It doesn't matter what Nana puts in soup; Mother won't eat it. She says a person had to make soup the old-fashioned way during the war when there was rationing, and when everybody had to plant a Victory Garden. Now she eats chicken noodle soup at Aunt Edie's from a proper can, which is the fashionable way to do it. Mother is always fashionable. Aunt Edie's husband, Uncle Edwin, is from the United States. Aunt Edie gets fashionable ideas for Mother from his sister in Seattle.

This *Saturday Evening Post* advertisement about black beans must have appealed to Mother in 1942. I wonder if she served it to her bridge club when I was a baby. She still lived in her own house. When she wasn't in the hospital, she served whatever she wanted.

The advertisement says... *"the smartest dinner soup in America today!"*

Mother's fond of things that are smart. One odd thing about all the magazine ads, they always say America and never Canada.

"New! Campbell's Black Bean Soup - once this distinctive soup was found only in the smartest hotels and restaurants...a specialty that contributed much to their fame. Now, right at home, you can have Black Bean Soup."

I've never seen a black bean. Nana grows green beans in her garden. If she grew fashionable black beans, Mother might come into the garden with us.

There's an article in this magazine that Nana must have liked. It's called "Making Something From Nothing". Nana's a great believer in making over. I can tell you, Historians, during the war there was a lot of making over.

Mother says there's no reason to carry on with makeovers in this day and age. She looks down her nose at people who wear makeovers. Nana says anyone worth their salt does not look down on resourcefulness.

Nana and I are resourceful. Nana makes over for me, but she does such a fine job that Mother never suspects. Like the housecoat Nana made for me out of Granddad Smythe's green brocade lap robe. His English cousins sent it to him before he died. It was too fine to hide away in a trunk. My housecoat is superior to anything from a store.

The makeover article tells about ladies from the Christian Church in Jerome, Idaho (that's in the United States) who clothed and improved the homes of 1500 people in seven months. They made comforters and clothes from cloth they took from discarded automobile seat cushions. I think that's clever. In one year they reclaimed velvets, corduroys, mohair, gabardine, broadcloth, cotton, velour, whipcord, serge, muslin, and leather. They made useful things for poor people. That was an important thing to do while the war was happening.

There's more to record from 1942, but this recording is taking longer than I expected. It's time to move on to 1943. The Post cost ten cents in 1943, and no more mention is made of Canada on the cover. I wonder why. I was two in the spring of 1943. 1943 is when papa and Uncle Joe went to the war in Sicily.

All the advertisements in this Post talk about the war, of course, and that's good for me. My family doesn't like to talk about it, and I have questions.

The *General Motors Truck & Coach Company* says Americans ate bacon and eggs during the war, but people in Japan only ate boiled rice. In Germany all they ate was ersatz. Nana says ersatz means a bad imitation. She doesn't know what bad imitation breakfast the Nazis made the German people eat. I guess up there in the future, you probably know the Nazis were bad people, every bit as bad as Communists.

The only time I ever hear talk about the war is at the farm when papa sits off somewhere with Uncle Metro. Even there they don't talk about it if they notice I'm listening. I've learned how to be quiet and not get noticed, but, no matter how much I hear, it's never enough.

On Remembrance Day, Fat Freddy, with a red poppy on the collar of his coat, makes a long, boring speech about the war at the cenotaph. Nobody likes it, but they have to let him do it because he's the mayor. His speech is full of brags about his uncles and nothing about the men in town who really went to the war. Nana says neither one of his uncles left England during the war. They fought Germans and Japanese only in their dreams. Fat Freddy calls Germans and Japanese, Jerrys and Japs. Nana and papa don't let us say those words or Chink or Nigger, either, or Bohunk. Those words are worse than swearing.

Mother disagrees. She says if papa had a real war wound, and a piece of steel in his head like her brother, Uncle Phillip, he wouldn't be high and mighty against calling the enemy what they deserve.

Papa got the shell shock from the war, and a broken arm, and bleeding in his stomach, but nothing that left a scar that we can look at, except on his leg, but that wasn't from a battle so Mother says it doesn't count.

Papa sat for three days in a deep hole with his dead brother beside him and two German soldiers who were wounded. He saved the life of one of the Nazi Germans, but he couldn't save his brother. Mother says only a madman would save a Kraut (that's another bad word for Germans).

Nana says there are many kinds of wounds a soldier gets in a war. Some of them are invisible. Nana says invisible wounds are painful in ways that can't be described to people who don't have them. Mother doesn't agree.

I know papa hurts. If a person takes the time to look at him they can see hurting in his eyes. That's the only place it shows. Nana says there's only one thing that can help. Time. Nothing else. I wish there was something else. Time takes too long.

Granddad Smythe had friends from the Great War who had the shell shock, but it wasn't called shell shock in the old days. The army called it cowardice. Nana says the men who got it were shunned like lepers. On the battlefield, some of them were shot by their own commanders. Can you imagine that?

Nana says the understanding about shell shock didn't change much in this last war, but it should have. She says getting the shell shock is every bit as serious as losing a limb, worse even, because with an arm or a leg gone, people know what to get used to. With the shell shock, people get bad dreams; they burst into crying in the middle of company. Nobody knows when it will come on. It's hard to get used to.

People with the shell shock forget how to feel happy. Nana says the happy feeling will come back, but it takes time. I hope papa can live long enough to remember how to be happy. I don't think any people think badly of him, except Mother and maybe Uncle Edwin.

I don't know why Mother doesn't understand the shell shock in papa. She gets her nervous breakdowns. They're invisible and nobody thinks badly of her.

Nana is the most upset with Uncle Edwin. Nana says if anyone should understand the debilitating effect of the shell shock it should be Uncle Edwin. It's his job to know about those things. She says when he was in school, he spent more time being a playboy than he did learning how to be a psychiatrist. She says he missed important parts of his education.

Papa tore his leg open on sharp wire when he was dragging poor, dead Uncle Joe across the battlefield looking for a hospital. His leg got infected, and the doctors nearly cut it off. Papa still limps.

Maybe that's why he never notices my limp. We make a funny pair, hibble-hobbling along together.

Mother says I was a wild baby who wouldn't stay put. Crawling around everywhere. Nobody could catch me. I climbed out of my crib all the time. That's how I got the cut beside my knee on the outside of my leg. I cut it on the baby bottle I threw out of my crib. It broke all over the floor. I still have a little white scar there. On the side of my knee. It's hard to understand how such a small cut can cause such big problems.

I'm rambling, aren't I? I wish I would quit doing that.

Anyway, back to business. Boy, reading the advertisements in this magazine you'd think the United States was the only country fighting the enemy. I hope you historians know that all the other countries in the world were busy fighting for victory for years before the Americans decided to join in.

Nana says the United Sates people sat back when everybody else was suffering from the bombings and the killings. Crazy Marion says they made nothing but money from the war. She says the United States people like to be heroes. That's why they saved themselves for the end. By the time they joined the war, everybody else was exhausted, and they were fresh and strong. To hear the Americans talk about Italy, Nana says, you'd think they were the only soldiers over there.

Crazy Marion says only about a third of the soldiers fighting the Bosch and the Eyeties in Italy were American. The other two-thirds were soldiers from other places, like the India ones who had turbans on their heads instead of helmets, and the Gooms from Algeria who looked like shepherds from the Bible. They sneaked around at night and fought with long knives. That's why it was called a world war, because the whole world was there, not just the United States.

Nana says the United States was happy to have a war. It made money for their industry. Saved them from the Great Depression. Uncle Edwin stayed away from the war with a desk job in the United States. His father's companies made scads of money from it all.

Aunt Edie thinks Nana picks on Uncle Edwin because of the money. Aunt Edie and Mother say making money isn't a sin. Nana says it's not the making of the money that's the sin; it's how the making gets done.

I like listening to Nana. She talks of things I don't hear from other people. I like that. It keeps my brain busy trying to make sense of it.

Mother doesn't like the way Nana thinks. She says Nana should let sleeping dogs lie. She should mind her own business. Nana says the welfare of other human beings is her business. She says it's everybody's business. It's in the Bible. Mother says it isn't in her Bible.

Nana gets mentioned in the newspaper for helping people. Mother has a high regard for people who get their name in the newspaper. Mother and Jeannie get mentioned in the paper, sometimes with a photograph. Especially when they dress alike. They have the best outfits at Easter, Christmas and at Halloween. They paint flowers on their nylon stockings for when they sit on stage waiting for someone to buy their decorated lunch at the church box social. When I grow up, I'm going to get my name in the newspaper, but it'll be for helping people like Nana does, or because I'm a famous historian or a lady writer.

Mother and Jeannie are butterfly people. All they have to do is show up and people are happy to admire them. Next to them, I'm a plain, night moth that nobody notices until it hangs on the screen door looking in. Then, people shut the door.

Nana believes in dressing for comfort. Her housedresses are wrap-arounds with good pockets. When she's in the garden or in ditches picking medicine weeds she wears papa's farm clothes. Mother won't be seen anywhere near her then. But, please, Historians, don't think Nana is plain. She's not. When she has a mind to dress up, she's magnificent.

Mother doesn't approve of what Nana wears for dress up. Neither does Grandma Walters. They think Nana dresses old fashioned when modern dressing is required, but Crazy Marion says Nana is the classiest broad around. Nana's day dresses all have long, pleated sleeves, buttoned cuffs wide skirts for easy walking. In the kitchen, after Nana's New Year's feast, Crazy Marion told Grandma Walters that glamour girls like Mother are a dime a dozen, but classy women like Nana are rare. She apologized for saying it, but Grandma Walters still went home in a huff. Marion says even when Nana dresses for comfort, she does it with flair.

I wear slacks most of the time to cover up my crooked leg. Mother says I look like a tomboy and they aren't much admired.

It isn't very crooked, my leg. It's a skinny along the outside below the knee. Skinnier than my other leg. The shoes I wear are homely, not the shoes a person wears with dresses and skirts. They're boy's boots and my slacks cover up most of them. I have plaid slacks and corduroy. This year, Nana bought me blue denim jeans with flannel lining. When I roll up the bottoms, the flannel shows. Nana buys girl blouses for me to wear with my slacks, but on me, even attractive blouses turn into ordinary.

Flair won't do me any good, so I've decided to be brave. That's another way I could get my picture in the paper. It would impress Mother. Then, she'd put her arm around me and pose next to me for the camera. You don't have to be pretty or elegant to be brave.

May 3rd, 1953

Dear Diary,

They've all gone to church with Grandpa and Grandma Walters. Except for papa, Nana and me. We went to the Church of England service this morning. That's the Anglicans. The others go to the Fellowship Baptist; they're dunkers. Nana doesn't hold with dunking.

It's a good thing Beanie and his Aunt Dorothy go Anglican too. Beanie and I sit together so we can escape right after church as soon as we wrap egg-salad sandwiches in wax paper and put them into Beanie's satchel. We don't bother with the church Kool-Aid. It's watered down. Nana and Beanie's Aunt Dorothy stay for sit-down sandwiches and tea after church, so they can argue about when women will get to be priests.

Today I let Beanie eat all the sandwiches. Mrs. Webb made them. She uses sandwich spread in her egg-salad instead of mayonnaise. I'm not fond of it. Beanie's gone off to find his friend, Russell to play submarine, so I'm up here in the eagle's nest in the Sunday peace and quiet with a peanut butter sandwich and Nana's magazines.

I've spread them all over my bed and dresser. I'm still stuck in the during-the-war magazines. There are more pages than you'd think there'd be in a magazine.

I didn't read the stories about Roosevelt and Churchill and the United Nations. Those are long and tedious. They're about things that you Historians already know about in the future. Instead, I read about feeding Europe's children. I don't know how to think about that. Do you know, up there in the future, that little children in every country were hungry in the war?

So many little children born in 1941, in all the Europe countries, born in the same year as me. Except, over there, they had no food when I had plenty. They were freezing in their schools. And their houses got blown up or stolen by the Nazis. They had to sneak away to live in barns and cellars. The Mothers were starving too, eating food that wasn't fit for animals.

Mother would not put up with being starved. I don't know what would happen if she got stuck in a war.

Now that the war is over, I hope those children have food. I hope they didn't die. Thinking about them makes it hard to feel sorry about having a gimpy foot. I do that. Fall into a blue melancholy when I dream too hard about being pretty and graceful like Mother and Jeannie. When I dream about being a dancer. Spinning around and around in tiny white shoes with a wide skirt floating like smoke around me. And everybody smiling at me and clapping.

But, what's a gimpy foot next to being starved? Having no house to go to and no bed to sleep in? No warm clothes in winter and no food? That's the worst part. If you have no food you can die.

I don't like to think about being cold all the time, and having bombs drop from the sky right into the town. All things dead around me, even the birds. I don't like thinking about it, but I have to now. That's the bad part about reading. You get to know things you didn't know before. That starts the thinking. Thinking is hard. It hurts the front of my head, the back, and even the sides. Once thinking starts, it's not easy to stop. Historians, I hope the world is finished with war up there where you are.

Another good example of hard thinking is in the middle of this magazine, covering up two whole pages. It's about the Stewart-Warner Corporation. They're telling people to buy war bonds. "*We live in the only nation on earth where the price of freedom is so small.*" They mean they had no bomb-torn streets and hell-infested skies. But we didn't either, here in Canada, or in Mexico, or in South America even, or in Australia or New Zealand, or in most of China, and I bet many more countries than that. The United States wasn't the only nation on earth free of war. Crazy Marion says the Americans like to think they're the only important nation on earth. I don't know why they don't tell the truth. Nana says that's what free countries do; tell the truth. According to this, she might be wrong about that.

In this family, there was a big price paid for freedom. Papa was in the battle with Uncle Joe when he died. Uncle Joe was the last of the brothers to die in the war. After that, the army said papa had to be L.O.B. (left out of battle). Nana says the army has to do that because they don't want all the men in one family to get wiped out. Papa tried to sneak back to the fighting. He got in trouble for disobeying. That's when the shrapnel exploded into his already sore leg. That happened when they were bringing him back.

I have a picture from Nana's Chatelaine magazine tacked on my wall. It shows a Mother, a father and three children all smiling in their backyard. They look happy. That's how families should be. My family's not like that; we're the happiest when we're not with each other. I try not to mind, but I can't help being curious about why some families fit with each other and others don't. I wonder why God makes mistakes when it comes to organizing families.

It's still May 3rd, 1953

Dear Diary,

I can't seem to finish this day. At supper I looked at papa. All of a sudden I felt wicked for being happy that he came back from the war. That's another thing that's hard to think about. The hundreds of children all over the world with no papa at their supper table tonight. That made me think of Josie Carter and her brothers and sisters. They live over by the grain elevators in a charity house. Their papa didn't come back from the war. And Mrs. O'Kane. She was having her baby when she heard about her husband being killed in the war, shot right out of the sky, and his body never found. It sent her into a nervous breakdown. Her sister took her baby away, and didn't ever bring it back. So that baby doesn't have a mother or a father. It's not good to think about those things at supper. It makes it hard for a person to eat and make conversation. Historians, I'm going to be writing quite a bit about the war, so you might not want to read this just before a meal.

Mother saved me from going hungry from too much heavy thinking. She got laughing about something Jeannie said. It was her good laugh, like Christmas bells. I don't like it when she laughs high and loud, but tonight it was the right sound to hear to cover up the sad thoughts pushing hard against my mind.

Jeannie tells Mother all about her dates. Even the date where Roger asked her to go steady. Mother's not happy about the going steady. She doesn't believe in it. They didn't have going steady when she was a girl. They only had being engaged. Mother says Jeannie is the only one of us girls who has a chance for a good marriage, but not to Roger. Roger's not marriage material for Jeannie. Roger's friend Gerry, whose father is the pharmacist, is a better prospect.

Roger uses his brother's car to take Jeannie and her friends to the new drive-in picture show in Vermilion. Gerry can't drive yet. Jeannie says Roger is a dreamboat. He has a face that makes her face look prettier. I don't know what that means. I can't explain 'dreamboat' either, Historians. I can understand the dream part, but the boat part? No matter how hard I try, the truth about many things escapes me. Especially when it comes to Jeannie. She makes my head hurt.

Mother says Roger comes from low people who shop from the economy section of the Eaton's catalogue. It's not good for Jeannie to get serious about someone like that. Nana shops the economy section, but Mother says that's different. Nana doesn't have to. Mother says she's contrary that way.

Mother and Grandma Walters agree that quality people don't shop catalogue, but I know for certain that Grandma Walters shops catalogue. She does it in secret. After Christmas, when I was there for lunch, Grandpa Walters brought a box from the post office. Grandma Walters grabbed it from him before he got his boots off. She took it to her bedroom. Later she came out with a tray of china ornaments, each one full of Neptune Fern. It doesn't need dirt to grow or water to stay alive. It's good that Grandma Walters discovered Neptune Fern. When plants that need dirt and water get full of bugs at her house, she throws them in the burn barrel. Nana's indoor plants never get bugs. She feeds them cold tea for shiny leaves and compost tea for sturdiness. She knows about plants from her books by Sir Albert Howard. I think he was somebody famous so you will probably know about him, even up there in the future.

I looked through Nana's midseason Eaton's catalogue. You can't guess what I saw. Every one of Grandma Walters' china ornaments. All on the same page! The rose decorated swan and the turbaned Hindu head sit on Grandpa's magazine end table. The bird on a nest, and the little girl and boy artists are up on the dining room shelf. Everyone one of them is poked full of fern. Nana smiled into her hanky when I showed her.

But I was writing about Roger. He used to be an outcast with the popular crowd at school. He wasn't allowed with Jeannie's crowd. After he graduated, he got a job. That's when Jeannie approved him. It's because his brother lets Roger drive his car every weekend. It's pretty. The car. Aqua with a beige roof. Jeannie says it looks better with her in it, because she's a blond. It has automatic windows in the front, power brakes and a radio. She picked Roger for a boyfriend because of the car and because he works at the gravel pit. That means he has money for presents.

Mother wants Jeannie to consider Gerry for boyfriend material, but that's where Jeannie is contrary. Mother says Jeannie will eventually come around to her way of thinking.

In our family, we go places in Nana's old black Ford. It doesn't have a radio. Mother rides in it only because she says it's better than papa's farm truck. His truck is last year new, and isn't full of oily rags and tools like in his old one, but it's not suitable for Mother's occasions.

Mother may not like Roger, but she's quick to ride in his car if she gets the front seat where she can dangle her arm out the window. I like Roger. He always says hello to me when he comes over. He plays checkers with me when Jeannie is upstairs sick with her monthlies or flung out in a pout. Nana likes Roger, too. She says he's a hard working young man with a good heart. She says he'll go far. Mother doesn't agree. She says someone like Roger can't go far enough to suit a pretty girl like Jeannie.

Laura doesn't care about pretty. You don't need to be pretty to be a doctor. Mother says if Laura insists on that foolishness, she'll be an old maid. A woman trying to be a doctor is a wild idea. Only Nana would be so bold as to encourage that. She's right. Nana does encourage it.

Nana bought Laura a microscope, because she's believes in education for girls. Real education. Not only to be doctors, but engineers and lawyers too. Mother says she's never heard of a woman engineer. And any woman who tries to be a lawyer needs her head examined.

Laura doesn't talk at the supper table. She eats fast and is the first to leave. She usually goes to her friend Linda's to do homework. Mother doesn't care where she goes or how late she stays out, because girls who keep their noses stuck in books are not in danger from boys.

Mother worries about dangerous boys. Going steady with a boy with a reputation for being fast can keep a girl from a respectable marriage. Because she thinks Roger comes from low people, Mother says he's bound to be fast. She tells Jeannie she better not become used goods. She says Roger is dangerous. Once he turns Jeannie into used goods, he'll jilt her for a floozy.

Early Morning May 6, 1953

Dear Diary,

Recording for the future is a hard job. Right now, my head is bulging with so many thoughts. I have to quit the magazines when that happens and move over to Granddad's spyglass.

I like watching people who aren't my family. I like watching them walk through their lives. You'd be surprised, Historians, how many families aren't what you think they are. You'll be surprised to hear how different they are when they think nobody's watching.

Nobody knows about me up here looking down on them. I'm at the window most nights, now. It's a good thing, Historians, that you're way off in the future. If you lived right here, maybe next door, I wouldn't dare write this down for you.

Especially about Fat Freddy. I expect he pulls on his willie to make it grow longer. Jeannie says it's important for a man's willie to be long and large. She says a man can't make good babies without the right sized willie. But Fat Freddy already has four perfectly good children. I don't know why he's after a bigger willie now.

Jeannie explained what a man has to do with his willie before a baby can be made. It's complicated. There has to be kissing in the dark. Nice words have to be said before any of it can begin. She says not just any willie fits inside a woman, only the willie of a man special to her.

I wanted to ask her how a woman finds out about a man's willie, but I didn't. I think a woman would have to sort through a lot of them to find the right match. I don't think men take them out for viewing. I'm sure I would have heard about that.

I've seen dogs do the thing they have to do to make babies. I've seen chickens do it. At least I think that's what the chickens were doing. It's hard to tell with chickens. With dogs there's no secret. They sniff everywhere. They lick each other. It takes a lot of concentration to get everything hooked up right. After they're done, they can't get unhooked right away. They have to stand in front of the whole world looking foolish.

I wonder how long people have to stay hooked up. It's hard to imagine going to all that bother. How embarrassing. I wonder what people talk about in the dark, while they're waiting to get unhooked.

There are so many mysteries about life. It's hard finding the truth about things.

After breakfast, May 6, 1953

Dear Diary,

I got up early this morning to write about what I saw last night. As usual, I got off on a side road. I'm famous for that. I always promise myself I won't take a side road, but before I know it, things push up against the front of my brain wiggling to get out, and off I go.

I'm working up to tell you about Dr. Masters. It's a puzzler. I feel awful about what I saw. It was hard to write it down right away. I let it slop around in my head all night and most of the morning.

Quite a bit is said in town about Dr. Masters' distinguished record in the air force, but Nana's sister from England says he was a drunken scoundrel who crash-landed his plane on purpose to avoid a dangerous mission. Mother laughed when she heard the story from Crazy Marion. She called her a meddling busy body, a used up old prune who is jealous of youth and beauty. But I think maybe he *is* a scoundrel. Here's why. I looked into his window last night. I saw young Mrs. Masters reach to take a glass out of Dr. Masters' hand. He yanked it away and he hit her.

Can you believe that? Oh, Dear Diary, he hit her.

I didn't remember to breathe when I saw it.

Right across the face.

With his hand.

She fell to a chair.

She put up her arms up to cover her head.

He turned his back on her. He drank what was in the glass in one gulp. He turned around, and threw the glass at her.

Threw it at her.

It broke all over her head and hand.

Oh, Dear Diary, it cut her. I saw the red blood of it. When she wrapped up her hand in a hanky, I saw the blood creep through the white and run down her arm.

Historians, she's in the family way. I don't know what's wrong with him. I don't. Why would he do that? Doesn't he know that doctors are kind and good? Do you think he has the shell shock? Who can I tell this to? If I tell Nana, she can't help. I think you have to kill somebody before it's against the law.

I wish I could tell Mother. Mrs. Masters is her friend. But what can a friend do? I don't know. It doesn't matter anyway, because Mother would never believe me. Young Mrs. Masters had a bruise on her face at the Christmas concert. Nana said she knew by the look on her face it was not caused by tripping over a rug. I didn't know what she meant, then. I think I know now. Nana says young Doctor Masters has the demeanor of someone who misuses his authority.

Mother is scandalized by bad talk against Dr. Masters. She says men like him never do unseemly things. Oh, Mother. Such things are done. They are. Poor, poor Mrs. Masters. I cried for her when I saw it. I want to cry again as I write this down.

I finally told Granddad. He was angry. Dr. Masters is lucky Granddad's dead. I told the Dead Uncles too. I wish they'd swoop down from the sky like avenging angels and shake the stuffing right out of Doctor Masters. What do you think, Historians, when you read about this? I hope things are better up there in the future.

Nana says human beings continually struggle to get more civilized, but it seems to me that people are not struggling hard enough. I hope Dr. Masters won't throw things when there's a tiny baby in his house.

After seeing all that, I didn't feel like watching the town any more, but the lights came on in the Oberg's living room. I looked in there before I thought the better of it. I'm glad I did. I was badly turned outside myself before I looked into that window.

Oscar Oberg came back from the war with burns on his face and his hands. He has no eyebrows, and not much ears left. He looks strange because of it. Sometimes he gets the shakes. Mother says it's revolting to look at him. She thinks he should have better sense than to show himself in public like he does, singing in the choir, taking his wife to the movies on Saturday night. Mother feels sorry for his wife.

It was the Obergs who smoothed me out. The Obergs made me cry again, but not because of being sad. They must have just bought a record player. Because that's what they took out of a box. They put it on top of the tall radio cabinet by the door. They put a record on it. Mr. Oberg opened his arms wide. Mrs. Oberg smiled at him, the smile you give someone who is most wonderful. They danced. Close together they danced. She wrapped her arms around him. One of his poor wrinkly, red hands smoothed her hair like he was petting a cat.

It was beautiful to watch. I imagined the music. Benny Goodman. Mother has Benny Goodman records that she and papa danced to before the war.

Benny Goodman made music in my head while I told Granddad about the Obergs. He laughed and he cried with me. When they stopped dancing, Mr. Oberg put his ruined hands on Mrs. Oberg's cheeks. She smiled up at him like he was the most handsome of men. He kissed her slowly. I didn't want to watch anymore. It seemed rude to look at them like that, ruder than watching Fat Freddy in his garage. I still haven't told Granddad about Fat Freddy.

Mother says that if Mr. Oberg were a decent man he would set his wife free to look for another husband. Mother thinks Claire is too pretty for a wreck like him. I don't think Mrs. Oberg thinks her husband is a wreck. Not at all.

Still May 6th, 1953

Dear Diary,

I haven't told you about Constable Kipp's wife yet. She's Mother's friend. Together they are wondrous to behold. She has red hair. Auburn, I guess I better say. Mother says only floozies have red hair. Mother's hair is so blonde it's nearly white, just like Marilyn Monroe.

Mrs. Kipp hangs on Constable Kipp's arm like a queen when they come to a Christmas concert or a church supper. She pats his hand and taps his chin with her beautiful long fingers. She tells everyone how brave he is. Nana says she's too old to talk in that little girl voice. Mrs. Kipp talks a lot. Constable Kipp doesn't say anything, just nods his head and gets red in the face.

So you can imagine what a surprise I got. When I saw Mrs. Kipp on a blanket in her back yard behind the hedge, I wasn't interested. Then I saw Mike from the Co-op store come to deliver groceries. He's a divorced man from Edmonton who lives with his mother upstairs over the meat market. He put the groceries on the back porch, and, instead of going back to his car, he crawled on his hands and knees across the yard. I guess it was so nobody would see him. He looked silly. He crouched down beside Mrs. Kipp, and rubbed sun tan lotion on her. He un-did her bathing suit in the back. Can you imagine? I don't know why she was wearing a bathing suit. It's not near warm enough for sun tanning yet. They wrestled around on the blanket. Then she wrapped the blanket around her shoulders, and went into her house. Mike crawled back across the lawn and went in the side door after her.

I bet Mother doesn't know about Mrs. Kipp.

Are you as puzzled as I am, Historians? Is this really the kind of daily life information you need? I don't know if a kid should know these things about grownups. They'd be embarrassed if they knew what I knew about them and maybe even mad. I wonder if Granddad wrote down what he saw through his spyglass? One day I'll be brave enough to ask Nana.

Not quite dark, May 6, 1953

Dear Diary,

This day is lasting forever. Jeannie says I can't understand woman things until I have my monthlies. I think she's right. There's so much I don't understand about women, or men for that matter. Then there are girdles. I'm surprised anyone understands girdles. There is an ad for girdles in a during-the-war magazine. Girdles and bras.

It says *"Don't shirk war work...still, don't let it harm your charm! Every woman's called upon to assume greater responsibilities today - even to do men's work, but no one asks that she lose her femininity! Quite the contrary, everyone agrees that preserving feminine charm is a big factor in maintaining morale."*

Preserving feminine charm means always wearing a girdle. It's hard to understand why a woman can't be charming without a girdle. Nana doesn't wear a girdle, and Judge Balder told Reverend Sykes at the Church Supper that Nana is still a charmer after all these years.

Finally dark, May 6, 1953

Dear Diary,

After yesterday I can't get warmed up to look in the spyglass. I'm tired of the magazines, but I'm still thinking about the war. Fat Freddy didn't go to the war. I heard Grandpa Walters say Freddy made his mother shoot off two of his fingers so he couldn't go to the war. He wanted his Mother to shoot off toes, but he chickened out at the last minute, yanked away and she got his fingers instead.

He tells people he lost them in a farm accident, but I don't think anybody believes him. Fat Freddy is older than papa by less than a year, but Nana says he isn't half the man. Mother says papa was more of a man before the war. Before the war, she says he wouldn't have let her suffer in this old house while he wastes his time and money playing farmer. Before the war he would have taken the first opportunity to become mayor, which is what a man from a better family should be.

Mother wants papa to build us a new house in town, or buy back our old house. She says it won't be long before papa tires of the peasant life at the farm and comes back to his right state of mind.

I think Mother's wrong. Our farm house is on the quarter section that Tarazenkos rent from him. They're Mary's people, the Tarazenkos. Mother won't go there to look at the new house. She says she didn't marry a farmer, and she has no intention of being a farm wife.

Papa says she wouldn't be married to the farm; she'd be married to him. I don't think Mother likes being married to him. She says the war took her husband away from her and sent back a stranger in his place.

Nana says people are like onions with only one part showing at a time. But all the other parts are right there folded over each other, all touching. She says bad things like war eat layers off a person. Papa came home with different layers showing. They're not the layers Mother was used to. I think the war ate off Mother's layers too. Maybe papa isn't used to the layers that are left showing on her either. You know, Dear Diary, the war has been over a long time (nearly eight years), but there is still misery because of it. You'd think it had ended yesterday.

I'm happy at the farmhouse. It's bigger than our old house, but not two stories high. It has thick walls, and it's shaped like a square with one side missing. A square C shape. I've never seen another house like it. Papa got the thick wall idea from the Tarazenko's house. He says thick walls are a good idea for the deep cold we have in Canada. Papa's house has real stucco on the outside with bits of blue glass stuck in it, and good plaster walls inside. Tarazenko's house is plastered with mud inside and out. It's fine too. Papa said Mother wouldn't tolerate mud walls, no matter how fine. For her sake he put real plaster inside and stucco outside. I wonder why he thinks it matters. She won't live in the house as long as it's on a farm, and it isn't the sort of house that would go good in town.

The windows are tall and skinny; the window sills wide enough to sit on. Papa put a big Ukrainian plaster stove in the living room instead of a fireplace, because he says it uses less firewood. It makes the warm stay inside the house instead of escaping up the chimney. Nana agrees with him about fireplaces. She closed off the fireplaces in her house in the dirty thirties, and put in Quebec heaters, which Mother says are primitive.

Nana has a gas furnace, but she doesn't use it often. She prefers the comfort of wood burning. Papa does too. He has a basement in his new house, with a furnace for oil and coal, because gas lines haven't come as far as the farm yet. But he likes to burn wood in the stucco stove.

There's a cubbyhole behind papa's stove where he sleeps when he stays over. Mother would never sleep back there. He doesn't use a mattress. Mother would hate that too. He has a pile of spruce branches to sleep on like Crazy Marion and the Kokum use. Once a month he puts them outside to burn and gets fresh ones. Over the spruce boughs he throws Granddad Smythe's old buffalo robe. He puts wool army blankets over that and then the feather bed Baba made for him. Finally two, fat feather pillows and a thick feather quilt. There's no place on this earth more cozy than papa's bed. I wouldn't blame him if he slept at the farm all the time.

I slept there once last winter. A blizzard came up, covering all the roads with snow, so we couldn't go back into town until the snow plows came out in the morning. It was heaven. The house didn't have electricity yet, but papa made a fire in the stove in the kitchen, and in the stucco stove, and he put coal oil lamps on the table. Everything smelled like Christmas trees and campfires and the light from the lamps danced yellow on the walls. We ate Aunt Olga's borscht, and soaked it up with the bread that Baba wraps in cabbage leaves and bakes in her outdoor oven, even in the winter.

Papa slept rolled up like a caterpillar in a wool quilt on a stack of spruce branches on the other side of the stove from me. He said he slept like a baby there. I also slept like a baby in papa's warm, dark cubbyhole. We couldn't hear the blizzard through the thick walls, and not a breath of cold came in to bother us.

Mother doesn't know how often I go to the farm with papa. The farm house is up against a long hill full of quaking aspens and Saskatoon bushes. Mother says it's like papa to ignore a fine view from the top of the hill and build at the bottom like a peasant. Papa says he did it to shelter the house from the northwest wind, so it would be pleasant in all weather.

The open C of the house faces the south with a wide veranda along all three sides. Papa planted hops that climb up the house for shade in the summer. When they fall down every autumn, the sun reaches in the windows again during the cold days.

Nana says papa's house design is ingenious. I agree. He sat on the hill for days at a time for over two years while he planned how to build it. The kitchen faces the east. It has more windows than most kitchens, because papa did another ingenious thing. The whole north wall of the kitchen is one long, deep pantry with four separate doors. You can walk into any part of it, close the door behind you and feel cozy. There are shelves and counters and a sink for washing vegetables and grimy pots. Inside the door near the east wall is the place for canning jars and jam and pickles. There's another door that leads into the root cellar.

The root cellar is most amazing. I think it's the only root cellar in the world you don't have to crawl down into. It's built into the hill with a dirt floor under a wooden grate and dirt walls and bins all around for the vegetables. There's a double door to the outside where you walk right in with the vegetables. You don't have to stoop. Baba keeps her vegetables there. She says she's never seen such a good root

UNDER THE MAIDENHAIR · 49

cellar. Nana sent all her roots there last fall, because she says it's the only place she knows that keeps potatoes right into July.

The Tarazenkos live on the other side of the slough from our house. They pay papa rent, grow grain in the fields, look after cows, chickens and sheep, and keep a garden. When papa was a boy, Tarazenkos owned their own farm, but Uncle Metro got the drinking sickness and lost that farm. Nana and Granddad Smythe helped him get over his drinking sickness and now Uncle Metro is saving to buy the farm from papa. The only part papa wants to keep is the part our house is on.

Papa says the rent Uncle Metro pays goes toward the purchase of the farm, but Uncle Metro says, no. He wants to pay cash money like a proper man. Nana says many people pay rent against the time they'll own, but Uncle Metro is contrary. Nana and papa will win in the end.

Mother wants papa to go back to his old job at International Harvester Farm Implements. Before the war he and Uncle Pete owned it. Papa did the books. Mother says if he doesn't want to do that at least he should work for Grandpa Walters at the elevators and have a little office where he could wear a suit for selling insurance to people. Or at the Windsor Salt Plant by Lindbergh.

Papa doesn't want any of that. He likes living in the country. He doesn't want to wear a suit ever again. He says it's a foolish convention to make some men seem better than others. He says he's no better and no worse than the next guy; the war showed him that. Mother slams things around when he talks that way. I think she makes noise on purpose to punish papa. It makes him jumpy when she drops things and yells.

Papa says everywhere he went in the war was full of stink, noise and too many people. Mother says he comes home from the farm smelling of manure and garlic, which is worse than any war smell. Papa says she's lucky she'll never have to smell the stink of war. As for me, I like the smell of manure. It smells like grass and hay. I don't tell anybody that but you, Dear Diary, in case they think I've gone soft in the head.

May 8, 1953

Dear Diary,

I went to the farm with papa today. We don't usually talk, papa and I. We roll down the windows to let bird songs come in. All the blackbirds in the sloughs sing at once in the spring. As we drove by the long meadow in the sand hills papa slowed down in case we might hear a meadowlark song.

No birds sang as we drove past the gravel pits. Into that quiet space I told papa how much I like going to the farm with him. I've wanted to tell him that for a long time, but there's a stillness about him I hate to muss up by talking. Nana says it's important for people to tell each other about the things they like. She says everybody is quick to mention things they don't like, until there's no room for mentioning the things they do.

Papa smiled. He nodded his head and got back to the business of driving.

"I quite like it myself. You're easy company, Tally." He nodded his head as we drove along.

He's a pacer; papa is, back and forth from room to room. At the farm he paces slower. Today we had tea at Mary's place. When papa got up from drinking his tea to pace the room Mary's Baba shook her finger at him.

"George a George. Always hurry, you. Always hurry. What's a matter? God give it time for every-ting, time for sit."

Papa said, "I know. I know." But he didn't sit; he gulped down another cup of tea and went to the barn to talk about seeding with Uncle Metro.

I got comfortable sitting in the corner listening to Baba mumble through her work. I didn't want to budge. When Baba mumbles she calls it singing.

"I like to sing it, all the time sing it, you little turnip."

Baba makes different noises: little squeaks, rumblings in the back of her throat like growling, and a rush of Ukrainian words that go up and down like a Catholic prayer. Not singing I'm used to, but I like it just the same.

If strangers watched Baba work, at first they'd think she was slow. Her feet shuffle like she has all day to do everything. But her hands tell a different story. I love to watch her hands work.

Today she made three washbasins full of *pear-oh-heh*, my favourite of all food in the world. *Pear-oh-heh*. I can't spell it. I don't pronounce it properly either. Mary can't spell it for me, because Ukrainian words are written with different letters. Anyway, *Pear-oh-heh* are little dough pillows filled up with different stuffing like mashed potatoes and onions and sour cabbage and cottage cheese.

Mother says they smell like rotting food. She's wrong about that. Everything about making *Pear-oh-heh* smells round and buttery. Baba doesn't have a maidenhair fern table for me to hide under, but she has a little stool in the corner beside the hot water reservoir on her big wood stove. I tuck myself back there and watch her hands fly like sparrows around the kitchen.

Today Baba made a beautiful ball of *Pear-oh-heh* dough. To cover it, she yanked a clean cloth off the clothesline that runs from the pantry door to the stove.

"She sleep little bit, now. She no good without little bit sleep."

I don't know what the dough does while it's sleeping. It doesn't rise up like bread dough. It looks the same when the cloth is lifted as it does when Baba covers it. Baba says the dough calms down under there. Mixing gets it excited. Excited dough makes the little *Pear-oh-hehs* angry and tough.

While the dough slept, Baba got sour cabbage from her cold room to put in the mashed potatoes that go into the little pillows. Sour cabbage has a fine, sharp smell that begs a person to drink its juices. That's what Baba, papa and I do. We drink it to keep us strong. If Mother would let herself get close to the cabbage she'd change her mind about the smell. But that's the trouble with Mother; she makes her mind up about things without ever getting close to them.

Kapoosta juice. That's what cabbage is in Ukrainian, *Kapoosta*. I like that word. The Ukrainian word for egg is a good word too. *Yi-chee*. Papa says that's the surprised noise a chicken makes when it lays an egg. *Yi-chee*.

When Baba brings the bowl of cabbage shreds to the table she has a jar of canned blueberries in her other hand. We drink the juice from the canned blueberries too. When we're done, the excitement is gone from her dough. She yanks the towel off, scoops up the dough, throws flour all over her big table, and drops the lump in the middle of it. There it sits looking like the first ball of a snowman in a backyard of new snow.

Baba doesn't have a rolling pin. She has a long, thick round stick. She rolls it all over the dough until the dough stretches to cover up the table. That's when she hollers for help. Auntie Olga comes running. She wakes up half-blind Wasy who sleeps in a chair by the big stucco oven.

Wasy is Mary's older sister. She was a baby when Auntie Olga came to Canada on a boat after the first Great War. She got sick on that boat. She nearly died. After that she was half-blind and slow in the head, but she's a good worker and everyone loves her just the same.

Together, three women's fingers are an army of spiders rolling up a big dough web. Baba and Auntie cut rounds from the dough with jar lids, each starting at one end of the table and meeting each other in the middle. Press, twist, flip. Press, twist, flip. Hands grab the round of dough one at a time and hands scoop up filling.

Baba wraps up the blueberry ones, because they're the hardest to do. Auntie wraps the sour cabbage. Half-blind Wasy does up the potato and onion, and the cottage cheese.

Plunk. The filling goes in the middle. Fold the round over. Pinch, pinch, pinch it closed. Roll it off the hand to the floured table. Quickly the giant dough tablecloth turns into rows and rows's of little dough pillows.

Baba finishes first. Then slam, slam, slam. The stove lids rattle as she shoves more firewood into the red-hot coals. Water in the galvanized pail on the stove is already boiling, but Baba doesn't want it to stop for a second when she throws the pillows in to cook. She looks at it so fiercely it doesn't dare stop boiling. Before Baba cooks the *Pear-oh-heh*, she takes her big knife. Chop, chop, chop, she cuts the left over dough into little pieces that will dry and be noodles for soup. Into the boiling water goes the *Pear-oh-heh*. Steam fills the kitchen.

Out comes the *Pear-oh-heh*. Scooped out with a big wire strainer Uncle Metro made from window screen bent over a willow hoop. The *Pear-oh-heh* slide into the big bread bowl, now shining with melted, yellow butter. Baba tosses them around in there. They slip and slide like tiny perch in a washtub, fresh caught for bait.

By then Auntie Olga has chopped and fried up a big roaster of onion, which she dumps into the bread bowl on top of the *Pear-oh-heh*. By then my stomach has turned over on itself in desperation for the first taste. My tongue wants to fly from my mouth like a snake's to lick buttered onions off the little pillows. My nose is full of the good smell of it. I'm close to fainting with hunger.

As the last of the *Pear-oh-heh* hit the boiling water, papa and Uncle Metro come stomping in. They know the right time to come. They wash in the basin by the door and holler for Dominic. I hope you have *Pear-oh-heh*, up there in the future. It's a most excellent food.

Dominic is Mary's brother. He's 16, but he still goes to school, because in Mary's family, education is for boys. He's always reading or writing. He never talks to me when I'm at the farm, but he does smile at me. Nana says he's smart, but he's shy. He's afraid his Ukrainian accent will offend somebody. Nana says he doesn't have much of an accent left, but he worries anyway. I understand that. Nobody wants to offend if they can help it.

I wouldn't mind if he spoke to me, but he doesn't. I used to see him at school at recess sitting on the grade ten school steps reading. I'm in grade seven. That means I can't go over to the grade ten schoolhouse. I should be in grade six, but Nana persuaded Mother to let me go to grade one when I was five, because I started reading early and was squirmy at home.

Next year the grade tens and elevens move over to the new high school. Dominic will be far away from me. I'll only be in grade eight.

Before we eat, Baba scrubs the table with stove ashes and wet sand and a big ball of straw. Auntie Olga washes off the grit with a big wet cloth. The table is nearly white with cleanness. Uncle Metro made the table from a grandfather spruce tree he cut down over at the mouth of the creek.

I know Mother loves her Arborite-topped table. Her long fingers like to rub over its cold shininess, but I think if she came to the farm, her fingers would love the warm, smooth polish of Uncle Metro's table. Mother misses so much by staying in town.

Early morning, May 9, 1953

Dear Diary,

Nobody's up for breakfast yet, and I can't sleep anymore. Back to the recording business. I see food in a during-the-war magazine about daily life that I should warn you Historians about.

Raisin Sauce. There's a recipe for meatballs and raisin sauce. I'm sorry Nana saw this recipe. She doesn't make the meatballs, but she makes meat loaf and pours raisin sauce over each slice. I don't like it. The recipe says raisin sauce adds a *"zesty flavor to most wartime meals."* It isn't wartime anymore. We don't need that much zest. In case there's a war in the future, when you Historians read this, I'm putting in the recipe. But remember; only use it in case of war.

Raisin Sauce

Cook 1/3 cup each of chopped onion, green pepper and celery and a small minced clove of garlic in 3 tablespoons of bacon dripping until soft. Add 1/2 cup Sun-Maid Seedless Raisins, 1/3 cup catsup, 1 tablespoon of vinegar, 1 cup of water and salt and pepper to taste. Simmer for 30 minutes. Serves 6. (If people don't like it, it will serve more)

All the women in this magazine are pretty like Aunt Edie and Mother. Aunt Edie made a good marriage. She doesn't have any children and doesn't want any. She only talks to me if she has to. Uncle Edwin never talks to me. Mother says he can't waste his fine mind on foolish children. Nana says he's the one who's foolish. So stuck on himself that he's not learned how to be interesting.

Nana doesn't waste time on boring people more often than she has to, to be polite. She doesn't like what Uncle Edwin does at his work, and she tells him so. He works for the government at a place where they keep dangerous defectives, people who don't commit crimes they can go to jail for, but who are not fit for living in society.

Mother says they shut away dangerous people to protect society. If they ran wild, they'd have flocks of babies that would grow up to add more danger to society. She says we have to keep danger from spreading. Nana says there's lots of danger in the world, but it's not caused by defectives.

At the place where Uncle Edwin works, they spay people like they do cats and dogs. Mother says it doesn't hurt. It's done to them when they're young. They don't know anything's happened. I'm young. I think I'd know if that happened to me even if they put me to sleep first. They have to cut right into a person to spay them. A person is bound to notice that. Mother says when they do it to girls they tell them their appendix needs taking.

Nana says we fought Hitler, because he locked away the people he didn't like, and that led to him killing people like rats. Mother says that's not why we fought Hitler. Besides, no one at Uncle Edwin's institution gets killed. They get rounded up and sterilized and kept out of sight. Mother says it's the modern way. It's what must be done to protect society. They can't be allowed to bother healthy people. Nana says rounding up people is what Hitler did and it's never a good thing.

Pearl S. Buck agrees with Nana. Nana has a scrapbook of newspaper writing Mrs. Buck did since she came back from China. She says Mrs. Buck is one of the bravest women alive today.

Mother says people like Nana and Mrs. Buck aren't modern. They don't understand scientific progress. She reminds everybody that Nana talked in favour of having a place for mental defectives before the war.

Nana says, "I was wrong, Lillian. I'm not too proud to admit it." That's Nana for you.

When Nana was young, she and Grandma Walters helped to get the vote for women. Can you believe it, Historians? There was a time when only men voted. Women can vote today, but not Indians or Chinese. I don't know why that is. Trying to get the vote for women happened at the same time that everybody got keen to protect the world from mental defectives. Nana says she hadn't learned to think things through completely. Besides, in the beginning, the mental defective had to say, "Yes, it's alright to make me sterilized."

Not like now, when nobody has to get permission from the defectives to do it. Nana says it's wrong. Back in the old days, Nana thought it was a good plan to make a safe place for Mongoloid Idiots like Beanie's friend, Russell. It would be somewhere for him to go if his family all died off leaving him alone. But now, she says it was incomplete thinking; there are better ways to look after people like Russell. Nana's not afraid to go against anybody's grain by saying so.

I heard the argument about defectives when I was younger. I used to be scared that Uncle Edwin would take me away to his hospital and sterilize me. I know sterilizing people is not like boiling jars for jam, but I was still scared of it. Uncle Edwin looks at children with a fierce frown. Mother says he frowns because he has heavy thoughts. Nana says he frowns because he expects people to cater to him, and nobody does it fast enough.

When I was little, I had dreams about Uncle Edwin in a butcher shop apron chasing after me. I ran all through the house, fast as anything, but he always caught me, yanked me off my feet and held me up by my heels over a pail of boiling water like a chicken about to be dunked for plucking. I always woke up before he dropped me in.

Nana says they don't sterilize people with physical defects like mine. If they decide to, she won't allow it. As long as I have Nana on my side I have no worries.

Mother doesn't know it, but I can run. I do it where people can't see me. I'm not a pretty thing to watch, but I get the wind against my face like any other person. I'm fast for a Gimp. Last year, when I started running at the farm I didn't go far before getting tuckered out, but you should see me now. I can last a long time. Beanie's the only one who has seen me run. He says I look funny, going from side to side like an old chicken, one shoulder ahead of the other for balance, but he doesn't make fun of me. He's jealous, because even without a gimpy foot, he can't run very long without puffing. He's a roly-poly person.

May 10, 1953

Dear Diary,

Today I went to the farm again, and guess what? Dominic runs too. Faster than I do, and much nicer to watch, I'm sure.

I ran behind him. Far enough behind he wouldn't notice. He makes a fine sight. I could watch him all day. Nana says he's a handsome figure of a boy for his age. She's right about that.
There's a place where he ran down a long hill and back and forth on the river flats. I had to drop down on my stomach on the top of that hill to watch him. That's what I'm good at. Watching.

He ran until he collapsed. Then he lay there, on his stomach, all flung out, banging the ground with his fist. After a while he rolled over and fell asleep with his arm across his eyes. It was peaceful up there on the hill. I got sleepy listening to the bees in the yellow buffalo beans, bird songs everywhere and quaking aspens rustling their tiny round leaves in the wind. With no chill in the wind today, I might have slept for hours.

I nearly missed Dominic coming back up the hill.

After lunch I took my book and went to the old well cribbing where he was reading. I was determined to make him talk to me. It was easier than I thought.

"Do you mind if I sit and read here?"

He looked surprised. "You would like to?"

"Yes."

Nana is right, his voice is perfectly fine. There's not much Ukrainian left in it. He moved to make room for me. At first I read beside him. That was nice. Of course, I didn't keep my big mouth shut. I blurted.

"I saw you run today."

He lowered his book and looked at me sternly.

"By the river."

"So, you see what a runner I'm not."

"No, I think you're a fine runner."

"For a Bohunk." He turned back to his book.

The way he lifted his chin and said Bohunk made me suddenly mad. "That's a damn, dumb, stupid, bird twit thing to say."

He looked up. "Dumb?"

"Yes, dumb. I know kids call you Bohunk at school. So what? Kids call me Gimp, and it doesn't mean anything except they are rude with no manners."

"But they are right about me. I am a clumsy Bohunk. I will never win the endurance against Rodney Clark."

"Why not?"

"You saw why not. I can only last for half the time it takes for the endurance."

"Oh, for Pete's sake. You got lots of time for practice."

He shook his head.

I was dumbfounded. "You're giving up, before you start?"

"I came in third, last year and Rodney was first."

"So?"

"You think it is easy?"

"No. Nothing like that is easy. But it's possible." I sounded like Nana.

"What do you know about running?"

That made me double mad. I yanked his book away and threw it on the ground. That's not one bit like me, Dear Diary. I don't throw things, especially books. I think I lost leave of my mind right then.

"I can't run fast, but I can run long, and that's only because of practice. I think practice for me is whole lot harder than practice for you."

He looked down at my foot.

I poked him in the chest. "I could outlast you right now. Because of practice."

"You could not."

I turned and ran. For once in my life I didn't care what I looked like. I went through the bush where I knew the trail and he didn't. It was the only way to keep ahead of him. I heard him puffing behind me. I made myself keep going. I caught my second wind running down the hill to the river flats. Then I started on the back and forth route he took earlier. He caught up to me down there, and I pooped out. Then, I got back up, and fell in behind his pace, and every time he looked like he was slowing down I yelled at him.

"Come on! The Gimp is still going. Are you going to be a quitter before the Gimp?" I was puffing pretty badly. I had no idea how long we'd been at it, but I gave it one last go. "Come on, get your chin up. Can't run anywhere with your chin dragging on the ground!"

Finally, the run was gone out of me. I collapsed in a heap. He ran a bit farther before he realized I'd quit. He ran back in a panic.

"Natalie. Are you hurt?" He fell to his knees beside me. My name sounded lovely coming out of his mouth.

I laughed. "No, you slow poke. I'm pooped, not hurt."

"Pooped?"

I nodded. He fell over on his back beside me, and laughed, flinging his arms over his head. The sound made *me* laugh. After a few moments we quit laughing, and lay there together breathing hard and looking up at the sky.

After a while I sat up. "Dominic."

He looked up at me.

"You can't let yourself care what those boys say. You have to do things in spite of people, not be a quitter because of them. My Nana tells me that all the time, and she's right. You can run. You're a beautiful runner. If I looked as fine as you when I ran, I would never walk. I'd run everywhere."

"Natalie, you shame me."

"Good. Every time I come to the farm I'm going to shame you, until you run the endurance past anyone."

"Why?"

"Why what?"

"Why would you do this?"

I shrugged. "I think it's a sin for you to be a quitter." I threw in the part about sin because I know his Baba is strict against sin.

"A sin?"

"Yes."

"And you think I could beat Rodney Clark?"

"I don't know for sure. But it's worth a try, isn't it? Quit being a cry baby and get practicing."

"You'll come and help me when you come to the farm?"

"Yes."

"You promise?"

"I promise."

It wasn't until we had walked all the way back to the farm that I realized that he had seen me run, and had not been disturbed by my gimp. That's a new thing for me, and it felt good.

Dominic told papa I was going to be his coach. Papa surprised me. He didn't think it strange for me to be a coach.

"Our Tally has determination. She'll make a good coach."

I liked the way he said 'our Tally'. I've never heard him say that before. Nana says it all the time when she is talking to people about me, but never papa. At least not where I can hear.

After supper, May 10, 1953

Dear Diary,

It's embarrassing to have to write, "*When the stork brought...*" all the time, but that's what we have to say in our house. I heard Mother say to Nana that children would be alarmed if they knew the truth about how babies are born. I don't think so. All the cousins watched kittens being born under Grandma Walters' bed at Christmas last, and no one was alarmed except Grandma Walters. The mother cat purred nicely and licked her ugly, gooey little babies clean.

It would be nice if mothers purred. Real mothers, I mean. Like mine. It would be easy to tell when she is happy, if she purred.

My teacher, Mrs. Morrill, says the most ordinary things become important after the passage of time. I'm guessing a baby shower is an ordinary thing. Mother had a baby shower before the stork brought Jeannie. I found photos of it in the leather photo album right after the wedding pictures. There are pictures of Mother on the hospital steps with baby Jeannie.

There are two baby shower pictures where she is receiving a baby quilt from her bridge club before the stork brought Laura.

There are no baby shower pictures of me. There is a picture of Mother and papa in the summer of 1942. It's my favourite picture from the war. She is saying good-bye to him beside the train in Edmonton. They are standing with their arms around each other as if they like each other. Mother has one arm across her stomach.

That's where I was, right under her arm before I was born. I like to pretend that's my baby picture. I want to draw an arrow to her stomach and print beside it - Natalie. Of course I was already a baby when that picture was taken, but it's the only picture of Mother where I can imagine a baby me inside her.

After that, papa went over to England to wait for his turn to fight the Bosch. Mother says papa and Uncle Joe waltzed around England having a big fling with English girls when other men were busy shooting Germans. Uncle Joe married an English girl over in England. They had a baby when I was two. Nobody here except papa has ever met them. Uncle Joe's wife died when a bomb fell on their house. Uncle Joe sailed off to Italy to die in in the mud with papa holding his poor broken head in his lap.

Nobody knew about Uncle Joe's wife until papa finally came home from the war. Uncle Joe's sister-in-law took the baby, and papa sends them money and a package every month. Papa has a photograph of Uncle Joe's daughter at the farmhouse. She was born in November and her name is Alexandra. She'll be ten this year. She wears a uniform for school, and she looks small, skinny and serious in the photograph.

Last year Papa let me put things into her birthday box. I put in pencil crayons, because papa says she likes to draw and paint, and I put View-Master reels in an envelope, because papa sent her a View-Master the Christmas before. I would like to write to her, but papa says that's not a good idea. He won't say why. Nana says he has his reasons.

Mother doesn't like anyone talking about Uncle Joe's English family. She says it was shameful the way English girls threw themselves at Canadian boys like they had no men of their own. She says the least Uncle Joe could have done was to send home a wedding photograph. Of course, she says, that's what you get for marrying low. When you marry English you might as well marry high, is the way she looks at it. Even during the war, high English people had wedding photographs taken. Mother sets a great store by high people and photographs of them.

Nana has one picture of papa, Uncle Joe and Uncle Joe's English wife. She wasn't as pretty as Mother, but in the photo she looks friendly and kind. She's standing between the two brothers, both of them in their soldier uniforms with their arms around her.

Anyway, I'm guessing there are no baby shower photographs of Alexandra either, because of everyone being poor in England during the war. Papa says people had to pick rose hips in all the hedgerows to make jam and tea for vitamins, because there was no fruit for years and years, and no sugar either, and no milk except for sick babies. Alexandra had to live in a cellar when she was a baby because of the bombs.

I don't know if there'll still be baby showers in the future where you are, Historians, but I know there will still be babies. In this 1943 magazine it recommends invitations for baby showers be made of paper shaped like diapers and held together with small safety pins. The napkins should be folded to look like diapers and pinned together too. The gifts are supposed to be wrapped in diapers. They make peanut shell storks with paper beaks and cotton swab legs to put beside each plate. All the guests are supposed to bring a baby picture of themselves and the one who can guess the most baby pictures wins war stamps for a prize. I don't know what they give at baby showers for prizes today.

I don't think mentioning diapers is a good idea at a baby shower. Mother didn't want a baby shower before she had me. She had two babies finished with diapers, and had grown to loathe all the changing and washing of them. Grandma Walters said that is part of the reason Mother had a nervous breakdown after she had me. It was because of too many diapers and no hired girl to wash them. She didn't have money for a hired girl to help her, and that made her nervous enough to be sick.

She did get a hired girl after she came home from the hospital. She had to give up going to the hot springs with Aunt Edie, so she could afford it. She also had to cut back her shopping trips to Edmonton.

I won't ever have a baby. Mother told Mrs. Kipp that I won't be allowed to marry.   And Mrs. Kipp said, "Of course not," like there was a law against it.

Jeannie says nobody will marry me because of my foot, but Laura disagrees. She says not every person is a snob like Jeannie. Besides, when she's a doctor she'll find a way to fix my foot. Jeannie says that's not possible. She says I better not have babies, because I'll have babies with wrecked feet. I don't think that's true. Laura says it isn't.

Beanie doesn't mind about my foot, but he's not someone to marry. Russell doesn't mind about my foot, but he is a Mongoloid idiot, and because of that he won't be allowed to marry either. Jeannie's boyfriend Roger doesn't seem to notice my foot, but he's a person who will marry someone pretty. Dominic's not put off by my foot, or maybe he's just polite. I don't know what girl he'll marry, but it won't be a person like me.

Dark of night, May 10, 1953

Dear Diary,

Oh, Dear Diary, I've gone and done it. It was because of the baby shower that I looked through Granddad Smythe's spyglass tonight. What am I going to do?

I can't believe what I saw.

I can't believe it.

This is more awful than awful.

I don't want to write it down.

This time I did tell Granddad. Right out loud, I told him. And I wished he was in his real body and here to help me. He tried to calm me down like always, but this time it didn't work.

I saw Fat Freddy steal jewelry from Mrs. Masters' jewelry case right up in her bedroom. Right off her high dresser. Right in the middle of the baby shower. What a thing. What a thing. There's not one person who would believe me. Not one person. Never. Not even Nana, I don't think. This is a serious secret. Playing with his willie is one thing, but stealing! Yikes! He's the Mayor of Deep Creek. He can't be a burglar!

I was up here in Granddad's old armchair, as usual. I had made a cup of cocoa, and set up the spyglass. Mother went to the baby shower at young Mrs. Masters' tonight, and I was curious to see what they were doing. I haven't looked in that window since Mrs. Masters got cut, but I didn't think Dr. Masters would be mean to her in the middle of a baby shower, so I was safe from seeing that.

I counted sixteen women going in, including Granny Barclay, who brought Mary along to help with the lunch. Mary's hired girl time is supposed to be finished after supper. That's when she likes to read, but Granny Barclay always takes her around the neighbourhood to help when she goes to visit. Nobody ever pays Mary for her work. Nana complains to Granny about it, but it doesn't do any good. Sixteen is a lot of guests for a newcomer, but Mrs. Masters is a doctor's wife. I suppose everyone wants to make a good impression.

Anyway, they put a silly hat on young Mrs. Masters, and she opened gifts. Mother sat beside her, writing down what everyone brought. There was orange juice in a pitcher beside her and three bottles of gin on the table, so Mother wasn't short on medicine. It was boring. If I hadn't been so comfortable I would have gone to read more magazines. Granddad's big chair does that. Lulls a person.

I was drifting off when the porch light went on at the Masters', and my eye had to find the spyglass again. There was Fat Freddy at the door. Men don't go to baby showers, not even the husband of the baby shower lady, but Fat Freddy doesn't want his little mouse of a wife to have one minute of fun (that's what Crazy Marion says). He probably came to fetch her home.

The shower had come to the food part. I bet it was Mother who sat Fat Freddy down in the kitchen with a cup of coffee to wait till after the lunch. She doesn't take kindly to interruptions. After a moment, he went upstairs – I didn't see him go, but I saw a light go on up in the Masters' bedroom, so I moved my spyglass up a notch. I knew it was a bedroom, because they have the biggest bed I've ever seen, and nice pictures on the wall. I was surprised to see Freddy in there. I knew he was up to no good. Slowly he walked across the floor. He lifted the lid on the jewelry box on top of the dresser, took long necklace things and put them into the inside pocket of his suit jacket. He opened drawers and pulled out silky little wads that he put into his pants pocket. It looked like lady's underwear. I don't think it was handkerchiefs. Why would he want lady's underwear?

After the shower, when Mrs. Masters put her brooch away, she discovered her jewelry missing. She was frantic.

Oh, this is awful. And there is no one to tell. Why did he do it? He's got more money than anybody in Deep Creek. He doesn't need to steal. Crazy Marion says he's pretty close to owning the whole town. And he's the mayor! Mayors don't steal. I don't know what you think of this way up there in the future. I wouldn't have believed it either, but I saw it with my own eyes.

After breakfast, May 11, 1953

Oh, Dear Diary, today is my birthday and there were presents by my plate at breakfast, but nobody was much interested in them. The robbery was the only thing on everyone's mind this morning. And on top of it all, Mother says Mary took the jewelry.

I breathed in milk, and had a coughing fit right there at the table. I blew milk snot over everything. Mother left the table in a huff when Nana told her to stop foolish talk. She came back to have another cup of coffee after Nana went to plant more garden. I should have left the table too, but I wanted to hear what Mother had to say.

Mother says Constable Kipp will arrest Mary and send her away to the place in Red Deer where Uncle Edwin works. The place for mental defectives. Mother says half-blind Wasy and Russell should be sent there too, and that stumble-dumb Kokum that Crazy Marion is so cozy with.

Beanie says once a person goes there they never come out. Russell's mother is old, and Nana says she worries about what will happen to Russell when his mother dies. She doesn't want him to have to go to the defective place. Russell's brother, Richard, went missing in the war. Russell's mother thinks he'll find his way home one day and look after Russell, but Nana says missing that long usually means dead.

When Russell's mother finally dies, Mother says Uncle Edwin's institution in Red Deer is the only place that will take a person like him.

Beanie says Russell can come and live with him, but Mother says Beanie's Aunt would faint dead away at the thought of it. I don't think that's true. Beanie's Aunt Dorothy is kind. She's the only one besides Nana who invites Russell into the house for cookies. She lets Russell push her lawn mower and he does a fine job of it.

Anyway, that place in Red Deer is worse than a jail. Mary would shrivel up and die if they put her there. I'm the only one who knows Mary didn't do it. I'm trying to think how to tell Nana. She'll know what to do. I have to save Mary from being sent away. But it's only my word, and I'm a kid. The word of a kid, even if Nana believed me, isn't much use to anybody against a mayor.

It is still May 11, 1953

Dear Diary,

I buzzed around downstairs all morning, doing extra schoolwork, hoping to catch Nana alone at the same moment when I knew what to say to her. The moment never came. Beanie came over at lunch with a birthday present for me. A pair of bobby socks. He used up his pop bottle money to buy them, so he didn't have money for wrapping paper. He rolled them up and put them into his lunch bag. The socks smell like peanut butter, but I don't think my feet will mind.

When he went back to school, I retreated to my spot under the maidenhair fern table. Good thing, too. Mother is insulted about the theft. She and Nana had a royal argument over it. Mother paced back and forth in hall outside the sun porch, smoking her long, elegant cigarette while Nana sat in her wicker chair by the screen door with her hands folded in her lap.

"Of course it was that Ukrainian girl." Mother stretched out *Uke-ah-rain-ee-an*, pronouncing each part of the word the way she does when she disapproves.

Nana made her worst frowning face. "That is absurd. Mary wouldn't steal a crumb of bread."

Nana doesn't approve of jumping to conclusions without considering all sides. Nana is famous for considering all sides. That's what makes Papa a pantywaist, Mother says. He's had the example of so much considering that he can't pick a side to settle on. Nana says she raised all her boys to consider every side of an equation.

Mother was in a rare mood when she argued with Nana today.

"This is one time where going on and on at me isn't going to make a difference, Marjorie. Those foreigners are sneaky. That girl can barely speak English, you know, and what she does know is a grammatical nightmare. She has had the benefit of good schooling too. She's been as far as grade seven, and with those people that is a major miracle. Little Tally has a vocabulary that outstrips hers by a mile."

Nana smiled and winked at me where I was folded up, sitting quietly.

"Our Natalie, my dear Lillian, is no longer all that little. She has been reading like a professor since before she was five and, may I remind you, she has had all the time in the world to do it. Young Mary Tarazenko has had to work like a farm hand since she was five, and you're right - considering that, it's a major miracle that she reads at all. But..."

That's when Nana reached into the magazine basket for a National Geographic. I knew she was riled. Nana says turning pages when she is angry helps keep her wits about her. Nana gave Mother such a glare. If I received that look I'd feel like she'd run me through with a sword.

"... Mary's lack of grammatical finesse isn't lack of intelligence; it's lack of opportunity for practice."

Mother stood in the doorway and blew a long stream of smoke. "Oh, for heaven's sake, Marjorie. I don't know why you defend those people. I think you do it to be perverse, and because you know that it annoys me."

Nana slowly turned the pages of the magazine. "I'd like to think that I do it to be just. And how often have I been right?"

Mother tossed her lovely hair like a movie star. "I suppose you're referring to Eddy Cutknife. I don't apologize for thinking the man was drunk. Those people are always drunk, and one old Indian in a diabetic coma doesn't absolve them all."

Then Nana said a strange thing. She leaned forward in her chair. "Lillian. Think carefully about everything that happened at the shower, before you start accusing people."

Mother's face turned red. "I don't know what you mean."

Nana sighed. "I think you do."

Mother threw her half smoked cigarette on the floor, and turned with a flourish on her heel. I like watching her in action. If I had my wish, I'd grow up to look like Mother and to think like Nana.

Nana is the good queen and Mother is the beautiful, willful princess. I'm sorry Mother's wrong again. But she gets to feel right until I can figure out what to do about telling. I want to tell Nana, but even if she did believe me, what could she do without proof? There's got to be proof for a thing like that, and Granddad agrees. Also, she would take away the spyglass for sure.

I explained my dilemma to the Dead Uncles. Uncle Wilton always sides with me. I never hear his voice, but I can feel him nodding. Uncle Pete never agrees with anything at first. His voice in my head told me to just spit it out. Tell Nana and the police. Uncle Joe reminded him that Deep Creek doesn't have real police. In the end, all the uncles agreed I need to find proof.

Early morning, May 12, 1953

Dear Diary,

I didn't sleep much last night. My brain burned like a box of lit matches with all my thinking. I have to find where Freddy put the jewelry. He has more money than God, Crazy Marion says, so I don't think he sold it. Besides who would he sell it to? Mother says the ruby bracelet is priceless. It belonged to Mrs. Masters' grandmother and the rubies are set in real gold. Old gold, Mother says, which is more valuable than new gold.

Nana says not to worry. Nobody can put Mary in jail or send her to Red Deer without proof that she stole the jewelry, but I'm not sure about that. Freddy has the jewelry. I think he'll find a way to make it look like Mary stole it. He'd do that. He would. Maybe hide some in her bedroom in Granny Barclay's shed.

I've thought through this awful business twelve ways past Sunday, and it's clear Nana might believe me without proof, but what could she do about it? I sat outside in the garden half the night beside the Dead Uncles and didn't get one inspiration.

Granny Barclay was in hysterics today, ready to drag Mary over to the jailhouse herself. That's the reason I'm up early. Granny phoned Nana before breakfast, and Nana had to go and calm her down. I heard Nana's car drive away and it woke me up. I went down to have toast until she got back.

Nana tried to persuade Mary to come away from that place, but Mary says she can't. She promised her father she'd never cause the family shame. Nana explained that being accused of something you didn't do isn't shameful, but Mary doesn't understand. She says being accused is shameful and quitting would make it a double shame.

May 14, 1953

Oh Dear Diary,

I've watched Fat Freddy's place for two days without seeing anything. I don't know what I hope to see. Maybe I hope he'll bury everything in his back yard or take it to his outhouse shed while I'm watching. I'm so stupid. I have to quit waiting for miracles. I've got to go down there. Sneak out and snoop in his garage and his outhouse shed. I don't think he'd hide things like that in his house.

I've talked it over with Granddad, and he agrees. Nana says Granddad was a true adventurer, quick to take action. I'll pretend he's with me. That will give me courage. Fat Freddy's not a person you want to get up close to. Of course, I'll go late at night when he's sleeping. I don't know what I'm fussed up about. I'm such a pansy. I don't know how I'll ever be brave enough to get into the paper.

May 14, very much night

Dear Diary,

You'll never guess what happened. Granny Barclay kicked Mary out. Her suitcase and everything on the sidewalk. At night!

It was because Constable Kipp came to Granny's three times today asking Mary questions about the jewelry, and searching her little room. Making Mary cry. Mary told him she didn't take anything. She told him she would never steal. He doesn't believe her, and Granny is worried people will accuse her of harbouring a thief if she keeps Mary on.

This is the stupidest, stupidest mess.

At first it seemed Nana and I were the only people believing Mary's not a thief. But, I am happy to tell you, Dear Diary, that papa believes it too. I thought he might. He argued with Mother over it. He's not an arguing man, but he knows the Tarazenkos. He knows firsthand they're good people.

Can you believe Mrs. Morrill thinks Mary did it? She loaned her books, and gave her hand-me-downs and handkerchiefs. Nana says Mrs. Morrill should be ashamed of herself. A teacher should know the character of her students, and I agree. But Nana's the most upset with Reverend Sykes. He's the United Church minister, and although Nana is Anglican, she's held Reverend Sykes in the highest regard. She's dropped him to a lower regard now.

He made a sermon on Tuesday at the Ladies' Aid meeting about stealing and about God-less immigrants. Nana didn't hear it, but Grandma Walters heard it and told Mother who was in quite a state by the time she got home. Mother told us about the ignorance of peasant people, and how we have to treat them with Christian charity, but we don't have to trust them.

It happened at supper as Nana leaned forward to sip her tea. That's when Mother started talking. Nana set her cup back in the saucer slowly and folded her hands in her lap. I knew she was readying herself. Nana is wonderful to behold when she readies herself. I put my fork down and waited. I felt sorry for Mother who was about to get her comeuppance, but I was eager to hear what Nana wanted to say.

Mother didn't notice the change in Nana. She never does. She reached her elegant hand across the table for a fresh dinner roll. She looked at Nana through her eyelashes while she spread butter.

"It's a peasant's way, Marjorie. Over in Russia it was natural to steal from their masters, but it's time those people learned they aren't in Russia anymore. We don't tolerate theft here."

Nana's voice was quiet. "Lillian. I would be careful about pointing fingers if I were you."

Mother flipped her hair, turned her head and looked out the window.

Nana picked up her tea cup. "The Tarazenkos are from the Kiev region. They are Ukrainian, not Russian."

"Don't nitpick, Marjorie." Mother dropped two sugar lumps into her tea. "Russia, Poland, Kiev, what does it matter? They're all the same. Beasts of burden. They've been bred that way for centuries. I don't know why we bother trying to educate them."

Papa looked up from his Yorkshire pudding. "Lillian." His voice trembled.

Mother swung around to look at him, with her angry eyes. "George. Don't start. There's nothing here that touches *your* life."

"Injustice touches everyone's life." His voice was quiet, but strong. For a moment he sounded like Nana.

I wanted to smile and encourage him, but for once I knew better than to interrupt. I made a trench in my mashed potatoes for the beef dripping to run through. I stared at it to keep my tongue quiet.

"Injustice?" I peeked at Mother. She looked up at the ceiling. "What do you know of injustice, George? You spend your time at that god-forsaken farm walking around in the muck with peasants. You're starting to think like them." Mother pointed her butter knife at Papa. "The injustice, my dear George, is that after everything we have done for those people, they pay us back by robbing us blind right under our noses, and they get away with it."

I looked at papa and I saw him take a deep breath. I thought for a moment he might yell. I've never heard him yell, and I wasn't sure how to get ready for it. But he didn't yell. He pressed his fingers tight against his temples for a moment.

He said, "I am sorry you feel that way Lillian, and I'm sorry there's nothing I can say that will change your mind." He gripped the table with both hands and sat up straight. "I know the Tarazenkos. They're proud. They're trustworthy. Not one of them would steal a kernel of wheat even if they were starving, and believe me, they have been close to that many times."

I wanted to leap up and fling my arms around papa's neck. Tears made my eyes blurry. I had to take a long drink of milk, tipping my head up, making the tears run back where they belong.

I glanced at Nana. She was trying not to smile. She pushed her napkin tight against her mouth, and I knew she wasn't wiping away

UNDER THE MAIDENHAIR · 75

food. Mother jabbed at a piece of roast beef with her fork. "That girl's not starving. Granny Barclay treats her like one of her own daughters."

Nana finally sipped her tea. She held her cup between her hands and rested on her elbows. I relaxed. Nana doesn't raise her voice when she holds her teacup with two hands.

Both Nanas' eyebrows rose up into her hair. "Like a daughter, Lillian? I was not aware that any of Mewsetta's daughters had to sleep in a coal shed and split their own firewood to keep it warm in winter."

Granny Barclay has a first name! Can you believe it? Mewsetta. I've never heard such a name. Nana told me later that Granny Barclay's mother was a hopeless romantic who invented sweet names for all her children.

Mother rubbed her forehead. "Oh, stop, Marjorie. Those people are used to living like that. And it isn't a coal shed any more. Granny Barclay had it cleaned and whitewashed inside. She put a cot in there and proper bedding, far superior to what she has at home, I'm sure."

Nana looked like she was going to answer back, but Papa cleared his throat, and Nana sat back sipping her tea.
"Lillian, when Mary is at home with her family she has a bed fit for a queen. A more comfortable place to sleep than you can imagine. She has a deep feather bed in a warm corner behind the stuccoed oven."

Mother flicked her hair away from her face. "Stuccoed? Oh George, you do like to romanticize their pitiful lives don't you? I know what they plaster everything with. Manure, George, manure. They plaster with manure. That's hardly stucco."

Papa looked down at his plate.

I've never seen papa angry. I clamped my teeth tight to be ready to endure him yelling. He didn't yell.

He shook his head slowly. I hardly heard his voice. "There has been no evidence against Mary and until there is, I won't tolerate accusation against her in this house." He dropped his fork on his plate.

It clanged like a school bell. His voice rose up and flung itself across the table landing right on Mother. "Do you understand?"

Mother stared at him. Her face got red. She stood up, threw her napkin on the chair and stormed out.

Papa said no more.

Jeannie mumbled, "May I be excused?" Her voice was so low you had to guess what she said. Her napkin fell to the floor when she left, and Nana didn't ask her to return to pick it up.

Laura frowned at her plate. She hates when people argue. Nana squeezed her hand and told her she was excused to do her homework. She went to Linda's.

Beanie was first to discover that Mary had been kicked out. He and Russell found pop bottles by the creek after school, but Beanie didn't have a chance to gather them up until after supper. He had to run clear across town to Henry Wong's confectionery to trade them in for candy before Henry closed up at nine. When he came out with his candy he saw Mary sitting on the green bench beside the Dominion Bank with her suitcase beside her. She was crying like a baby.

Beanie tried to give her candy. That's the way he is. He pretends he doesn't care about anything, but he's the first one to help, even at school. I like that about him. Anyway, Mary didn't want candy, and she wouldn't stop crying. Beanie rode his bike up the hill to get me. I sat behind him, hanging on to his sweater like a bur.

I sat on one side of Mary. Beanie sat on the other. Beanie's dog Stella put her big head in Mary's lap. We huddled there while Mary heaved with sobs. Finally, Mary wiped her nose on the hem of her dress, and rubbed the tears off her face with her sleeve.

There's no telephone at Uncle Metro's. She thought she had to walk all the way home in the dark night in her disgrace. In the night, if you can imagine! I wanted to tell her that I knew she didn't do it, but I swung my feet fast under the bench, because I worried the whole story would then come gushing out. Beanie opened her hand to give her a big jawbreaker and candy corn.

"Mary, I know you didn't steal nothin' from nobody. I know you didn't do it. And Aunt Dorothy says it too." He sat up straight on the bench, put his hand to his chest, leaned his head back and spoke in his aunt's voice.

"She a fine gel, young Mary is. I'd give her my own silver to take home to clean, and not be worryin'."

That made Mary smile but it made me mad. I should have been the first to say she didn't do it. Beanie gave her candy. His favourite candy. Beany usually isn't one to share. I didn't have anything to give her and my telling was spoiled by saying it in a rush. I told her I knew she didn't do it. I told her papa and Nana knew it too. I nearly had to bite my tongue in half, to stop from blurting more than that. I hate that about myself. Once a few words leak out, other words I want to hold back try to follow. It's a curse. I know I shouldn't be mad at Beanie, but sometimes I can't help it. Mary got cheered up, put the jawbreaker in her pocket and ate the candy corn.

I told her papa's going to the farm tomorrow or maybe Saturday. She could sleep at our house until then. That made her cry again. She's scared of Mother. I don't blame her. I left her there with Beanie while I rode his bike up the hill to get Nana. Nana, of course, knew what to do. She came down with her car, and she moved Mary into her own rooms. I wanted Mary to sleep with me upstairs, but she doesn't like it up there.

There's a davenport bed in Nana's sitting room where her sister sleeps when she visits. It's perfect for Mary, and Nana has her own bathroom where Mary can wash up without bumping into Mother. I brought soup, hot milk and cinnamon buns from the kitchen. We sat there, the three of us, all cozy together.

Mary didn't want to wear her own nightdress in front of us. She says it needs patching. Nana smiled and said that some of hers need patching too. She made Mary wear one of her new nightdresses. She said it needs breaking in. I told Mary I often help Nana break in her nightdresses.

Nana's flannel nightdress covered Mary like a revival tent. She wrapped her arms around herself and burrowed down into it.

I asked Mary if it was warm sleeping in the coal shed.

"Yes. Nice warm. In winter I wear my brother wool underdrawer before my nightdress. I have good wool stocking for the bed and wool head scarf."

Nana asked if she had a hot water bottle.

Mary shrugged. "No, nothing for hot water, but Granny allows rocks in the oven. I wrap in a gunny sack and it makes my bed warm. It is good when there comes snow. I make big pile around my little house and the wind can't come in to find me."

Tears ran down her cheeks. She likes her little house. She made curtains from sugar sacks and embroidered beautifully on them. She put pictures from calendars on the walls.

And can you imagine this, Historians? She showed us things she wove from wheat straw. It's hard to believe such a thing can be done. She made a holder for her brush and comb that hangs on the wall. The straws are pressed flat and are all woven together in the most cunning way and she wove a beautiful cylinder that surrounds a tin can for putting flowers in.

She got happy again when we ooo-ed and aah-ed over them. Nana will pay her to make dozens of them for Christmas gifts. Mary was amazed by that. She doesn't seem to know how lovely her straw things are.

"Mrs. Smythe, I can also for you make…" She stopped and frowned. She couldn't think of the word. I get that way. A perfectly good word that I've always known flies from my head when I want it. It doesn't return till I don't need it anymore. Words can be contrary that way.

Anyway, she made a frame in the air with her hands and pointed to a frame around a picture of Granddad Smythe. "Like this. For around picture." She blushed and sat down. "No, you wouldn't want it. It is not nice like these." She waved at all the photographs on

Nana's wall. Nana has more pictures on her walls than most people, because she's clever with her camera. She likes her photographs up where she can see them. Grandma Walters thinks it makes a big clutter all over the wall, but I think if she really looked at them she would change her mind.

Nana has a photograph on her wall of Grandma Walters wading in the lake when she was a young woman, lifting her skirt up so dainty, her hair hanging down. Grandma Walters hates that picture. I can't figure why. Anyway, Nana laughed and squeezed Mary's hands and told her that she would be delighted to have woven straw frames for her photographs.

Papa is going to take Mary home tomorrow, and Nana will find another place for her to work. If she doesn't get job in town she'll have to find work in Vermilion, and then I'll never see her. I won't see her if she goes to the Red Deer Provincial Training School for Mental Defectives, either. That's its whole name. Provincial Training School for Mental Defectives. I don't understand why they would send Mary to such a place. There's not one part of Mary that's defective.

Mother says stealing is a big clue that a person is defective. When people steal, especially young girls, it's proof of a mental defect lurking inside waiting to make her a danger to herself and society. Defects lurk along with germs, I guess. Also Mother says that young girls who steal will soon be promiscuous and have illegitimate babies they won't be able to feed.

Nana says that's ridiculous. She was happy to spell promiscuous for me. I looked it up. It says - *involving indiscriminate mingling, not restricted to one sexual partner.* For Pete sake. Mary doesn't mingle. She doesn't even have a boyfriend.

I asked Nana if they'd do it. Send Mary to the defective school. Nana sighed deeply, took off her glasses and pinched the bridge of her nose. "Oh, Chickadee, I wish I could tell you that such a thing is as impossible as it's ridiculous, but in complete honesty, I cannot. Human beings can think of many ways to bring injustice down upon each other, and that idiotic school is one of them."

Now, I'm scared. Nana will try hard to stop anyone from sending Mary there. Papa will too, but Mother will work against them, and so will Aunt Edie and Uncle Edwin once they get wind of it. Mother has probably already given them wind of it.

I should be down there snooping at Fat Freddy's place, but it's late and I've taken too long to write this. I thought recording for you Historians would be a cinch. It's not. It's hard to write it all down when a person has to be busy watching. I guess I won't be sneaking out tonight. Maybe tomorrow.

All the lights in his house are out now. Everybody's lights are out. And here am I, not sleepy. I guess I'll start in on a stack of Nana's Reader's Digests. *Reader's Digest* is a United States magazine, but it says right at the top - printed in Canada. There's not a lot of information about everyday life in the Reader's Digest. Mostly articles about brave people and banks and other countries and what's wrong with the world. I'm going to read the most boring one to put me to sleep. Good Night!

Oh, Dear Diary,

I thought I was done writing tonight, but I read an awful story. It's in September 1945 *Reader's Digest*. I was four then and papa was still in the hospital in England.

The article is about DPs. Displaced Persons. All those people, chased away from their towns and their homes by the Nazis and the war, and for such a long time they didn't know how to find their way back. The roads were blown up and the bridges too. Everything mud and slop and stink. Where did they sleep in the war? What did they eat? I don't know. In this article the people get to walk across a bridge to freedom. That's what it says. It also says that young people are like old people, skinny from having no food. They can't stand up straight, rags instead of clothes, no baths - for how long? - weeks? Years even? It was nearly eight years ago when they walked across that bridge. If they were young people like fifteen or sixteen, they would be twenty-three or twenty-four. Did they live? Might they be dead now? It's bad enough for soldiers to be dead, but regular people too.

I would like to write the whole thing down here. The whole article. But it would take too long. There is one part you have to read. One part. When papa says "the stink of war" he gets such a look on his face, and that word, *stink*, hisses and spits out of his mouth. Now I have an idea why.

"The stench is appalling. Heavy on the hot air, it fills our throats, sinks into our clothes, the same awful smell that hangs like a plague around every prison camp. They stand or lie, human cattle in stinking rags, these who had been the decent men and women of France."

The picture that draws itself in my mind is too awful. On the map of Europe there are many more countries besides France, and all of them full of broken people with wrecked houses and stores burned down to the ground and roads full of deep holes made by bombs. And no spring smells and no summer smells and the birds all gone. A person could die from that.

Papa was in the middle of the smoke and the fire that caused all that. He walked for days over rocks and rubble and through the mud, soggy and wet, breathing in that stink. And I thought stink was just another word. Funny how words are. You think you know a word, but you don't know it until you climb into it, and close the door behind you.

Stink. The article pushed me inside that word. Shoved me there. Dirty body smells. Pee smells. Old pee. And poop and vomit and infections like boils. Pus. Dead-gopher-puffed-up-in-the-sun smells. Dead mouse, dead and rotting behind the cupboard smells. Dead smells everywhere. On you. In your hair. Stuck to your skin. You can't get away from it. No water to wash with. Not even if you go to the next town. And the smoke from burnt things on top of every-thing. In your eyes and down your throat and everything around you dirty. And nothing around you living, except worms and flies and vermin. I'm not sure what vermin is, and I'm too tired to look it up, but I guess vermin must be slimy creatures that live where things are rotting.

Now I know why papa doesn't want to tell people about the stinking war. Who would believe it? Who would want to hear about it? I bet Mother didn't read this article. I bet Nana did. Oh, Dear Diary. I'm lucky to live here in a safe place. No wonder Uncle Joe's Alexandra seems serious in her photographs. I want to bring her here to live with me, here where the smells are good and there's lots of food. I feel terrible. I can't even cry.

Now I can't go to bed until I find a happier story. I'll never go to sleep with a long line of suffering people walking through my mind, the stink of war wrapped like a rope around them.

I found it. November 1945, *Reader's Digest*. I read the whole thing to Granddad. He liked it every bit as much as I did. It pushed the stink away.

"My Ninety Acres" is fine writing about a man and his wife who make a farm together. It's from a book called *Pleasant Valley*. After the wife dies, the man thinks about her all his life and is gentle with his farm like he was with her. I think that's how papa would like it to be on the farm for him and for Mother. I can see papa thinking that way. I can see Mother not knowing how to understand him.

May 15, 1953, early morning.

All that reading about war, Dear Diary, got me thinking about papa. Got me remembering when papa came home. The Bosch took him prisoner in France after he sneaked into another battle after Uncle Joe died. Before he got rescued from prisoner-of-war camp he got tuberculosis, and had to stay in a hospital in England for a long time. Mother said he didn't want to come home. Nana said he was too weak to travel.

He was supposed to come home for Christmas in 1947, but he surprised us and came earlier. Nana got the telephone call. Mother had gone to Edmonton with Jeannie and Laura to get dresses and shoes for the Christmas pageant, so they would be the most beautiful angels. She left me at Nana's. When I heard my papa was on the train, I got so excited I nearly threw up. I had dreamed and dreamed of the time my papa would come home.

We saw him standing on the train platform when we stepped off the sidewalk that goes past Deep Creek Hotel. Tall and so thin. Nana gripped my hand tight. When we got to papa, Nana flung her arms around him and burst into tears. He rocked her back and forth like a baby. They forgot all about me at first, but I was used to that.

Then Nana turned around and lifted me up, even though I was too big to be carried. "This is your Natalie."

Papa stared at me. I stared back at him. All I remember now are his eyes. Big and dark and full of tears. Then he smiled. Just a little smile like his face was sore, and he put his hand against my cheek.

"Natalie." He whispered my name, gruff and deep. "Natalie."

"Are you my papa?" I knew he was, but I had to ask. I wanted to hear him say yes. I put my hand on his rough, pale cheek. It felt cold.

He nodded his head, "I'm your papa."

Then he hugged me tight like I was a big doll. I liked it so much I didn't want him to ever put me down. I was too big to be lifted and hugged like that, but I didn't care. When he put me down, he let me hold his hand, and we walked all the way up the hill, Nana on one side with her arm through his, and me on the other with my hand lost inside his big one.

I don't remember ever being so happy. Papa said nothing about my limp, and although I did notice, I didn't say anything about his. We went to Nana's house, because Mother and my sisters would not be back for two days.

Papa had chocolate in his kit bag for us girls, and silk stockings for Mother, and rolled up inside one of his wool socks he had a painting of a river with a stone bridge across it. He painted it when he was in the hospital in England. He painted it for Nana, because it's close to where she grew up. She cried when she saw it.

Jeannie and Laura were not happy to see him. That surprised me. Nana says it was because they got used to not having him around. He was happy to see them, but Jeannie burst into tears and told him to go back to the stupid war. Laura, who always pretended to be so grown up, even back then, looked him up and down and told him he was too skinny to be her father.

I don't remember what Mother said.

After Christmas he had to go back to a hospital in Edmonton, because he got sick again. Nana and I went to visit him every week on the train, but Mother never came with us. I used to pretend she went by herself, but I know she didn't.

And now, Historians, the misunderstandings in this house are going to get worse. Mother brought up the idea of television with Nana again, and I know she'll bring it up with papa soon. Aunt Edie's sister-in-law in Seattle has a television set, and as soon as they can get better reception, Aunt Edie and Uncle Edwin in Red Deer will have one too. They put a big antenna up against their house in Red Deer. Mother says it reaches higher than the chimney.

Television, Historians, is a small movie screen where you can see the news and musical concerts and variety shows right in your house. I wonder if you'll still have them up there in the future. Mother says television will put the movie theatres out of business, but progress is progress and nobody can stop it.

Nana isn't interested in television. If she wants to go to a movie, she'll go. If she wants news she'll listen to the radio or read the paper. Her life's too busy for idleness. With a radio, a person can walk around doing things, and still listen. With a television, a person has to sit in one place and not move. I don't think television will be popular. People will get sore bottoms from so much sitting. No work will get done. People will get fat, and everybody will be in a temper. Nana can bake and cook while she listens to the radio, but what would she do while watching television? I know papa won't want that interruption either. Mother likes to sit around. Maybe television will suit her. Maybe she can put one in her room. I think she's got herself into the wrong family by mistake. I don't know how things like that happen.

Nana's sister said it was Grandma Walters who insisted that Mother marry into this family, because she thought it was the best family in town. That was because Granddad and Nana came from England, not because she liked them. Grandma Walters has the idea that people from England are better people. Except for Crazy Marion. Crazy Marion came from England the same as Nana, but she doesn't believe one kind of people is any better than any other kind of people. She says thinking like that is what starts wars. She also says Mother didn't need Grandma egging her on to marry a Smythe. She says Mother had plenty of petty ambition of her own. That's the way Crazy Marion talks. She doesn't like Mother and Mother doesn't like her.

Mother says she wanted to go to University to study to be a Home Economics teacher, but she married papa instead. Crazy Marion says that's a naked lie. She says Mother didn't finish grade eleven. She wants to sound important, hoping people will believe that marrying papa wasn't her idea, since it didn't give her the life she planned. Crazy Marion says Mother's only ambition was to be the wife of the mayor of Deep Creek.

Nana says papa would have paid for Mother to go to school to be a Home Economics teacher if she wanted to. Maybe Grandma Walters told her not to. Grandma Walters says married women of means do not attend school like pathetic spinsters, and they certainly don't work out. She says working women lose their femininity, and their natural appeal to their husbands. When a woman works out, her sons become hoodlums and her daughters have illegitimate children.

Mother got in the family way with Jeannie, and that was the end of that. I'm sorry Mother didn't get to be a Home Economics teacher, if that's what she truly wished for. I think it would be easier for her to be happy if she had work she liked. She used to sew for herself and Jeannie and for Aunt Edie, but she doesn't do that anymore. And of course, there's the cooking. Home Economic teachers do have to cook. Mother doesn't like to cook. Now, she says she doesn't cook, because it's Nana's house and she doesn't like Nana's rules in the kitchen. She didn't cook much in our house either and in that house all the rules were hers.

Before supper May 15, 1953

Dear Diary,

I'm out of breath. I don't know how I can settle down to write, but I have to. If I don't write all of it down tonight, I won't remember it in good order. It's lucky I don't have to go to school anymore, because I have no time for school.

Papa didn't take Mary home today like he planned. Everything is changed. He's taking Mary home tomorrow. Guess what? She's coming right back to our house to stay. She's going to be our hired girl. Our own hired girl. Right here in Nana's house.

Mrs. O'Kane told Nana she's decided to marry Bachelor Harrison this summer. That means Nana needs another hired girl. That means we get Mary! Living right here with us where Nana can protect her from being sent to the defective place. Freddy can't frame her when she's safe in our house.

Until Mrs. O'Kane leaves, Mary will be her helper and learn all the things she has to know to be our hired girl. She'll sleep in Nana's room for now, and later she'll have Mrs. O'Kane's room off the kitchen. Mary is excited. She loves Mrs. O'Kane's kitchen bedroom. It isn't big, but it has a nice bed, a bed table with a lamp, a dresser, a closet, a sofa chair by the window and a writing table with shelves above it. Nana says Mary can arrange it however she likes.

Mary said she'll be like a queen in that room. I said she'll be more like an empress. When I said that I was thinking about the empress in Pearl S. Buck's books, and my picture of her is bright and colourful, dressed in reds and gold. The empress that Mary thinks of is more of a Czarina. That's the queen they had over in Russia, before the first Great War happened. Mary's picture of being an empress is full of ivory lace, long white stockings, white shoes, white gloves, big white hats with white ribbons and fancy teas every day.

Just goes to show, doesn't it, how many different pictures can be made from the same word? I love when that happens.

The kitchen room used to be Granddad Smythe's office where he did farm books and town work. After the first Great War, when he was mayor, there wasn't a town hall or a town secretary or anything. Nana says Granddad Smythe pretty much ran the town business from his house all by himself, with help from her and Crazy Marion, of course.

Mother is sizzling mad about Mary coming here. She flung her ashtray into the honeysuckle bush off the porch she was so riled. She thinks Nana is hiring Mary to spite her. Nana, of course, told Mother that hiring Mary has nothing to do with her; it has to do with justice, and with getting good help.

Mother says Nana uses justice to explain all the stupid things she does. She says harbouring a criminal is completely unexplainable. Mother says it's fine for Nana not to care what people think, but it's Mother who has to hold her head up in the community and pretend that her family is normal.

Nana told Mother that if she insisted on redefining what's normal every six months she'd have to live with it.

"Marjorie, you're an imperious old woman without a shred of decency. If George had any sense at all he'd have you committed."

After that, Mother went through the house slamming doors. Papa had just come in from the farm. I saw him scrunch his eyes like there was a pain in his head and he went right back out again. He'll probably drive down to the river and sit on the hill for a while. Nana says watching the big, old North Saskatchewan River moving slowly past calms him like few other things can. Mother took her gin and a can of orange juice to her room.

Mother and Grandma Walters have a different idea from Nana about how people should act in society. Nana says she left England to escape society nonsense, and she does not tolerate pretensions in this country.

Isn't that an odd thing, Dear Diary? Nana and Crazy Marion escaped England to get away from pretensions, and Mother and Grandma Walters would like to bring English pretensions here. I think we are all DPs. Every one of us lost and trying to find our right home. I wonder why Mother and Grandma don't escape to England where things are more suited to them. Nana says escaping to Canada was the smartest thing she and Crazy Marion ever did.

Mother and Jeannie are taking the train tomorrow to Edmonton. Jeannie has been begging to go shopping for weeks. Of course she'll miss school again. She always misses school. They want to buy Jeannie's and Mother's graduation ensembles. Mother says it isn't a moment too soon. It takes time to get everything right. Mother wants Laura to go too. She wants all the ensembles to match.

Laura suffers being in the same grade as Jeannie. Jeannie was supposed to graduate last year, but she was absent too many days and had to be held back. She's missed a lot of days this year too, but Laura helps her with her hand-ins now that they're in the same grade. Laura doesn't care about matching, and she detests trying on clothes.

Laura says she isn't going to miss school just to stand around watching Mother and Jeannie prance about in every outfit in the store.

Besides, she already bought material and a pattern. Nana and Mary are sewing her graduation dress.

Mother is steamed about that. She says Laura wants to ruin Jeannie's graduation by wearing an unsuitable dress that won't fit in the photographs. She says she won't tolerate Laura turning up in an unattractive housedress. Mother likes to exaggerate. Laura would never wear a housedress to graduation.

Believe me, Dear Diary, the pattern Laura chose is nothing like a housedress. It's wonderfully handsome. Mother thinks the material is too dark for a young woman, and too plain, but she's wrong about that.

I expect Mother and Jeannie will be gone for at least a week, so we'll have peace and quiet for a while.

Look at that. I thought I had a lot to write about and I'm done already. I should be getting more information from the magazines, but I don't have the patience for it right now. My mind is too busy with Mary's problem.

Evening, May 15, 1953

Dear Diary,

I've been watching Fat Freddy's without seeing a thing for so long that I nearly missed it tonight. I can't put off the snooping now. I don't want to do it. But I have to.

After supper while Mary helped Mrs. O'Kane with clean up, I peeked into Fat Freddy's windows. I watched them eat their supper. We always eat at five. They eat at six or later. Do you know they eat fried Klick? Nana says canned meat is for dogs and poor soldiers on the march, not for people with real food to choose from. Fat Freddy has lots of money, but Crazy Marion says he never spends a nickel where it doesn't show, and I guess what you have for supper doesn't usually show.

I saw Freddy bang his cup on the table. That made the hired girl jump up get the coffee pot. While she poured coffee for him, he put his hand up her blouse. It looked like he was laughing when he did it. Freddy's wife turned her head away from the table. I'm so embarrassed for Freddy's children. I could only see the backs of their heads. What a thing for them to see. What a thing for him to do. It gave me a bad feeling in my stomach. I made the spy glass search around for something else, then I saw Freddy's porch light go on.

I saw him come out of the house and go into the garage. I watched through the little side window as usual. It's not as easy to see into small windows when it isn't dark, but I was lucky, because the sun sits low after supper and shines right into the other side window and makes everything orange. I saw him open the passenger side of his car, and put wadded up cloth into the glove compartment.

It looked like underwear to me, but there might have been jewelry too. Maybe this is my miracle. It's not a good idea to jump to conclusions, so I'm going down there to investigate. I think after all this time it's probably a wild goose chase, but I'm driven to do it. It'll plague me to Hell and back until I do. I sure know how to get myself deep in the pickle juice.

Very late, May 15, 1953

Dear Diary,

I'm not a good spy. First of all, it took such a long time to get dark. Nearly nine o'clock these days. I'm surprised how slow time moves when a person wants it to go quickly. To pass the time I read to Granddad Smythe some of what I am saving to put down here for you Historians. He loved every word of it. Nana says he had the deepest, richest laugh, and today I heard it.

The first part of the spying was easy. All I had to do was go quietly down the back stairs into what used to be the coal shed before

Nana got natural gas piped in. Once down the stairs I crawled through the dead spot in the cotoneaster hedge, and that took me right under Beanie's bedroom window. He does love climbing out his window at night. At the last minute I decided to invite him on my spy mission.

I don't know why I wanted to take Beanie. I go out in the dark by myself all the time, but spying on Fat Freddy alone was too scary for me. Pretending Granddad with me wasn't enough; I needed a real person.

Of course, I had to tell Beanie the whole story. That Beanie. He has to know all the facts before he'll do anything. Usually I like that about him, but it wastes time. I didn't want to mention the spyglass, but I had to. Then Beanie made me rub dirt all over my clothes and my face. He wouldn't budge an inch until I did it. He wasn't satisfied until we used the good black dirt from the garden. He says that's what soldiers do on a spy mission, so no one can see them in the night. I guess it was a good idea, but I'm going to catch it from Mrs. O'Kane on washday. I'll have to think up a story to explain my grubby clothes.

We had to leave Stella behind because she likes to chase cats. That meant keeping her busy, so she wouldn't whine and howl and wake Beanie's aunt. More time wasted. Lucky for me Nana keeps raw hide strips in her garden shed to give to give to Stella for treats. We gave her two for good measure.

Walking in the shadows next to hedges, sheds and garages all the way to Freddy's house was easy. We pushed close against the big lilac bushes when we got near Fat Freddy's garage. I thought we'd dash into the garage quickly, see if the jewelry was in there, and get right back out, but when we got to the corner of the garage, we heard Freddy's back door slam. Freddy walked down the path.

Beanie rolled under the lilac bushes to stay out of sight. I hid behind the maple tree that grows up over the lilacs. It has a good, thick trunk.

Freddy came down the path to the burn barrel. He walked so close to me I nearly yelped. He held something over the trashcan, and

lit it with his lighter. Something soft and small like ladies' underthings. I thought for sure he'd see me when his lighter flamed, but he
stared hard at what burned in his hand. He dropped it into the burn
barrel, and stood like a statue watching it.

Beanie thought it was the underthings too. It blazed up and for
a second I saw Freddy's face. It was mean and scary. I breathed faster,
even though I tried not to. If he had listened, he would have heard me
breathing and my heart pounding loud. But all his attention was used
up with the burning. He didn't once turn his head toward the maple
where I crouched.

After the fire went out, he lifted his head and was still for a
moment. I don't know why he didn't feel us watching him. Then he
went to the garage. He stepped quietly through the side door and no
lights came on.

A heavy quiet pressed against me and all sound stopped. I
stretched my listening fiercely to hear through it. When I could hear
again, noises were muffled as if the town beyond us had rolled itself
up in cotton batting. A car door slammed way off on Main Street. A
dull, sleepy sound. Somebody over by the ball diamond yelled at a cat.
A low shout, hardly worth uttering. Mr. Jepson's cows called to calves
in the field across the railroad tracks with a mournful mooing.

It was strange. Like Beanie and I were the only people wide
awake in the world. The only ones who knew a bad thing was happening.

Except we couldn't yet prove it. That's why I had to creep
over to the garage window. Every step I took crunched underfoot. I
saw a glow in the window like from a candle. I'm too short to see in,
and Beanie is even shorter. I spied a wheelbarrow in the garden. I
pushed it over to the window to climb on. I motioned for Beanie to
come and help. He shook his head. I know he wanted to go home, but
I knew if I went home I'd never get the gumption to come back.

Finally Beanie crawled from under the lilacs, and held the
wheelbarrow while I climbed on it. Beanie is a chatterbox most times,

but tonight he didn't even whisper. When I inched my face over the windowsill I saw Fat Freddy sitting in the passenger seat of his car, the door open, looking down. The coal oil lamp on the workbench had a dirty chimney. The light flickered back and forth from bright to dim.

Fat Freddy put his head back against the seat and draped something over his face. At first I thought it was a handkerchief. He sat there, so still, his round head draped like furniture hidden for spring cleaning. I saw elastic and I knew that it was underdrawers. Ladies' underdrawers. Most likely the ones he took from young Mrs. Masters.

On his head? I don't know what to make of that. Underwear on his head, over his face? What a thing. I didn't tell Beanie. I won't be able to tell Granddad either. I stayed still a long time, until Beanie poked me.

"What? What d'you see?" He tried to whisper, but it sounded like a steam train hissing.

I whacked at his head to make him keep still. He whacked back. Fat Freddy pulled the underdrawers off, and looked at his watch, and then everything happened fast.

He shoved the drawers into the glove compartment, got out of the car, slammed the door shut and walked over to the lamp. His back was turned to me when I tried to hurry and get down from the wheelbarrow. Good thing, too, because I slipped and banged against the garage. I yelped before I stopped myself.

If anyone had been watching, they would have seen me run like the wind. I got around to the alley side of the lilacs before I heard the garage door shut. Beanie was right behind me. He can't run as fast as I can. I threw myself to the ground and rolled under the lilacs. I grabbed Beanie's ankle as he came close. He fell like a tree. I heard the wind whoosh out of him. I tugged hard on his foot.

"Come on. Quick. Get under here."

He moaned and wiggled towards me.

"Hurry."

"I...am."

"Hurry faster."

When he got close I grabbed his sweater and rolled him like a log. I wiggled back as far as I could go. I got leaves in my mouth and sharp sticks in my back, but I didn't care. Beanie was still breathing hard. I shushed him sharply. He gave a little squeak, but he did manage to quiet.

"Who's there?" Fat Freddy's voice sounded harsh and low. "Who is it?"

His feet crunched on the gravel. The sound came closer. I shut my eyes. I know that's silly, but I always feel safer with my eyes closed.

He stood in the alley not far from where we lay. I heard him breathing. Could he hear us? I thought for a moment he could, but he turned and walked back into his yard. I pushed Beanie into the alley and rolled out after him. He made little mewing sounds when I helped him to his feet. At first I thought he was hurt, but he was just scared. I grabbed his hand and pulled him through the darkness towards Main Street. I figured we'd better go the long way back.

I was wrong about Freddy giving up. He'd gone to get a flashlight. The light from it hitting the side of Middleton's garage caught my eye, and before I knew what I was doing I shoved Beanie in behind Vasyli Turk's woodpile, and pressed myself against the rough wood beside him. I bit my fingers hard to make myself stay quiet.

It's a tall woodpile with the wood all in straight, even rows. We stood up behind it. If Old Turk had looked out his window he might have seen us, but at that moment, riling him seemed better than getting caught by Freddy. Old Turk is the shoemaker, and he does as fine and careful a job as can be done on shoes and saddles Nana says, but with people he is rough.

The flashlight beam shone on the woodpile. I saw it between the log ends. I pressed my palm against Beanie's mouth and stared between the logs, willing Freddy to turn and go away. But he didn't.

He shone the light right into my eyes. I was too astonished to close them.

"Who's there?"

I thought our potatoes were baked. Suddenly Old Turk's big orange tom jumped down from the woodshed roof. It stood bent up and prickly as a Halloween cat, hissing at Freddy. He swore, picked up a handful of gravel, and threw it at the cat. As the little pebbles rained down on our heads, and the tom ran for the house, Freddy turned off the flashlight and grumbled as he disappeared down the alley to his place. "Goddamn cats. Someone should poison the lot of them."

I like a close call in the movies, but I can tell you, Dear Diary, it's not fun in real life. I had to crouch down after that, because my legs were soft as cooked noodles. I stayed down there so long my legs are still sore.

Beanie cried all the way home. He made me swear I wouldn't tell anyone he'd cried. I told him I wouldn't tell anyone about the crying if he didn't tell anyone about the spyglass. It's a good thing he cried. He can be a blabbermouth, and now that he knows about the spyglass, it'll be hard for him to keep quiet. I won't let him use it; that would be too much secret for him to keep, but I told him about it. I had to.

I don't know what to do now. Wake up Nana? Tell the police? We didn't see jewelry, just underdrawers. I guess I have to go right into the garage and see for sure. I don't know where I'll get the gumption for that. And it won't be tonight. I'm going to bed!

Late, May 16, 1953

Dear Diary,

Boy-oh-boy, when it's daylight it seems silly to be scared of Fat Freddy. And maybe now, with Mary living with us, everyone will quit trying to blame her for the theft.

I went along when papa took Mary home today. At first Auntie Olga and Uncle Metro were stern when they heard about the theft, but Papa amazed me. Maybe he's getting better from his shell shock. He stood beside Mary with his hand on her shoulder. He said straight-away that she had done nothing wrong. He spoke firmly to Uncle Metro about his belief in Mary's innocence. Papa took charge. He gave me a chance to speak up for her, too. Grown-ups don't usually give me a chance to give an opinion.

Dominic got steamed when he heard about people wanting to blame Mary. He paced.

"Those big shots always think we don't know how to behave. Always think we don't know what's right. We have no manners. We are animals. Like cows. Not worth training."

Papa paced with him.

"I know it's maddening, Dominic. But you'll have the last laugh. You already excel, ahead of any of the other children, including our Laura. There's no question. You'll have the best education in town."

Dominic stopped and stared for a moment at the floor. "Yes, I will. But we were talking about Mary. What about her? She is smart too."

Uncle Metro took in a quick breath, and he lifted his shoulders. He glanced at papa, then banged his fist on the table. "No more talk like that. No education for girl." He glanced at papa again, but papa had his head turned away. Papa believes in education for girls, so he won't agree with Uncle Metro, but it would be rude to say so in Uncle Metro's own house.

"She read everything. She write everything. What more she do at that school? Who want to marry girl with too much school?"

"Papa, the world is changing. She would be a good help to a husband if she has an education."

"She has education. Big education. Woman not need it."

"You are wrong." Dominic stood up straight, taller even, than Uncle Metro. I wonder when that happened?

An ugliness came over Uncle Metro's face. "What do you know about life?" He stepped closer to Dominic who did not step back. I held my breath. Uncle Metro got red in the face. I thought he might burst a blood vessel.

Uncle Metro grabbed Dominic by the shirt. "*Sheet* on it! Life? You know about life?" He shoved Dominic away. "You boy. You know nothing."

Baba swatted Uncle Metro with the broom. "*Svenya*! You *peeg*, Metro. Leave it the boy."

All that time Mary did not say a word, but while Baba diverted Uncle Metro she touched Dominic's arm. She whispered. "Don't stir up papa. It's better with me now, Dominic. I have good work with good people. They let me read. Every day."

Uncle Metro pushed Baba away, and tried to grab Mary. Dominic stepped in front of her. That got Uncle Metro riled.

"What you say? Secrets? You tell secrets in front of me?"

Dominic held up his palm. He tried to smile. "Papa. There are no secrets. Mary does not want me to fight with you. She tells me she is happy with her work."

"Metro." Baba stepped right up close to him. "Go out. Cut wood. You matchstick. Make *beeg* fire for nothing. Go. Get out."

He slammed his cup down on the table, spilling *kvass* all over the place. He stomped out, slamming the door. Auntie Olga quickly cleaned up the mess, brought papa more *kvass* and a plate of fresh cut bread.

Auntie Olga is shy, but she likes papa. "I sorry the Metro." Her voice is soft like a whisper. "He sometime mad."

Papa patted her hand. "I know. Don't worry. I know Metro."

Baba waved her dishtowel. "Oh, dat one. He make *beeg* noise, but his water not boil no more after he sweat with the wood."

She laughed and poked Auntie Olga who laughed behind her hand. Half-blind Wasy smiled like she always does. She doesn't know many words and all of them Ukrainian.

After Uncle Metro took his storm outside, everybody got calm again. We had a celebration. At least it felt like a celebration. Mary and I were allowed *kvass* too and Dominic sat with us at the table. Historians of the Future, you might not have *kvass* up where you are. Papa says not many women bother to make it anymore. It's like iced tea without so much sugar. A gooey creature like a vinegar mother, makes the *kvass* in little crocks in Baba's pantry. The mother sits on top of the juice like a cooked egg white, building itself up into layers. From time to time Baba peels off the old tired layers and feeds them to the chickens.

Vinegar mothers are delicate, silken threads, near the bottom of the vinegar jug, but the *kvass* mother is round, firm and solid, like Baba. The liquid it floats on is a mix of strong black tea, beet juice and a little bit of honey. There's alcohol in the *kvass,* which is why papa doesn't approve of me drinking it, but today we all had a cup. We toasted Mary for her new job, Dominic for getting the highest mark in math, Auntie Olga for her excellent bread, me for rescuing Mary, and Baba and half-blind Wasy for their delicious prune buns. It was like a party. No one mentioned Mary going to school, and Uncle Metro did not come back in.

After more *Kvass*, papa went off to do farm jobs with Uncle Metro, and Dominic played geography with Mary and me in the grass by the old well. I started with Afghanistan. Mary didn't get a point, because she couldn't name a country next to it. Dominic got the first two points by naming Iran and Pakistan. Then he picked a country, and so on. I'm good at geography, but Dominic is better. He won easily, but he doesn't gloat like Jeannie does when she wins at something.

Evening May 17, 1953

Dear Diary,

I think things have settled down. It's terrific having Mary here. I can hardly wait for Nana's feast. Tomorrow. It's her first summer feast. She's having it early, because she says we all need it.

Nana has a feast in her garden once a month right from the end of May to September, sometimes October if the weather holds. Nana and Crazy Marion have been having summer feasts in the garden since papa was a boy. Since they're outside feasts we don't have to dress up. Nana says we can play bullfight on the porch after we've eaten. Beanie will be glad about that. Bullfight is his favourite game. Russell's too. Russell gets to be the bull, and charges at Beanie's towel.

Crazy Marion and the Kokum are coming, of course. They never miss a feast. Nana says we can bring the record player to the porch and play Bizet's Carmen for inspiration for the bullfight game. Mary has never been to one of Nana's feasts. I know she'll love it.
Mrs. O'Kane is gone until Tuesday, Mother and Jeannie are still in Edmonton, and Laura is off to her friend Linda's tomorrow. It will be a perfect feast with no grumblers.

We listened to Wayne and Schuster on the radio tonight, and Mary loved that too. She doesn't have a radio at her house, and Granny Barclay never let her listen when she worked over there. Tomorrow evening after everybody goes home we might listen to the Toronto Symphony Orchestra at Massey Hall while Nana shows Mary and me the proper way to tat edging for hankies and pillowslips.

I'm glad Mary's here. I hate handwork, but Mary loves it. Handwork would be impossible without the radio.

Nana and I listen most nights after supper, and, no matter what Mother says about hired help getting above themselves, Mary will listen with us. I don't know why Mother says things like that.

Always wanting to pry people apart. She has coffee with Mrs. O'Kane most afternoons. They crochet together, and she calls her Helen like a good friend. She says it's different in her case because she went to school with Mrs. O'Kane. In fact, Lloyd O'Kane married Helen the same summer that Mother and papa got married and they stood up for each other. Lloyd O'Kane was in the air force and got killed over France.

Mary and I were in school together. I bet Mary and I will stand up for each other if either one of us gets married.

Anyway, Nana says Mother is determined to be difficult over Mary working for us, and we are to pay her no mind. That won't be too hard. Mother doesn't come into the kitchen much.

May 18, 1953

Dear Diary,

Fat Freddy and the jewelry problem seemed far away today. I can imagine I saw the whole thing in a movie. Nana says people will get over blaming Mary, that sooner or later, the real thief will be found out; she seems sure of it. I have to remind myself that Freddy is the thief. The thief that's not a stranger in the night.

Mary made the soup for the feast. All by herself. Root soup. She used every kind of root left in the pantry bins: potatoes, carrots, parsnips, parsley root, oyster root, turnip, beets. The onions and garlic she brought from the farm. She used herbs too, from Nana's bundles. I cut a big piece of roast beef into tiny squares for her. Mary fried the bits of beef in butter with the onions and garlic and celery, and the good smell of that alone made me weak with hunger. She dumped that all into the soup pot, and used flour in the dripping in the frying pan to make a good thickening. She also cooked up barley to add to the soup for good measure.

Beanie and I cleaned off the potting shed table and dragged it over to the grass under the maples. Russell helped us carry the old wooden kitchen chairs from the garage, and he wiped all the dust off them. Mother wants Nana to send those chairs to the nuisance grounds, but Nana pays her no mind. She keeps the chairs high and dry in the garage, each hanging on their own big spike on the wall. She needs them for her summer feasts, and for summer garden company. They have little rubber boots on each leg made from cut up inner tubes, and held on tight with wire. It's so the chair legs don't get wet and rotten from sinking into wet grass and dirt.

Nana brought out the big bed sheet, two bed sheets actually, sewed together to be a tablecloth for the feasts. It has every colour of paint on it. When I was in grade three, Nana and Crazy Marion hung it on the clothesline and spattered it all over with left over paint they collected from everyone they knew. They let me help. They did it to make the cloth cheerful and to hide the stains from all the feasting. It gets washed after the feasting, of course, but some stains don't come out. Nana says we shouldn't have to worry about a thing like that. Besides, some of the stains hold stories. Like the long, grey stain that used to be blue. Uncle Joe made that one with a spoonful of blueberry pie he threw at papa. Near one end of the table cloth there are many round circles made by Granddad Smythe's coffee cup. He learned to drink strong, black coffee from Old Vegard Sorensen, who is still alive and living with his daughter south of the river.

There's a long hem all around the edges of the sheet that we thread through with binder twine. When the cloth is on the table we pull the twine tight and tie it up under the table. That way the fiercest wind can't blow it off. The potting shed table is good for eight people, and at first there were only seven of us. Mondays, papa usually checks on his farms over by Stony Lake, but he didn't go today. Beanie and Russell said the toreador would take the eighth place. I didn't say so out loud, but I knew Granddad would sit there.

Crazy Marion brought fresh fry bread, a roaster of smoked perch and whitefish that the Kokum made, and two big paper sacks of spruce buds for Nana to dry for winter tea.

Mary was impressed with the feast. She's never had smoked fish before, or fry bread, or spruce bud tea, and none of us had tasted her good root soup that scooped up on your spoon like stew. It was wonderful for everybody.

Mother says Crazy Marion and the Kokum smell bad, but she's wrong about that. They smell friendly good. The Kokum burns sage twists and sweetgrass. Those are the smells that follow them. Soft, sweet and lovely. Better than the Tweed perfume that Mother sprays on her wrists and hankies. When Mother's Tweed smell is fresh on, it makes me choke.

Beanie, Russell and I picked armloads of marsh marigolds to put in Nana's stone crocks to festive up the table and the porch. I can't remember a more handsome feast.

Mary laughed and laughed, and so did papa. The Kokum smiled. Papa carried Nana's phonograph to the porch. She played Bizet's Carmen. Papa clapped and the Kokum, who sat beside him in Nana's wicker rocker, clapped too.

Suddenly Crazy Marion jumped up from her chair and started dancing. She leaped in the air like a wild gypsy, her hands over her head, and her feet stomping in the grass. Nana jumped up and joined her. Nana kicked off her shoes so hard that one landed in the garden in the potato row and the other in the beans. She danced in the grass in her stocking feet. Crazy Marion took off her hat and flung it high in the air. It landed on the porch roof. Beanie was allowed to climb up to get it and fling it back down to her. It's an old hat, worn and droopy. Her dead husband's hat.

Sydney. He was Granddad's friend in the first Great War, the friend who helped him doctor horses in the mud and mire of France. Nana said Sydney had a way with horses like none other. He coaxed every single horse through the horse dip with only a halter. He was the one to call when gas masks had to go on the horses, because most horses wouldn't stand for them.

Nana said Sydney cried harder when one of his horses died than he did when he lost a school chum. Crazy Marion says he never got over it when they had to leave horses behind at the end of the war. They had to leave them behind to be food for the starving people. Crazy Marion was a nurse over in that war. After it was over, she married Sydney and they came to Canada for a new life. Sydney came from money, but it didn't ruin him the way it ruins some people.

He got the mustard gas in the war too. The first winter in Deep Creek in their new built house, the Spanish Flu found him. He died because the mustard made his lungs weak.

That's why people call Marion crazy. Instead of going back to England to find another man she stayed on the farm. She dressed in Sydney's clothes, and raised horses all by herself. She says after having the best of men, she would never settle for a second best man.

I've never before seen Marion without her hat on. She has amazing hair. Very curly. I know she's old like Nana, but with short, curly hair and no hat she seemed younger.

We all danced except for papa and the Kokum, but they clapped. Mary was shy to do it at first, but once we got her whirling and twirling on the grass, she didn't stop until we all fell down out of breath. After we rested, Mary hummed a little tune, and then she did the most astonishing thing. She danced a Ukrainian dance for us, graceful and beautiful. She was a butterfly girl, until she got embarrassed and covered her face with her apron.

Crazy Marion marched over to her chair, and saluted her just like a soldier. Papa came and saluted, and then Nana. Beanie loves everything soldiers do. Of course he saluted. Russell does what Beanie does, so he saluted, and so did I. Mary forgot about being embarrassed. She giggled. We all got to giggling. The laughing. The dancing. My sides still hurt from it.

Mary, Beanie, Russell & I did up the dishes. People say Russell is too dumb to be useful. That's not true. Beanie hates drying dishes, but he did it so Russell would have someone to follow. Together they did a capital job.

After the feast, papa went into his study to read like he always does, but when we started up the phonograph again he came out, and sat on the porch swing. That was grand. Never before have I seen papa on the porch swing.

Mary made the toreador song play over and over for a proper bullfight. Russell was the bull. Papa showed Russell how to scrape his foot, and how to put his fingers up by his ears for horns. It was so funny. Russell charged, and he charged again.

Papa is six years older than Russell. The difference is, papa's mind grew up and Russell's didn't. Pearl S. Buck has a daughter who is like Russell. I don't think she's a Mongoloid, but she's a girl who can't ever grow up. That's what happens when you're a Mongoloid idiot. You never grow up in your mind, and you stay short.

Russell doesn't care about that, and neither do we. Nana says women who have late-in-life babies often get Mongoloids, because their insides are too worn to finish off a baby. Nana says Russell and half-blind Wasy are gift people who remind us about what is important - like laughing, playing and loving each other. I like being reminded of that.

Mother says they're freaks of nature. In the wild, the weak and defective go off and die or get eaten. If I was a deer in the bush with a gimpy leg, I'd be eaten by wolves. I don't like that thought.

I won't ruin such a day with dark thoughts. It isn't ten o'clock, but I think everyone's asleep except Nana, Crazy Marion and me. Mary's up here with me and is deep asleep. Papa is in his old bedroom on the second floor next to Laura's room. He gave up his bed to the Kokum. Crazy Marion will sleep on the davenport bed in Nana's room. I'm glad they're staying over; it stretches the feast right into tomorrow breakfast.

Still May 18, I think.

Oh, Dear Diary,

I'm a snoop and my ears are burning right off my head from what I heard. I told it to Granddad in a rush, in the bathroom, where Mary couldn't hear. I cried like a baby into a towel. I am wide awake, now. I'll try to record this the best I can.

The windows up here are all open tonight to let in the good spring air. After I slept for a while, I woke up. I thought I heard crying. Down in the garden. I shut the window so Mary wouldn't wake up. I crept down the outside stairs. I sat at the bottom in the shadows and I listened. It was Crazy Marion, sitting under the wild cucumber trellis with Nana. Nana had her arm around her and was rocking her like a baby. They were too far away for me to hear what they were saying, but lucky for me they came inside and sat at the table in the sun porch. All the big windows were open. There's an up-turned bucket next to the rain barrel by the sun porch stairs. Nana uses it for watering. It makes a perfect listening chair. The shadows covered me and I heard them as plain as day.

You know, Dear Diary, I used to feel guilty when I eavesdropped. Nana says it's rude. Yet, she knows I listen under the maidenhair fern table and she doesn't send me away. Anyway, after tonight I vow never to feel guilty or bad about it again. Nana is right about secrets. There should not be any. When people keep secrets other people will make up stories about whatever it is. Those stories will most always be wrong.

I think writers are meant to eavesdrop. How else did Pearl S. Buck know what was whispered about in old China? Or Charles Dickens? How else did he know what people said to each other in private?

I heard such things tonight. Such things. They're tumbling in my mind like marbles shook up in can. New, beautiful, smooth marbles and old, ugly, chipped marbles all in there together.

Nana brought up a full jug of chokecherry wine for the feast. Usually Crazy Marion doesn't drink anything but Adam's Ale (that's what she calls water), but she had two or three glasses of Nana's wine at the feast, and when Mary and I said goodnight before we went up to bed, Nana was filling the glasses again. It's not surprising Crazy Marion sounded drunk.

"I drank enough to stagger a horse, Marge."

"That you did, my Marion." Nana did not seem the least bit upset.

"Will you allow me another glass?"

"There's enough here to stagger two more horses and I'll help you do it."

I heard the sound of wine poured into glasses, and a clink.

"Here's to Delphine. The Queen. She's a queen, you know. A goddamn queen."

Nana's voice was soft. "Yes, she's a queen. To Delphine."

Another clink. Delphine is the Kokum's name, but few people call her that.

"I was angry with you." Crazy Marion didn't sound angry.

Nana laughed. "Yes, I know."

"Having your feast on the anniversary. A goddamn happy feast. We vowed never to be happy on the anniversary."

"We did vow."

"Jeezly smart aleck you are, Marge. I didn't want to come. I didn't know if she would come."

"Ah, Marion. If we'd had our brains working right, we'd have finished our morbidity long ago. It's a pity a person has to wait this long to get smart."

"You're lucky she came. I didn't tell her it was the feast. She thought it was the anniversary like always on this day. Hadn't been for

George she would have bolted. And him escorting her in. Sitting with her. Did you put him up to that?"

"No one puts George up to anything. I told him I'd had enough of marking misery. He agreed. Today for Delphine's family. Next month for Wilton, and then for Sydney, and Pete, and Joe, and William, and then all over again. Picking off the scab every time it starts to heal."

"Didn't start like that."

"No it didn't. We needed to mourn in the beginning Marion, but we carried it on too long. We know better. We do. We give good advice to other people. All those people we sit with after they lose someone they love."

"We do know how to tell them. Cry like a banshee, as long as it takes. Wail. Howl. Then get on with your life. We're such hypocrites."

"You're right about that. Remember William in his last days? 'Celebrate Marjorie. I want you to celebrate. I had a fine life. I want you and the boys to remember how much I enjoyed it.'"

I heard more wine pouring.

"Of course, he didn't know how soon three of his boys would follow him. He couldn't know that. I agreed while he was still with me, because I didn't know how angry I would be after he was gone. Leaving me alone like that. And then my other men gone and George wrung out like a sink rag. Lillian off in her make-believe world, and those poor little girls bounced around like India rubber balls. I was happy to pour salt in my wounds on the anniversaries, and pretend to celebrate life at the feasts."

"So, we're hypocrites. Why change now? I like wallowing in misery. I'll miss it."

"You won't miss it, and neither will I, my girl. Delphine enjoyed today. We resisted it more than she did. We need real enjoyment again. George needs it. And Natalie, and Laura, and funny little Beanie, and Russell. And we have Mary to think about. Who knows what other strays will turn up."

"I don't like it when you're right. You know that don't you?"

"I don't like it when I'm wrong."

"Cheeky. You've always been cheeky."

"An old broad has to be cheeky to get by. Isn't that what you always tell me?"

"So, when did you start listening to me?"

Nana snorted. A funny sound coming out of Nana. They went back and forth like that. I forgot to listen for a while. Until I heard my name.

"It was during Lillian's birthday party. You remember, don't you?"

"What do you mean? She crawled into glass from a broken baby bottle. Everyone knows the story."

"Yes. Everyone knows the story." Nana sounded sad. "Lillian's twenty-seventh birthday. September. The Italians had surrendered. The war was still in a tangle, but we thought that victory was possible."

Crazy Marion swore. "I remember. You'd just received word about Joe and you decided not to tell Lillian or her mother that night. You didn't want to spoil the party. I remember being angry at you. I left you to grieve alone. Not my finest hour."

There was a long silence. I thought they'd fallen asleep. I wanted to burst in, yell at Nana to tell the rest of the story. It's a good thing I didn't because I would never have heard it.

"Marge. Get to it."

"I should have told you long ago. I don't know why..."

"You know goddamn well why you didn't tell me. You knew how I felt about those little girls. You knew I would do something stupid."

"What will stop you from doing that now?"

"Old age and too much chokecherry. Spit it out. Quit dangling it in front of my face like a carnival prize."

I can tell you, Dear Diary, my heart beat loud and strong. I was afraid I couldn't keep it trapped there under my ribs. One minute I wanted to hear Nana. The next minute I wanted to run away, so I wouldn't hear a thing.

Good thing I didn't run. I discovered I wasn't a stubborn brat like Grandma Walters says. I wasn't a willful child the day my foot got ruined. It wasn't one bit my fault. I can hardly believe it. It was not my fault. I didn't throw my bottle in a tantrum and break it and crawl through it. It wasn't my baby bottle that cut my leg. What I don't understand is, why did everybody say it was?

"Lillian invited me to the party, but I knew she'd be happier if I didn't come. After I received the news about Joe, I didn't want to stay in the house alone. Doc rescued me. He made a big production of having to drive out and check on Mollie Little Chief. She wasn't due for months, so I knew he was maneuvering me. I let him. We drove along the river road. Sat by the rapids in silence. Good man, Doc. He knew when to start talking. He remembered things about Joe. I remembered things. He held my hand in those big paws of his while I howled like one of the damned. I felt remarkably cleansed by the time he brought me home, but I couldn't sleep.

I started thinking about Natalie, the wee thing in that big crib, in that dark room with no one to rock her at night or sing to her or read her a story. That's why I went over so late. I knew the party would still be in full swing. I took Lillian's present over. I don't remember what it was.

She'd been drinking, of course. She snatched up the gift and made a big production about opening it. I sat with a cup of tea in my lap and a stupid smile on my face, counting off the minutes before I excused myself to go up to the bathroom. I must have known. Marion. I must have known.

"I would have gone straight to Natalie's crib except for Lillian coming up the stairs behind me. I ducked into the bathroom. I heard her calling to those below that she was going to show them what she got for herself for a birthday gift. My mistake was to use the toilet. I thought I might as well. Give her time to retrieve her gift and powder her nose. Then, I heard her yell. A door slammed and she ran back down stairs. I was slow to get out of that damn bathroom."

"You think that the few seconds you wasted pulling up your drawers would have made a difference."

Nana spoke sharply. "Quit interrupting."

"All right. Lips sealed. See. Sealed."

"There was no broken bottle, Marion. Natalie's diapers were soaked. She didn't need diapers at night any more if someone would put her on the pot once after ten. Naturally she climbed out of her crib. She'd wiggled out of her diaper in the hallway and would have gone down stairs next if that stupid figurine in Lillian's bedroom hadn't distracted her. A porcelain figurine. A Wallendorf Swan Lake ballerina. I don't know where Lillian got it. She didn't have money for anything like that. Once the whole thing was over, I was too distracted to try to find out.

"Of course the baby picked it up to admire it. What baby wouldn't? Stupid trinket, laying there on the stool in all that tissue."

"So, Lillian grabbed it and threw it — ...sorry...I won't say another thing."

"Lillian told me Natalie had it by the leg and wouldn't let go. That's what she said in her defense. When she yanked it from Natalie's grasp it fell and smashed to pieces. Lillian slammed the door on that frightened little baby and ran back downstairs to her party."

"My gawd!"

"When I wrenched open the door to Lillian's room, there was Natalie laying on the floor screaming. She had knelt in the shards trying to pick up the pieces. Her little hands were bloody from clutching them. I had an awful time prying her little fingers open."

"I didn't see the cut on her knee then. I thought all the blood came from her hands. Only later at Doc's, when we cleaned her up to see where she needed stitches, did we see the gash on the side of her knee."

Crazy Marion swore. Man swears. I can't write them here.

Nana wept. "I want my Natalie whole again."

Oh, Dear Diary, I have never, never, never heard my Nana weep. Never. And she was weeping about me.

Nana cried. Crazy Marion swore. They drank more wine while I sat like a stone. I'm surprised it isn't morning. Oh. It is morning. I've been writing so hard and fast I didn't see the sun come up. Now, I'm tired. My head is drained like a sink. It wasn't my fault, Dear Diary. It wasn't my fault.

May 21, 1953

Dear Diary,

This has been such a busy week that I haven't had time for you. I thought certain Nana was right about people forgetting to blame Mary.

Mother hasn't forgotten. She just got back. She and Nana had a fight right off when she tried to get snotty with Mary. Mother thinks everyone should be fussing over Jeannie's graduation. She doesn't notice it's Laura's graduation too. She wanted to have a reception at Grandma Walters' house with ribbon sandwiches and meringues, and other fancy things. She's irked because Grandma Walters said no.

Grandma Walters said, since Nana's combined dining and living room are bigger than hers, and since Nana has a lovely garden for spillover, the reception should be here. Nana agreed, but she isn't happy about it. She wanted it to be a simple lunch buffet, not a reception like for a wedding. She wanted to ask people to drop by, not send formal invitations. Mother wants formal invitations.

That all happened right after breakfast with our house full of Grandma Walters and Mother talking at the same time. Jeannie with dozens of boxes and bags she wanted to open in front of everyone. Laura's lucky she has school to escape to.

I wouldn't mind going back to school. I miss walking down the hill with Beanie. Even though Beanie is a year older than I am, we're in the same grade, because I started early. Every day he tells me what goes on at school, but, I have to say, Historians, he's not very good with details.

Mother said Jeannie has to rest up. She's off to Grandma Walters' to get her new everything's pressed properly. The Kokum does all the pressing in this house, but Mother doesn't let the Kokum press her things or Jeannie's. They get Grandma Walters' hired girl to do it. Grandpa Walters comes up the hill once a week to fetch a basket full, and brings everything back on hangers.

Mother never noticed me and that's a good thing. Now that I know the truth about my ruined leg, I feel so different. I'm sure it shows on my face.

Sometime after Lunch May 21, 1953

Oh, Dear Diary,

Nana was wrong. It isn't just Mother who is still blaming Mary for the stealing. Constable Kipp came over to our place right after lunch to try to arrest Mary. Can you believe it? Right in our house. Nana wouldn't let him, of course. She said he had no reason for doing it. He stood in our doorway trying to bend his hat in half, and mumbled with his head down. When Nana told him to speak up, he turned red as a beet. Nana took pity on him and invited him into the breakfast nook and offered him coffee.

I went into the kitchen and held hands with Mary while we listened with the door open a crack. She nearly broke my hand in two she squeezed so hard.

"Leroy." Nana spoke kindly to him. "I know who sent you. I'm sorry you're pressured from those quarters, but you know you cannot arrest a person without evidence."

Constable Kipp sat near the edge of his chair. One of his legs shook up and down like a milkshake machine. He held on to his hat with both hands, so he couldn't drink his coffee.

"I gotta arrest the girl. The mayor says I gotta."

"Or he'll fire you?" Nana smiled.

Constable Kipp wouldn't look at Nana. He nodded.

"You go back and tell the mayor that I obstructed the arrest. If he'd like to take this further, tell him I'll be here all afternoon."

Constable Kipp shot off that chair and out the door like fire-crackers. That's that. I knew Nana could protect Mary. She did it magnificently. Fat Freddy might be mayor of the town, but Nana is in charge of this house.

May 21, 1953 Late afternoon

Oh, Dear Diary,

Constable Kipp came back with Fat Freddy who tried to bully Nana into letting them take Mary away. That scared us, I can tell you, but we didn't need to be scared. He should know better than to try to bully Nana.

She was polite at first. Anyone who knows Nana, knows when she gets over-polite it's time to watch out. She didn't invite the men for tea; she told them that they *would* have tea with her in the sun room, and discuss their problem like civilized people. Constable Kipp got busy trying to bend his hat again, and stared at his feet twisting back and forth on the linoleum. Fat Freddy blustered and blared. He said Nana was standing in the way of justice. Nana ignored him.

I can't believe his nerve. I'm sorry I didn't speak up. I wanted to. I bit my tongue hard. But I'd have made a fool of myself blurting without proof.

Nana sent Mary and me to the kitchen to help Mrs. O'Kane, but Mary was too scared. She tried to help but she couldn't. Her apron got all twisted up in her hands, and when Mrs. O'Kane swore at her, she folded herself in half in the chair by the pantry, and cried into her apron, rocking back and forth wailing in Ukrainian.

Mrs. O'Kane called her a stupid Bohunk. I've never seen Mrs. O'Kane that riled. I thought she was a kind person, but I was wrong. She glared at Mary like she was a stinkbug to be squashed. I grabbed Mary's hand and pulled her off the chair. Mrs. O'Kane frowned at me. I frowned back. I made Mary come upstairs with me. In Granddad's room I sat with her on the bed until she calmed down. It took a while. She rocked back and forth, shaking her head and moaning.

I told her I knew she didn't do it, but she didn't hear me. I blurted that I'd seen Fat Freddy take the jewelry. Mary stopped moaning instantly and stared at me. I had to tell her the whole story and let her use the spyglass. I feel better having someone besides Beanie knowing about this crazy business. She understands why we can't tell anyone until we know where the jewelry's hidden, but she thinks, because Freddy is mayor she'll get blamed no matter what we find. She thinks we can't stop her from being sent to live with the defectives in Red Deer.

She said Mrs. O'Kane told her that bad girls are sent to Red Deer; the law has no choice. That made me mad, I'll tell you. Nana won't be happy when she hears about this. She can't abide talk like that.

I showed Mary where to listen to the grownups down in the sunroom. In papa's old bedroom on the second floor there's a cold air register. If a person lies on the floor and is careful not to let anything fall through the grate, you can see right down over Nana's tea table and hear everything undetected. Mary didn't want to do it. I told her to a least shush, so she wouldn't give me away. She nodded her head and curled up on papa's old bed like a puppy in a snow bank. She pulled her apron over her head while I stretched flat on the floor. My hot cheek felt good on the cold metal frame of the register. The cool hardness stopped my insides from simmering, and helped me get still. I hadn't missed anything important.

Nana was finishing what she calls her niceties. She always prolongs her niceties when people insist on being difficult. She says it's much more annoying for them than if she's rude. She had her best teacups out. They're small and dainty. Constable Kipp hunched over the table with the teacup handle between his big thumb and his pointing finger. He held the saucer in his other hand. It shook like the station windows when the freight train goes by.

Fat Freddy sat with his ankle on his knee and his arms folded over his pumpkin stomach. I saw the round bald spot on top of his head. His hand with the two fingers missing hung over his arm. It's his little finger and the next one that's gone and some of his hand too, I guess. If his mother had managed to get his toes instead, I wonder if he'd be a gimp like me. Strange, isn't it, how having a wrecked hand isn't a defect, when you're the mayor, but having a wrecked foot is, when you're a kid.

Nana's teacup made a dainty clinking sound when she put it back in the saucer. She reached for her napkin to tap her mouth. "Gentlemen. Now that we have had an opportunity to calm down…"

Fat Freddy uncrossed his arms, and leaned forward.

Nana looked at him. She didn't say anything, but he crossed his arms again and sat back. She continued. "I know how distressing it is to have an unsolved crime on your hands, but nothing can be gained by accusing an innocent girl."

Freddy sprang forward. "Innocent! There's nothing innocent about that lying little Bohunk."

"Frederick." Nana's tone was sharp. "You will refrain from using that language in my home." She folded up her napkin and laid it carefully beside her plate. She sat slowly back in her chair. "What evidence do you have for your accusations?"

Constable Kipp rattled his cup and saucer to the table, and his hands sprang away from them like they were on fire. "Mrs. Smythe, we don't exactly have any hard evidence, but she was the only person there that night who could have…"

Nana's voice was soft and calm. "Really, Constable. How can that be so? There were at least sixteen other people at Dr. Masters' home that evening. Seventeen if we count you, Frederick."

Freddy jumped up and leaned on the table. "Me? You would accuse me?"

Nana stood up too. "Sit down Frederick and behave yourself. I accuse no one, and nor should you, until you have reason to."

"They are born thieves. All of them. Stinkin' ignorant immigrants…"

"Frederick." Nana sounded dangerous.

Freddy kicked his chair away from the table. "You think you're all hoity toity, Marjorie Smythe, protecting thieves and bums. I warn you. We're going to watch those Bohunks so close they won't take a shit without somebody counting the turds. Sooner or later one of them's going to get rid of stolen property. If there's a hint that girl was involved, you'll face serious charges."

Nana voice was cold. "Don't you threaten me Frederick Bugle. Constable, remove this man from my home."

She sat down and poured herself another cup of tea. Freddy nearly pushed Constable Kipp off his chair.

"I go where and when I please, and don't you forget it." He strode out of the sunroom with Constable Kipp stumbling over his feet to catch up with him.

Nana sipped her tea.

Still May 21, 1953, much after supper

Oh, Dear Diary,

Dear Diary. Where's Nana? She needs to come home. Now. Right now. She's with Doc Rawson at Mrs. Sawchuck's to help him bring in the new baby.

They have no phone.

I can't phone her.

I can't sit here.

They've taken Mary. To Jail. And Mother helped. I can't believe she helped.

I have to calm down. Nana will be back, soon. Nana always comes back. I'll write everything. From the beginning. I got to take a breath.

Tell it from the start. Write it down. Don't miss anything.

Oh, please God, get Nana home soon. Please. I know Nana says we aren't supposed to bargain with you, but this is serious. Very serious. Please hear me, God. Please look down and see what is happening. Please. Talking to Granddad is no help. There is no help without Nana. None.

I have to stay calm. Write what happened.

After Freddy and Constable Kipp left this morning Nana took Mary and me down town for a float. She doesn't want Mary to feel like she has to hide. She wanted to take Mary's mind off being scared. Can you believe Mary's never had a float? Nana had an Orange Crush float. I had Ginger Ale float and Mary had a Coke float. We traded back and forth until Mary tasted them all. The creamy goodness of the floats helped her forget to be scared for a while. We had fun until Doc Rawson came for Nana.

Mrs. Sawchuck's baby is trying to come early. He always takes Nana when he goes to the country to deliver a baby.

I can't do this.

I can't sit up here writing things down like it's an ordinary evening. And Mary down in the jail all by herself. Papa's off to Lloydminster with Uncle Metro to get seed wheat. Nana's not here. Mother has forbidden me to leave the house. This time she is paying attention to where I am.

I can't imagine Granddad anymore. He's disappeared and I can't get him back.

Mother snooped in Mary's things while we were at the café. Mother and Mrs. O'Kane. They went right into Nana's rooms and snooped in Mary's things! They found the money she's saved from her Saturday cleaning, and from making straw frames for Nana. They think it's money from selling the jewelry. They think it's perfect proof of her guilt. After Nana and Doc Rawson were gone they called Constable Kipp. Mary and I didn't know a thing about it until we heard banging on the kitchen door. Nana had left us in the breakfast nook, reading Pearl S. Buck before supper. When the loud knocking started, Mother ran into the kitchen. Mother never goes into the kitchen. As soon as we heard Fat Freddy's big, mean voice, Mary dropped her book, and covered her mouth with her hands. We didn't have time to run.

They came into the breakfast nook so fast I barely got my arms around Mary. I thought if I held her tight, they'd at least have to take me with her, but they didn't. We hung on to each other, but it was no use. Mary started shrieking when Fat Freddy jerked her away from me. I leaped on him like a cat. I bit his arm. Hard. I got his horrible blood in my mouth. He yelped like a dog, and flung me away. I fell on the floor and spit out skin. I've never bitten any one before. It doesn't leave a good taste in your mouth. I yelled at him at the top of my lungs. I called him every swear I know. Even Crazy Marion's best swears.

When I got up to go at him again, Mother grabbed my arm and tried to pull me across the room. I twisted around and yelled at her.

"You witch. You horrible, horrible witch. You can't let them take Mary. You can't."

Mother was the reason they came to get Mary. Mother was the reason my foot was wrecked. I've never before had such anger in me. Boiling like water for tea. Boiling over. My yelling surprised Mother for a moment, so I was able to yank away. Mrs. O'Kane grabbed me and wrapped her arms around me, nearly squeezing my breath out.

I hate her. I hate Mother. I hate them both. I thrashed and squirmed. I'm surprised how strong I am when I'm riled. But not strong enough. I did manage to kick Mrs. O'Kane in the leg with my heavy shoe. I'll never for my whole life be one bit sorry. I wish I'd kicked Mother, too. I know that's wicked, but I don't care. She deserves a kicking.

Mother shook me, flopping my head around, hurting me. "You little brat. You horrid little brat. You be quiet, instantly. Do you hear me? Instantly."

I think the whole town must have heard the ruckus. Mary wailing, me yelling at Mother, Mother yelling at me, Fat Freddy yelling at Mary, Mrs. O'Kane yelling at me. The only one not making noise was Constable Kipp. He had to concentrate on dragging Mary away. She threw herself around like a wild thing and howled mightily. When the screen door slammed behind them, I was forced to stand there between Mother and Mrs. O'Kane, pinned like a bug, listening to Mary howl all the way to Constable Kipp's car. They held my arms behind my back.

The fight leaked out of me when the car door slammed shut. For one awful moment everything was quiet.

The kitchen filled up with heavy breathing. Mother's, Mrs. O'Kane's and mine. My heart raced so fast I thought it would burst my chest. As soon as they relaxed their hold on me, I twisted away and ran for the door… But my stupid, heavy shoe slowed me down. They caught me and slammed me down hard on a chair. They shoved my chair up against the table. Mother stood behind me like a big, black vulture. She wasn't magnificent. She didn't look like a movie star. Her face was ugly. Bad witch ugly. And mean. I don't know why I thought she was beautiful. She's not. She's like a wicked stepmother. I wish she *was* a stepmother and not my real mother.

My mother. My own mother. I know she doesn't like Mary. She doesn't like me. But to let them take Mary like that. To jail. I never dreamed Mother would do such a thing. I hate her. I can't help it. Even if I go to Hell, I hate her. And Mrs. O'Kane and Fat Freddy and Constable Kipp. I have so much hate boiling in me I don't think I'll feel the fires of Hell when I get there. I'm hotter than Hell fire. I might as well go there. I'm hot enough to melt the devil.

I don't know how long Mother yelled at me. I didn't hear her after they shoved me against the table. Every part of me that wasn't held down by my body flew off to the jailhouse with Mary. Poor, poor Mary. She's so scared. And so am I. Maybe Nana can't save her now. Or papa. Maybe Freddy's racing her off to Red Deer right now.

When Jeannie and Laura got home from school Laura ran into the breakfast nook to find out what happened. Mother yelled at her and hit her across the face. Mother hit her. She hit Laura! Mother's gone crackers. Mother always talks mean, but she doesn't hit.

I was truly scared of her at that moment. As soon as they let me, I fled up to my room and slammed the door. I think Laura's gone to Linda's. I heard Mother yelling after her. "Don't you leave this house. Don't you dare leave this house. Laura. Come back. Right now."

This is the worst day of my life.

It's after midnight, so I guess it's May 22, 1953

Oh, Dear Diary,

I'm tired. So tired. But I have to record this. Who knows what morning will bring. I guess it's already morning. It feels like we squeezed a week into yesterday. The whole house is sleeping except me. Nana didn't get home until late. As soon as I heard Doc's car coming up the lane I flew down the stairs. Nana came in through the kitchen like she always does. I got to her first. I flung my arms around her and wailed like a baby.

Mother rushed out of her bedroom in her nightgown, not putting on a robe or slippers. She had hair falling around her face. Mrs. O'Kane didn't come out of her room even though we were standing nearly in her doorway. Mother and I started talking at the same time. Nana grabbed a pie tin from the drain rack, and bashed it against the refrigerator. That stopped us.

I feel silly thinking about how I clung to Nana like a baby monkey. I'm twelve, but at that moment I shrunk to four or five. A little kid lost on the way home. With Nana's arms tight around me I was able to quiet down. I shut my eyes tight, and listened to Mother's voice tell about the taking of Mary. She hissed and spit like a hateful witch.

"Marjorie, for once, you're wrong. Helen (that's Mrs. O'Kane, Dear Diary) and I found the little Bohunk's hiding place and all the money she's hoarded from selling Dora's (that, Dear Diary is Mrs. Masters' name) precious accessories. Ignorant little savage. Can you believe she sold those priceless heirlooms for less than a hundred dollars? We're sick over it."

Nana's hand stopped stroking my hair. We stood quiet, her and I. I felt her gathering herself up. I confess to you, I nearly fainted with relief. I imagined a lightning bolt flying from Nana's eyes, burning a hole in Mother. I did. I'm not sorry.

"Where's Mary?" That is all Nana said. Her voice was dangerously soft.

I felt Mother smile. "In jail, of course, where thieving liars like her belong. And Edwin himself is coming tomorrow to escort her to Red Deer."

Nana said nothing at first. She gently untangled me from around her waist, and walked into Mrs. O'Kane's room.

"Helen." Nana's voice was cold as a winter stone. "Get up. Get your things, and get out of my house. Now. When I get back I want you gone. Anything you leave behind I'll throw into the street."

I'll never forget Mrs. O'Kane's face. She sat up in her bed blinking like a surprised owl.

To me, Nana said, "To the car, Tally."

I was out the door and into her car before I breathed another breath. Mother followed us out, yelling. I put my hands over my ears. I don't want to hear anything she has to say, ever again.

I don't know what time it was, but the whole town slept, except the jail. I saw the windows in the courthouse lit up. Fat Freddy's station wagon was parked outside beside Constable Kipp's police car.

"Tally, I can't believe this. They've gone too far, this time."

I don't think Nana thought about me after that. If she had, she would have told me to stay in the car. She left the car so fast she forgot to close her door. I got out. I didn't close mine either. I didn't want the closing of it to remind her she'd given me no instructions. I followed her like a shadow, and was twice as quiet. I lifted my wrecked foot high, and put it down slow.

Constable Kipp sat at his desk reading a magazine, and drinking coffee. Nana snatched up his magazine, and flung it against the wall. Nana was magnificent.

"Leroy. Release her."

She sounded like the wrath of God. Big and booming.

Constable Kipp had to lift his head to look up at her. "Mrs. Smythe...ah..."

"Don't Mrs. Smythe me, you despicable mound of refuse." She reached across his desk, and grabbed a handful of his shirt. Grabbed his shirt like cowboys do in the movies. He stood up to follow his shirt. I thought for a minute he was going to cry.

"Release her, this instant."

"I can't. Really Mrs. Smythe. Freddy's still questioning her. He's…"

"Frederick Bugle is the mayor, you ignoramus. He has no business here."

We heard Mary shriek. Nana left Constable Kipp hanging over his desk like wet laundry. She yanked open the door to the jail cells and yelled, "Frederick Bugle. Get out here, now."

When we got to Mary's jail cell, she was scrunched up in the corner at the head of a mean little cot with only a mattress and no bedding. Freddy was standing beside it with her sweater in his hand. His shirt was rumpled, and his pants were a puddle at his feet. Mary's head was a wild nest of hair, her face was swollen from crying, and she had an angry red welt on her cheek under her eye. Her blouse was up under her armpits and her brassiere was pulled down with one broken strap dangling. Her hands jammed her skirt tight between her legs, and her eyes were squeezed shut.

I jumped up on the cot beside her, and wrapped my arms around her. She didn't cry or moan. I wish she would have. It was terrible having her so quiet. She trembled, like she was cold. I rubbed warm into her back like Nana used to do for me when I was little.

"Obstructing justice again, Marjorie?" Freddy used one hand to pull up his pants like it was an ordinary thing to do. "Not a good idea, even for a former mayor's wife."

Nana walked right up to Freddy, and talked close to his face. I thought Freddy was a scary man. Nana was scarier.

"I'm here to see that justice is served." It's amazing how reasonable Nana sounds when she's angry. "Do up your trousers and get out. Now!"

Freddy didn't move. "We caught her red-handed, like I told you we would…"

I couldn't help myself. I blurted. "Nana gave her that money. For cleaning. For picture frames. She never spent it. Never. She was saving it to give back."

Nana looked at me with surprise. She smiled for a moment before she got her mean face back on. She yanked Mary's sweater away from Freddy.

Freddy didn't give up right away. "You can't prove that you gave her that money."

Nana stared at him real hard. "Oh, but I can."

He backed away. I helped Nana get Mary off the cot. We wrapped Nana's coat tight around her. Mary still had her shoes on. Nana put her arm around Mary's shoulder. I put an arm around Mary's waist. We nearly carried her from the jail cell leaving Freddy standing there.

He yelled after us. "She's a slut. She offered herself. Skinny little Bohunk slut. I'd a bin doin' her a favour if I took her. Do you hear me?"

Nana turned and shouted at him.

"Frederick, shut your filthy mouth."

She slammed the big jail door right in his face. By the end of it all Nana had slammed quite a few doors. Magnificent door slamming like I've never seen before.

Nana tried to make Mary go to the car with me, but she wouldn't budge. She didn't say a word, but clung to both of us like she was glued.

"Give me the money, Leroy." Constable Kipp squinted his eyes and bit his lip.

"I can't. Really I can't Mrs. Smythe. It's evidence."

"Right, you pathetic idiot. It is evidence. Evidence of this girl's honesty and integrity. Give it to me."

Constable Kipp didn't move. Fat Freddy burst through the door yelling.

"Don't you give her nothing, Leroy."

"Don't make a bigger fool of yourself than you already have, Frederick. Have you examined the bills you stole from this girl? I can tell you, right now, they are all five-dollar bills. They are from William's collection." (William is Granddad Smythe.)

"I finally found a good place to use them. And I'll make a bet each one of them is still in their little cellophane envelope, the way they were when I gave them to Mary. And if that doesn't convince you I'll provide the serial number from each one. You know William was a fastidious man."

Constable Kipp's mouth hung open. Fat Freddy swore with words I can't write down. I gave him my meanest stare, and spoke as fiercely as I could.

"She didn't take the jewelry, and you know it."

His head swung around, his face red and his eyes on me like a snake. I nearly swallowed my tongue.

"You. You little Bitch."

He yanked up his sleeve. I was happy to see the big messy mark of my teeth there. I hope he gets double infection. I hope it fills him full of boils that rot until his arm falls off.

"She's probably rabid, the little cripple. I otta charge her."

I wanted to yell out, "You took the jewels, you liar, you took them." But I couldn't. First off because he scared me. Then because I knew I couldn't prove it. I felt Nana's mighty fury burning. Fat Freddy doesn't know how lucky he is Nana has remarkable self-control.

"You'll charge no one, Frederick, unless it's yourself, with profound stupidity. Go home."

He didn't like being dismissed like a child. He made an awful face, but there was nothing he could do. Nana got all Mary's money back, and we went home.

Mrs. O'Kane was gone when we got there. Nana told Mother to get out of her sight. We took Mary into Nana's rooms, and put her into a warm bath.

Nana told me to shush when I tried to get Mary to say something. Nana said she would talk, in time. I don't know what that means. How much time? I hope it's soon. It's bad with her so silent.

Nana stayed with her in the bathroom for a long time. I helped put her into one of Nana's big flannel nightdresses. She stood like a droopy statue, and did whatever Nana asked her to do.

"Lift your arms, sweetheart. That's it. Move your head a little. There. Are you cozy in there?"

Mary has her own nightgowns here, now. New ones. But Nana said she needs comforting. Nana's smart about those things. Nana's nightgowns are made from the thickest, softest flannel. I wear them when I'm sick. Carefully we put zinc ointment on the places where Mary's face got scratched from rubbing against the rough walls of the jail. Nana made chamomile and skullcap tea. She put drops of stinky valerian root tincture in Mary's cup. I know it's to help her sleep, but what a smell. Mary didn't notice. Nana tucked her into her own big bed, and we lay on either side of her with our arms around her until she went to sleep.

Nana kept saying over and over, "Don't worry, Mary. Don't worry, child. You did nothing wrong. You have never done anything wrong. We won't let them hurt you again. I promise."

Nana is a true protecting angel. I'm glad to be her helper. When Mary finally slept deeply, Nana told me to stay and sleep too. Oh, Dear Diary, I wanted to, so bad, but I knew if I waited, I'd never get this all down. Now, I'm going to sleep. Good night.

May 22, 1953

Dear Diary,

Will this never end? I woke up early. About 6:00 am. I don't know what got into me. I should have slept till noon, but there I was, wide-awake. I decided to go down stairs to see if there was tipsy pudding left from yesterday, and part way down the stairs I heard Nana talking to Mother. I sat right down, right there. It's the part of the stairs before the railings start, and when the lights are out on the second floor no one can see me sitting there unless I make a noise. I'm half sorry I listened. I'm wrung dry from all this listening. At first Mother was blustery and loud because Nana had taken away what she was drinking. She swore like I've never heard before.

"Take my damned drink. Take it you goddamn cow. Take everything. Piss in my face while you're at it."

She was drunk. I know that. But those words sounded like somebody else's words coming from somebody else's mouth. I want to know, Dear Diary, if that was my real mother, whose mother have I been hoping for my whole life? I sound crazy, don't I? I feel crazy. My mother's not my mother. I'm not myself. I don't know what it means. I don't. My brain is a rock. There's no thinking left in it. None. I'll just record. I'm a recording machine. It's my job.

"I need a cigarette."

Nana still held Mother's drink. Her voice was hard. Not a Nana voice.

"I don't care for a moment what you need. What you did was unconscionable, Lillian. Completely unconscionable. If you ever enter my rooms again without permission, I will have you arrested."

Mother stared at Nana. "You wouldn't dare."

"If you're that foolish, try me." Nana paced. I've never seen Nana pace. "You have not only violated my privacy and accused an innocent girl, you're also party to battery and attempted rape."

Mother jumped off the couch. "Rape! That's ridiculous. Who would do that?"

Nana's words froze hard, each one of them ice as they fell heavy from her mouth. "Sit down. You know who would. That's not the point. The point is. You. You gave him opportunity. You."

Rape. I thought I would faint. People don't rape girls like Mary. Run-away girls get raped. Girls in cities who go to the bad part of town get raped. Fat Freddy? He's a thief and a liar. But a raper, too? My stomach hurts. It's trying to digest all this, because my brain can't do it. It's not fit food for a stomach. I moved Granddad's rocker beside my desk. I want him to sit beside me. Close beside me. I'm pretending he is rubbing my back for me. Rubbing my back while I try to write all this.

Oh, Dear Diary, Jeannie told me what rape is, but I don't understand it. It's the same thing men and women who love each other do together to make babies. Then it's a good thing. Fun, even, Jeannie says. I don't know how it could be fun.

Rape is not fun. Rape is mean and hurtful and only the vilest of men do it. I don't know why anyone wants to do it. I feel so stupid. So many things I don't know.

How will Mary ever talk again? I don't think there are words invented for talking about that horribleness. The thought of Fat Freddy wanting to make his horrible little willie burrow down inside of Mary. I want to throw up. He should be sterilized without being put to sleep. He should have Uncle Edwin in a butcher's apron chase him every night in his dreams. Every night with the biggest butcher knife. Chopping at him. Chopping at his disgusting little willie. Every night for the rest of his life. I know why Mary wants to roll up into a tiny ball. I want to roll up in a ball with her.

Oh, Nana. How can that kind of thing happen? How can it, Granddad? How? And, because of Mother.

"Marjorie. You can't take the word of a girl like that." Mother sounded whiny. Whiny like Jeannie when she doesn't want to take the blame for what she's done.

"I would take the word of Mary over yours any day. Only she hasn't said a word. Not one word, and I don't know when she will. She is completely traumatized. She's covered with cuts and bruises. Her clothes are torn. We found Frederick in the cell with her. What do you think he was trying to do? What do you think he would have done had I not arrived?"

Nana still paced.

"I'm not so naïve as to think we can make a case against him. The letter of the law is on our side, but the intent in this jurisdiction is not. He will say she tried to seduce him, and that old fool, Judge Balder will fall all over himself to agree. Any attempt we make to obtain justice for Mary will call unwarranted public attention on her. She won't be able to bear it.

"You invited them into this house, so they were not trespassing. You're responsible for a terrible crime against an innocent child. You, Lillian. It's completely beyond the pale. Completely. Intolerable." Nana stopped and pressed her hand against her chest. "I can't remember a time in my life when I've had to contain such anger."

Nana paused. It was quiet for a few moments.

Mother closed her lips tight. They nearly disappeared into her face. She folded up on the couch, and wrapped her arms around her legs. For one awful minute, she reminded me of Mary huddled in the corner of the cot in the jail. I might have felt sorry for her then, but she opened her eyes, and she was back to angry and mean. Nana said other things. Oh, dear Diary I can hardly believe what I heard.

"Now, listen carefully, Lillian. I want you to know that I have willingly gone a long way toward protecting you against public discovery of your petty theft, and your drinking. I did it out of sympathy for my son, and my grandchildren, but now you're on your own.

I will protect you no longer. I know William had a soft spot for you. He paid for your indiscretions as he discovered them. I have continued this in his memory, but even he would call a halt now. I will not make one more trip to the city to pay for your ridiculous thievery. I will phone the shops that know you and inform them that from now on, they're to phone the police, not me. We were wrong to shelter you. It was not a kindness. You have a sickness. I'm sorry for my part in preventing you from seeking help. That you must do now. I have the name of a good man in Edmonton who understands this ailment. I give you two weeks to seek his help. If you do not, I will talk to your brother-in-law, and ask him for a referral.

Mother burst. "You wouldn't dare!"

"I would and I will. I know you don't want your sister and brother-in-law to know about this part of your life. I'm willing, God knows why, to spare you that if you take steps to seek help on your own. I'm also willing to give you time to speak to George about this. You must tell him what you've done, and you must tell him soon. I also know it's possible you took the jewelry. If you did, I don't want to know about it. Just make sure it's returned."

Mother whispered, "Marjorie, how dare you accuse me." Mother never whispers.

Nana sounded tired. "I'm not accusing. I'm suggesting. You know I have good reason."

Mother whimpered. "I need a drink. Marjorie, for God's sake have pity."

"My pity is no use to you, Lillian. Not anymore. Nor is a drink. I poured everything down the drain. Everything. The only hiding places I'm not familiar with are in your room."

Nana stood tall and straight in front of Mother who was slumped on the sofa.

"I've never invaded any person's privacy for any reason before, and I won't now."

Mother got up from the couch, and threw a cushion at Nana before running down the hallway to her room.

Nana picked up the cushion, hugged it tight like it was a teddy bear. She stood there, facing the hallway where Mother had disappeared. I wanted to run down and fling my arms around her and say, "There, there." Like she says to Mary and me. But I didn't. I wasn't supposed to hear any of it. If Nana knew I heard, she'd feel worse.

I sat on the stairs for a long time after Nana went to her rooms. Fat Freddy stealing is hard to understand. But, Mother? Mother doesn't need to steal. She can buy whatever she wants.

I said I hated Mother. I do. But I can't imagine her being as vile as Fat Freddy. She isn't. I know she isn't. But she got Mary arrested. She said girls who steal should be sent to Red Deer. Will Uncle

Edwin send Mother to Red Deer? If he finds out about the stealing? I don't know how to think about this.

Dear Diary, it's completely morning now, but the house is still quiet, and I am so tired. I want to sink into sleeping and never wake up till Christmas. I'm going back to bed.

May 22, 1953 late in the afternoon!!

Dear Diary,

I slept terrible. I kept waking up. All of a sudden I'd be wide-awake thinking about Mother. Then I'd be sleeping. Then I'd wake up thinking about Mary. Then I'd wake up hearing Nana crying. So much crying. Finally, I got up and wrapped up in the feather quilt and sat in Granddad's chair. I felt his strong arms tight around me and humming in my hair. I slept.

When I woke up it was past lunch. Can you believe it? The house is quiet. Mother is still in her room, I think. Nana took Mary to see Doc Rawson in his office. My mind's too tired to think anymore, so to give it a holiday I went back to the magazines. Historians, you'll never guess what I found.

LIFE Magazine, April 14, 1947 - 15 cents or five dollars and fifty cents for a year. In it a man wrote advice for lady tipplers. I think that's what Mother must be, a lady tippler. The lady tipplers in 1947 don't sound like Mother, but I should put this advice here anyway. So you'll know in the future how it was back here. When you read this you'll call this the old days. I like that. Maybe there won't be lady tipplers up in the future where you are.

The man who wrote about the tipplers, Noel F. Busch, says that in 1909 (Nana was young then, and already had two babies) lady tipplers were rare. Ladies who tippled hid in their attics and were ig-nored by society. In 1947, he says, there was a spread of female alcoholism, so maybe that's when Mother caught it. She was thirty-one and had a house full of children. You catch things easier when you're tired.

Mr. Busch says in 1947, modern women, generally, were emotionally upset. People thought it was because they didn't have parity with men. The dictionary says parity means equality or similarity, so I'm not sure what he means. Equal and similar in what way? Mother is emotionally upset, because she didn't have a happy life during the war. And maybe also, because she's mad at papa. I don't know if she worries about being equal or similar.

Mr. Busch says the other reason most women were emotionally upset in 1947 was because they were all mixed up, and should go back to cooking, sweeping and attending their children. I think he's wrong there. I don't see how cooking, sweeping and attending to children would un-mix Mother or any woman, even back in 1947. Anyway, Mr. Busch gives advice to lady tipplers, and I can tell you, Historians, maybe it was good advice in 1947, but it isn't any good in 1953.

He says, *"The bar is a men's club, not a hospital for housewives with the fidgets."* Mother doesn't go to the bar, and I don't think she has fidgets. What she has is worse than fidgets.

"When she enters the bar, the lady should do so without fanfare. Taking a table near the door so that she can leave without annoying other patrons, she should then order some simple potion like beer, wine or whisky, which will not distract the barkeep from his major duties. While drinking this she will see to it that articles of personal apparel or adornment do not fall into disarray. If a gentleman accosts her she will reply graciously, as the circumstances indicate, taking good care of her manners."

The dictionary says *accost* means *'to solicit someone for immoral purposes'*. I don't think, Dear Diary, anyone should have to keep up good manners when someone accosts them for immoral purposes. Where are the good manners of the person doing the accosting?

Nana knows more than anyone about good manners, and I don't think she would keep them up if she were accosted.

"The lady should not grab other people's fruit, olives or pretzels. She must refrain from patting dogs, cats or other pets that may appear, as these animals are often temperamental."

I think Mr. Busch was the one mixed-up. There are no cats, dogs or other pets in a bar; at least I am pretty sure there aren't. We have a beer parlor, here in Deep Creek, but I think that it's the same as a bar where Mr. Busch lives. It has two doors. One says, 'Men'. One says 'Ladies and Escorts'.

"Hat, coat and gloves should not be dropped to the floor. The handbag will be opened if at all only to pay the bill, and there should be no arguments about this matter.

If drunken political discussions start, the lady will refrain from taking part in them. She will eschew gossip, critical remarks and impetuous rejoinder. No more than a half an hour after her arrival, she will get up and go home. Drinking in the home, of course, poses other questions, but at least it does not constitute a public menace."

What lady would ever constitute a public menace? I think Mother's constitutes a private menace, not a public one, at least not in a bar.

Tuesday, May 26, 1953

Dear Diary,

Four days have gone by. Fat Freddie went off to a mayor's meeting in Edmonton. It would have been an excellent time to snoop around his place, but I haven't had time. I'm all caught up with helping Nana and Mary do Mrs. O'Kane's jobs. I like it. Three women together. I know Mary and I are not exactly women. But we three are like Baba, Auntie Olga and half-blind Wasy, working together, making a perfect tune.

I told Nana that if what we did together was made into a song, it would make fine listening. Nana laughed and gave me a fast hug.

She said, "Tally, you have a unique way of seeing things. That's a gift to be cherished."

That reminded her of a time I was listening to music on the radio with her. She says it was the Pier Gynt Suite, the part about morning, which I still love. I was a child, still not in school. I told her the music gave me a balloon heart. That is exactly what beautiful things do to a person, fill up the heart till it feels light and stretched and ready to float away. Nana is kind to give me a compliment for telling about it, but I'm certain every person knows when they have a balloon heart.

Nana told the story in front of Mary this morning. It didn't exactly make her smile, but she did whisper. The first words she's said since that awful time in the jail. I couldn't hear what she said, but it must have been asking to listen to the morning piece from Pier Gynt's suite, because that's what we did while we ate. Nana brought the phonograph into the breakfast room and the music filled it up.

Mary sat with her eyes closed, listening. Nana put her finger to her lips to tell me not to bother her, and I didn't. Nana whispered to me later that Mary has plenty of time to catch up with eating. If she doesn't want to eat yet, we aren't to bother her about it. She drinks Nana's medicine tea without quarrel. Nana made a special tea for her with the St. John's weed in it. The weed Nana picks at her sister's in B.C. Also there's chickweed in there, and raspberry leaves. Mary drinks it three times a day. I think it must be for getting over bad happenings. She sips soup too, and oat and barley water, so I guess she won't starve.

Mary smiled with her eyes closed. She whispered. "Sweet music, Peter Gynt. If it was taste, it would be honey on my tongue."

What a good way to say it. Nana agreed that Mary also has a unique way of seeing things. I wish she was my sister. Mary would make a fine sister. We fit together, Mary and I.

Beanie and I aren't fitting together anymore. After school he came over, like he usually does. We ate cookies on the porch, while Stella chewed on the ham bone Nana saved for her. Beanie wanted to know why Mary won't come to sit with us.

"I guess she thinks she's too good to be seen with me."

That was a terrible thing for Beanie to say and when I told him so, he grabbed cookies off the plate, stomped to the bottom of the porch steps and shouted at me.

"And she's making you stuck-up too, Natalie Smythe. See if I care. See if I care one bit."

I told him yesterday that Mary wasn't feeling well. I can't tell him what really happened, but it shouldn't matter. I'm his friend. Mary's his friend. He's mad and mean and I don't know why. Everything is so inside-out.

It's probably too late to find where Freddy put the jewelry. I'm sure he's got rid of it by now. Sold it or buried it or threw it in the river. Nana says the Masters have plenty of insurance, so they can buy more jewelry. I hope everything will settle down now.

I don't know if Mother told papa about her trouble. I don't know if she found a doctor to go to, but she seems like herself again. She's even polite to Mary.

I don't know if papa knows what happened to Mary. I think he doesn't. Nana says, for Mary's sake, we must not talk about it to anyone. Nana says that's how gossip spreads. No matter what we say, people will think badly of Mary, even though nothing is her fault.

I'm jealous of Russell for not having to grow up. I don't think I'm going to like being an adult.

May 28, 1953

Dear Diary,

Mary is saying a few words. Only to Nana and to me, but she's back to reading her part of Pearl S. Buck. Her voice is getting stronger. At first I barely heard her, but Nana told me not to bother her about it.

Mary won't leave the house without Nana. Not even into the garden. I don't think she'd leave even if the house was burning. She's easily startled, like papa. She's sure Freddy can pin the theft on her somehow, and she worries any moment he will bang on the door. I don't blame her for that. I know Nana will keep her safe, but Mary still has all those bad things so new in her mind. Though she misses her family, she doesn't want to go back to the farm, not right away. She wants to wait until her bruises are gone. The one on her face is the only one that shows up, but she's afraid of what Dominic might do if he finds out.

Beanie has not been back and I feel awful, but I've got no room to worry about it right now. Laura is particularly crabby lately. Mother says she's nervous about her graduation. What's to be nervous about? It's ceremonies and formalities and boring ones at that. We all have to go and endure it. Laura is the valedictorian, but she speaks at the podium all the time during public speaking. She wins prizes for it, so I don't think she's worried.

Jeannie's been fighting with Roger. Mother is pleased about that. When he left last night he slammed the door. He refuses to buy a new suit for graduation. Jeannie says if he loved her he would want her graduation to be perfect. He said she's a spoiled brat. He says there's nothing wrong with his suit. It was brand new when he graduated two years ago, and he only wore it once since. Jeannie is insulted. She says she'll break up with him the minute graduation is over. I asked her, why wait? She threw her movie magazine at me.

"Mo-ther. Get her out of here. She's always nosing around making fun of me."

That's not true. I never make fun of anybody. Mother yelled at me. Laura yelled at Mother. Yikes. When things get going badly there seems no way to stop it. The evil in Mother isn't gone. It's hiding behind her eyes. I try not to look at her eyes. She gets up early now, like she's never done before, singing little songs to herself as she gets ready to go down town to arrange everything for the graduation reception. Nana's washed her hands of the whole thing. She says Mother's being silly, treating a simple grade twelve graduation like a royal wedding.

It's easy to avoid Mother. She's too busy to notice me. She drags Jeannie and Laura around after school. She doesn't notice Laura getting grumpier and grumpier. Something is going on with Laura, but I don't know what it is. Worrying about Mary and about Beanie, and about Mother's tippling makes my stomach hurt, and now I'm in a stew about Laura.

Today Freddy is supposed to go on the train to his lodge meeting in Fort Caskey. He goes the last Tuesday of every month. Nana says it's shameful for him to snub his local chapter here in town, especially when he's the mayor. But he started doing it before he got to be mayor, so I guess he won't stop now. He never comes home till Thursday morning (Crazy Marion says he has to sleep off his hangover, first) so at least I have time to check in his garage one last time. I know it's silly to keep at this like a dog on a bone, but it would be a great relief to have Mary free from suspicion. Mother too, I guess.

Later, May 28, 1953

Dear Diary,

I hid in the caraganas by the train station, and saw Fat Freddy get on the train. I got thinking, squashed in there with prickles against my face. I got thinking, if I found the jewelry, and told the police, and Freddy went to jail, I might get my picture in the paper. Mother would clip it and put it in her scrapbook with all the newspaper clippings of her and Jeannie. She'd write under it in her beautiful handwriting. . .

"Tally, Our hero!" Mother likes to put little sayings beside her newspaper clippings. The one with Jeannie in her tap shoes when she won the talent night contest says *"Jeannie, Our little princess."*

I don't know why I care what Mother thinks of me. I still have boiling in my head and in my stomach over what she did to Mary. And then I turn around and wish she'd smile at me. I hate that. I am seven kinds of crazy.

Roger and Gerry came over after supper to take Jeannie for a ride. Nana was sorting seed packets on the garden bench by the wild cucumber trellis, and I was sitting on the porch swing when they came. Jeannie wouldn't come down from her room, so Gerry sat and talked with Nana. She says he's a vacuous boy who spends time with grown-ups because he wants to make an impression. She says he's harmless, but tiresome. Mother says he's a young gentleman who has the most high regard for women. She doesn't understand why Jeannie can't see he is the best choice for her. She still thinks Roger is a hooligan in the making like his brother and his oldest sister, Suzanne. The way Mother talks, they sound like criminals.

Nana says Roger's brother Don raised his brother and sisters after their mother died from falling down a well, and their papa died likkered up in a snow bank. She says he did as good a job as any human could have under the circumstances. He's a man to be admired.

Roger's oldest sister Suzanne, has a beauty parlour over in Fort Caskey. Nana says it's a crime she had to go to another town to do it because the people in Deep Creek are so mean about her little girl not having a papa. Suzanne helped raise Roger while other girls her age were having fun. She quit school early and went to work to help her family.

Roger came up on the porch and sat beside me on the swing. He said, like he always does,"How're ya doin', short stuff?" He put his arm along the back of the swing, right behind my neck. If I had dared lean back, my neck would have touched his arm.

I wanted to lean back. Oh, Dear Diary, I did so want to. It was the strangest feeling. But not a bad feeling. Not a bad feeling at all. I wonder if boy crazy is starting to happen to me. Roger smells good. Warm and spicy. Of course, it doesn't do me any good to get boy crazy over him. He's way too old and he's also going steady with Jeannie. I'm only in grade seven, not ready for a boyfriend. In fact, I would still be in grade six if I hadn't started school when I was five. Anyway, if Jeannie breaks up with him, he'll never sit beside me on the porch again. I'm sorry for that.

I can't ask Beanie to come with me to Freddy's this time. He's still not speaking to me, and anyway, I don't think he's over our last adventure.

Truly dark and truly late, May 28, 1953

Dear Diary,

It wasn't as hard as I thought it would be. I didn't smear dirt on my face or my clothes. I stayed in the shadows. I took my time. I lifted my knee with my hand to make sure my foot didn't drag.

Freddy's gone, so I wasn't in any danger from him, but I didn't want to be discovered by anybody else, because I'd get reported to Nana for sure.

He must oil the hinges on his garage door. It opened smooth and quiet. I had a pocket full of candles and matches. I lit a candle. I didn't think I'd find jewelry and I didn't, but I what I found. Oh, Dear Diary, what I found. Dozens of ladies' underwear in the glove compartment. Not just Mrs. Masters' underwear. Underpants of every size, and brassieres and even a garter belt. Little, tiny underpants and great, big ones. I had a hard time cramming them all back in.

Before breakfast May 29, 1953

Dear Diary.

Can you believe it? I had to begin another new scribbler to-day. This is my fourth one, and I'm writing on both sides of the page. I guess I'm lucky to be able to give you Historians so much daily life to use, but I was not so lucky last night. It turned out all right in the end, but it scared me cuckoo, I can tell you. I don't think I can ever tell Beanie the whole story. I'm glad he wasn't with me.

After recording last night's adventure to Freddy's garage, I fell asleep in Granddad's chair and didn't wake up until three this morning. My feet were cold, and I got mad all over again at Mother for being a witch when she should be a princess. I got mad at Freddy for being so vile, and for making so much trouble.

Freddy is cruel and mean and nothing bad happens to him. It's so unfair. I don't usually wake up grumpy and mad. I needed to shake it off. But how? Granddad finally gave me an idea. I have his fountain pen, but I don't use it much, because I smear. Granddad was right; if ever there was a good place to use it, it was now. On plain school pa-per, I made a note to Constable Kipp.

"Dear Constable Kipp, Frederick Bugle took Mrs. Masters' jewelry and her unmentionables. Look in the glove compartment of his station wagon. It is in his garage. Yours truly, anonymous"

I wasn't sure how to end it. I usually end letters with - 'your friend Tally' or 'your granddaughter Natalie'. I wrote the note left-handed to make it extra crooked and messy. Ink smeared, of course, and I tore the paper in a few places for good measure. I don't think anybody will guess who wrote it.

I know there's no jewelry in the glove compartment, but I didn't think Constable Kipp would bother to go there for just under-wear. When he sees how much underwear is in there, I hope he'll cause a ruckus. I hope there's a law or a rule against stealing under-wear. Even if there isn't, I think Freddy might be in trouble, because of some of the underwear belonging to Mrs. Masters. But how will

Constable Kipp figure out what underwear belongs to whom? I don't know if I helped anything, but it was the only plan I had.

I delivered the note last night before I turned chicken. I put my green bathrobe over my nightgown. That's just about as good as taking Granddad with me. I was going to wear my winter slippers, the ones with rabbit fur inside for comfort. I didn't. My boot is the only thing that holds my foot straight enough so it doesn't drag behind.

The whole town was quiet by then, and everybody's lights were out. The peacefulness of people sleeping calmed me. Frog songs came up from Tremolo Pond, and all around me pressed the strong scent of lilac. Widow Olson's mama cat rubbed against my leg, and walked with me for a while until she heard a mouse in Granny Barclay's woodpile.

A thrill trickled through me. There I was, in the middle of town, in my nightclothes, waltzing down the back alleys like a dancer in a big music show, and nobody knew. I got so comfortable with myself I nearly strolled up to Constable Kipp's front door and knocked like I was a regular visitor.

I stopped myself just in time. The big safety pin I brought to pin the note to the screen door made my job easy. After that, nothing went right. I tripped over plant pots at the bottom of the steps. Then I knocked a box of tin cans off the potting table when I tried not to fall down. What a noise. I think the whole town heard. A light came on in Constable Kipp's bedroom. I heard his wife shriek for him to wake up. I stumbled through his raspberry bushes. Boy, have they got sharp stickers. I got behind his outhouse just before his porch light came on.

"Bowser! You good for nothing hound dog. You git right now, and leave my garbage be."

Constable Kipp thought I was Reggie Pierce's dog. My relief only lasted a minute, because the Ostrum's put their back porch light on. It shines on the back of Constable Kipp's outhouse, and I had to crouch down quickly, and crawl into the caraganas. Try crawling in a nightdress and bathrobe. Boy, what a trial.

That might have been the end of it, except Ostrum's rabbits were in the caraganas. They got scared and ran for their den under Ostrum's porch. When Mrs. Ostrum saw them coming she hollered at Constable Kipp that the damn dog was after her bunnies. He jumped off his porch, and ran through his garden in his long underwear, leaping over the little onion shoots which are about the only plants up.

I hiked my nightdress up over my waist, scrambled out of the caraganas, and scrunched down behind his woodpile. It's a small woodpile, I had to lie on the ground to stay hidden. It was wet and slimy there, stinky with punky poplar bark.

Mrs. Ostrum screamed and pointed. I peeked up and saw something on the rim of Kendrick's garbage can. I thought it was a cat. Constable Kipp had his gun and he yelled. "I got you this time you black bastard. I warned you."

Poohm! He shot the garbage can. He ran over, reached in, and a big old skunk jumped out of there, nearly on top of him. That part was very funny, but I didn't dare laugh. He swore, tossed his gun into the hedge, and dashed over to his ash pile. He jumped up and down, rubbing ashes all over himself. That's how you get rid of skunk smell.

Constable Kipp and his wife yelled back and forth at each other, then he sat on an up-turned bucket in the garden, and put his head in his hands. I stayed put. Finally Mrs. Ostrum shut her light off. Constable Kipp's wife came out and told him he had to sleep in the garage. She threw blankets, a pair of long underwear, and a coat on the grass. When she turned her porch light out I nearly made a break for it, but then she came back out, and told him to burn his skunkie underwear.

Constable Kipp walked by the woodpile to get to the burn barrel. If he'd looked down he might have seen me. I should have shut my eyes when he peeled off his underwear to burn it up, but I didn't want to. I'm now used to seeing men in their all-together, and after looking at Fat Freddy's sad little willie, I was curious to know if Constable Kipp had a willie big enough to make babies, since he and his wife don't have any yet.

Not that I saw much of him in the dark, but when he lit the stuff in his burn barrel it flared up, and I saw a lot of hair all over his skin, even on his back. When he turned to put on his other underwear I thought I saw his willie, but I don't know how to tell if it's big enough. It dangled there like a wet tea bag between his legs. I'm glad I'm not a boy, having to put up with all that business hanging around loose in my pants, bumping against my leg. How uncomfortable. I've decided it's better to be a girl with everything tucked up tidy.

After he dressed, he picked up an old canning kettle from beside his burn barrel. I thought he would turn it upside down and sit on it. But he didn't. He carried it over and put it on top of the woodpile. He came so close I could have spit on his big toe. I nearly died about then. It's a good thing I had on my green bathrobe, I can tell you. Even so, I don't know why he didn't see me, but he didn't. He strode over to the hedge and yanked out his gun. I bit my thumb, hard, so I wouldn't squeal.

Poohm! He shot the canning kettle. I tried to sink into the ground. The enamel from the kettle crackled and snapped and shot bits all over me. I figured he was going to shoot again, and I was just about to holler for him to stop when his wife turned on the porch light and came out.

"Leroy, you cut that racket. Granny Barclay's on the phone thinking there's another war." She was riled.

Constable Kipp picked up his blankets and trudged into his garage. His wife went back into the house, but she didn't turn off the stupid porch light, so I had to wait again.

My nightdress and my bathrobe are in a paper bag under my bed. They are filthy. I don't know what to do about it, but washday is not till the end of the week, so I'll have a plan by then.

After lunch May 29, 1953

Dear Diary,

I'm going to fill up this scribbler pretty fast. Luck is with me again. Can you believe it? I got to see what happened after Constable Kipp finally read my note. I think Granddad must be talking to God, the fates, and all the angels to keep the good luck stuck on me.

Nana sent me to Harry's Hardware first thing this morning to get new clothes pegs. She doesn't like to use rusty clothes pegs to hang up her unmentionables. All I could think about was Fat Freddie, snatching them of the clothesline and putting them on his face. So there I was at the back of the store. I'm short and quiet. People forget I'm there, in stores, and other places. I used to hate that about myself, but it's getting to be useful.

I stood at the back of the store trying to decide whether Nana would like pegs that come with their own peg bag, which she can hang on the clothesline or just a plain package of pegs. I had just decided on the plain package when Constable Kipp burst in the door. He grabbed Mr. Hornby (that's Harry) by the arm and dragged him into the store-room. The storeroom door was very close to where I stood. They didn't close the door all the way.

Naturally, I peeked in. There was a cardboard box tipped over near the door. It used to have a stove in it. Easily big enough for me to crawl into. A rip in the cardboard let light in, and when I held my eye right to it I could see out.

Mr. Hornby pushed Constable Kipp away. "Kipp. You smell like a nuisance wagon. What'd you do, sleep under the porch with a skunk?"

"Shut up, Harry. Poke fun at me later. We got serious business. Look at this." Constable Kipp was out of breath and sounded very excited. "Look what I found on my screen door this morning."

He shoved my note at Mr. Hornby. My heart beat fast. What if they knew who had written it? My teacher can tell my handwriting. But, like I said, luck stayed tight against me, as close as my skin.

"Freddy Bugle?" Mr. Hornby hit his palm with the paper. "I'll be damned."

"Could be a joke. He's not the most popular bastard."

"What's this about unmentionables?"

Constable Kipp turned his palms up. "Beats me."

"So, what are you going to do?"

Constable Kipp put his hands on his hips. "We. We, Harry. What are we going to do? This is too serious for one man."

"Oh no." Mr. Hornby turned away. "I'm not having anything to do with this. Freddy's got a mean streak as long as a train." He waved his arms around. "I'm not crossing him."

"You have to help me. Come on, Harry. Listen, I have to look in his garage. I have to. He's not even home right now. If we don't find anything we don't have to tell anybody we were there."

"Don't we have to tell him we're going in? We need a search warrant, don't we?"

"Don't need one, not for a car. Don't know about his garage, but I do know for a fact he's out of town. His missus and the kids left on the morning train to her Aunt Viv's in the city. The hired girl went home to help with seeding, so we could say we knocked and nobody was home...if we have to."

Mr. Hornby shuffled his feet through a pile of shredded paper packing. "I don't know. This isn't petty theft, you know. Doc's wife's jewelry is old antique stuff. Real gems and what not. Shouldn't we tell the judge or somebody?"

"Are you crazy? If this is a hoax, do you want it to get around town that we were snooping in Fred's garage? I don't know why people with valuables don't keep them in a safe." Constable Kipp sounded grumpy.

"This isn't the big city, Kipp. We don't need to lock things up here. All right. I'll come with you, but I don't think we'll find anything. Why would Freddy steal jewelry? He's a horse's ass, but he owns half the town. He doesn't need to steal."

"Yeah." Constable Kipp sounded relieved. "You're right."

When they left, I had to wiggle out of the box quick, pay for the clothes pegs, and dash them home to Nana, then race back down the hill to Freddy's to see if they looked in the glove compartment.

My good luck made everything go perfectly. I saw Beanie in his back yard building on his secret hideout with Russell. I waved. He waved back and went on hammering. He's going to be sore he missed it all. It's a good thing he didn't come. It's harder hiding in the day.

I took a chance and slipped into the outhouse beside Freddy's garage. Freddy's got indoor plumbing now, but he still uses his outdoor for storage. It's full of old papers, spider webs, and a thick, unpleasant poop smell, but I didn't let myself get worried about that. Constable Kipp had gone home to put his uniform on, so I had time to squeeze in there before they showed up. I don't know why he bothered with his uniform when he didn't want to be noticed. Nana's right. Most people don't bother to think things through. I watched through the cracks in the door, and saw them go into the garage. I heard the car door open.

"Holy shit." I heard Constable Kipp as clear as anything.

Mr. Hornby shot out the garage like a spitball from a peashooter. He stood on the boardwalk twisting his hands together. "Ohmygod this is bad news. Very bad news." He looked around like he was scared somebody might see him there.

Constable Kipp came out of the garage carrying underthings at the end of a stiff arm like they might burst into flames. "I don't believe this. I friggin' don't believe it. Now, what are we going to do?"

Mr. Hornby grabbed his own arms, rubbing up and down like he was cold. He glanced around like he thought Freddy would jump out of the bushes at him. I don't know why they were so scared. Constable Kipp has a gun.

"We can't arrest the mayor, Kipp. Isn't there a law against that?"

Constable Kipp shook his head. "It's against the law to steal, Harry. Even for mayors. Theft over fifty. The young Doc is still pretty steamed about the whole thing, and whoo-ee, he's going to blow his top clear to Mexico if any of these belong to his missus."

Mr. Hornby rubbed his head with both hands like it was sore. "What's the matter with that damn fool? Why'd he go and do a thing like this? Stupid. Just plain stupid."

"There's only one piece of that jewelry in here, Harry, just the bracelet, but it matches the description Doc gave. Real rubies, worth a whole year's salary, they say. A whole year of my salary, at any rate." Constable Kipp shook his head. He didn't seem so timid anymore with the real proof in his hands. "Can't ignore this Harry. Can't. We have to show it to the Doc. We have to, Harry. This's pretty queer. I dunno. Freddy's always been a little off the mark, but panties and such? The Doctor's wife's panties?" Constable Kipp talked like a machine gun. I didn't know he could say so many words at one time. He held up several pair of underthings between his finger and thumb. He shook his head. "Pretty fancy. Didn't buy these at Semeniuk's Five to a Dollar store."

Mr. Hornby stared at the underwear. "Stealin' jewelry's bad enough. I can just about understand that, but the Doc's wife's... his wife's. Oh, God. Goddamn it Kipp, put them out of sight."

"Come on, Harry. Calm down. Jesus H. Christ, I need some help here. That glove compartment's crammed tight with these things."

Mr. Hornby shook his head and started walking away. "I'm not touching them. Get the Doc. It's his mess."

"Harry, come back." Constable Kipp hollered at him, but Mr. Hornby kept on walking, faster and faster.

Constable Kipp pulled a crumpled paper bag from his pocket. He shook it and put the underthings he held into the bag. He stood there staring into it for a few minutes before he took a big breath, and walked back into the garage for the rest. He came out with two paper bags full, and some hanging out of his jacket pocket.

Boy, good thing I wrote the note. I didn't know about the bracelet. I wonder what Freddy did with the rest of the jewelry? It doesn't matter now. Mary will be free from blame even if they can't put Freddy in jail for only one bracelet. And Nana won't have to worry it might have been Mother.

Evening May 29, 1953

Dear Diary,

I didn't think I'd use the spy glass again, once Fat Freddy got caught out, but I've found another mystery that needs solving. It's the puzzlement about Laura. Nobody else has noticed. She goes every night to study with Linda, and I bet I'm the only one who knows she doesn't always go there.

Twice, after Laura left for Linda's and came home late, I passed my spyglass by Linda's house. Once I saw Linda curled up in a chair in her living room beside the radio with a book for the whole evening. Not once did I see Laura. The other time I saw Linda making pies in the kitchen with her mother, and her aunt Ruth, for the Church Supper. And no Laura to be seen. I don't know where she goes. It's not like her.

I had to tell someone, so I told Beanie. He just shrugged and said she's probably sneaking to see a boy. That's not possible. Laura doesn't even like boys. She says they're immature and stupid. Beanie says I'll be boy crazy next. I told him I was never going to be boy crazy. It was too damn much trouble. I guess we're still not back on track, Beanie and I.

Morning May 30, 1953, Thursday

Oh, Dear Diary,

Everybody is in a state this morning, and it is very hard to stay quiet. As usual I'm glad I've got you, Dear Diary. Mother got a phone call this morning from the Deep Creek station agent's wife, and she shook her head all through breakfast while she told us about Fat Freddy getting arrested.

Mary, of course, is the most relieved. In fact, she is a little bit cuckoo. She's flying around the kitchen doing everything at once. She chased Nana and me out this morning. She says she doesn't need help any more. She can do it all. Nana laughed and hugged her, and said she would check now and then to make certain she didn't overdo it.

"And when I say it is time for you to take a few hours or a few days off child, don't give me any argument. Do you understand?"

When Nana said that, Mary burst into tears and flung herself to her knees in front of Nana, grabbed her hands and kissed them all over and blubbered about being her servant forever. Nana pulled her up and sat her in a chair, gave her a hankie and a good talking to.

"Mary, my girl. I don't need a servant and you don't need to be one. Right now, you need a job, and I need a hired girl. You are already twice the help of anybody I've paid good money too, and if you don't slow down and mind what I say, I'll be forced to pay you more."

Nana had a very big twinkle in her eye when she said it, but Mary doesn't know Nana enough to know when she is teasing.

Mary gasped and shook her head wildly. She already feels she's getting a queen's salary, and feels guilty taking it. Nana pays her enough, so she can send money home, and still have some left to save for her education, but Nana says it is no more than she has ever paid for good help.

Mother reported that Constable Kipp and Mr. Hornby were waiting at the train station when Freddy got home this morning, and boy did he make a fuss. The men tried to talk quietly, and they kept apologizing all over the place about what they had to do, but Freddy yelled and kicked his suitcase halfway across the platform. He wouldn't let anybody get close enough to touch him. Except Constable Kipp has to touch a person for the arrest to be right. That's the rule. He had to chase Freddy all over the platform, and Freddy kept swatting at him with a rolled up newspaper. Nana says he should be charged for obstruction, but she says he won't be.

Freddy only stopped the ruckus when Doctor Masters got out of his car, from where he'd been watching the whole thing. He came up on the platform and punched Freddy right in the face. Then he dared Freddy to lay charges against him, got back into his car, slammed the door, and drove away making a huge cloud of dust.

Freddy had a bleeding nose, and a cut under his eye. Mother said he whimpered and sniveled all the way to the Constable Kipp's car. There's going to be a trial, but nobody believes he'll get much more than public humiliation. He insists one of his enemies planted the jewelry and the underthings, and goodness knows he has enough of those. Enemies, I mean.

Now that Mother is freed up from suspicion you'd think she'd be happy, but things are not back to where they were. Mother is still one way on the outside, and another behind her eyes. I can feel Nana is still displeased with her. I'm not so pleased with her myself. And then there's Laura. She's usually a quiet mouse in the house, but lately she has been picking fights with Jeannie and with Mother. She put her Philco radio in the kitchen where she goes every day after school to bake with Mary. I have to confess I'm a little bit jealous. I'm not much interested in baking, but just the same, they're having great fun. I've never known Laura to be interested in the kitchen. Very strange. I don't know if Nana has noticed. Maybe now that Fat Freddy's been discovered Nana will turn to solving family trouble. Nana is the only one who knows how to do that.

Tomorrow I'm going with Nana to visit poor Mrs. Bugle. Nana says Freddy deserves whatever he gets, but that poor little thing doesn't. Nana says if she visits in broad daylight others will follow suit. That's the way with Nana. A lot of people want to copy her. Tomorrow Freddy has a court appearance, and Nana wants to make certain nobody condemns Mrs. Bugle along with Freddy.

May 30, 1953, still Thursday

Gerry and Roger came over after school to see Jeannie, but she's still playing hard-to-get in her room. Mother made jokes about it and insisted Gerry and Roger play Monopoly with her. I don't know why. She doesn't like Monopoly. I knew Roger didn't want to stay, but Gerry winked at me and said, "It would be fun, Mrs. Smythe. I haven't played monopoly in a while."

They played monopoly with Mother for over an hour, and she giggled every time Gerry said even one word. Roger tried to make jokes about Freddy, but Mother didn't laugh at one of them. She ignored Roger, but she talked to Gerry like he was a grown-up.

Mary and Nana were staking peas in the garden, so Mother sent me to the kitchen to bring Kool-Aid and cake. Roger helped me. He pulled my hair and called me 'short stuff'. Oh, Dear Diary, I really like him. Do you think that makes me boy crazy? I know he's too old to take an interest in me even if he didn't have Jeannie, but it's fun to imagine it happening. Do you suppose, someday, if there was a boy my age, and if he didn't care about my foot, do you suppose Mother would change her mind and let me marry?

You know what, Dear Diary? Maybe Mother won't be the boss of me by then. When I'm twenty-one, I'll be grown-up and can do as I jolly well please. Go where I want, and marry anybody in the whole wide world if I take a notion to.

June 1, 1953

Dear Diary,

I've got over an hour before I go with Nana to Fat Freddy's, so I better record for you Historians, instead of wearing a ditch in the carpet walking back and forth like a horse in a pen. I feel like I have a cap gun inside me ready for someone to pull the trigger. I'm such a busy body. I never get enough of hearing about everything.

So, back to magazines. *'Writing is fighting too'*. Isn't that a good sentence? It's from an advertisement for Wearever Zenith fountain pens. Mother has a Wearever Zenith pen and pencil set on her tall bureau. I don't think she's ever used it. Nana says she didn't write to papa when he was overseas. Crazy Marion says Mother hoped papa would die bravely, so she would get a decent pension and be a merry war widow. Maybe that's true. Mother says the war ruined papa. I asked Nana about it and she didn't answer me until she had crocheted a whole round on the big tablecloth she is making for somebody's hope chest.

"War is an awful thing, Chickadee." She stopped for a moment and wrapped the crochet cotton round and round her hand. "Good men know it, the ones who survive."

I knew she was thinking about Uncle Joe, Uncle Pete and Uncle Wilton who didn't come back from the war. And maybe Granddad.

"Good men are easily ruined by war, because it isn't in their nature to participate in such destruction." She paused again and stared out the window. "Men with a mean streak come away from war the same kind of bullies they were when they went in, only by the time war is finished with them, only the bullying part of them is left."

Oh, Historians, I hope you don't have war up there in the future.

Speaking of bullies, Fat Freddy had to stay in jail for two whole days and one night because he wouldn't call a lawyer. He wanted to defend himself. Judge Balder is steamed. He doesn't like it when his life is interrupted, and this is too much interruption for him. He was fishing up at Muskeg Lake. He wouldn't come back until Freddy agreed to get himself a proper lawyer. Nana said Judge Balder told Freddy, *Amicus Curiu*. Aren't those grand words? *Amicus Curiu*. Those are special judge words. Nana says they mean, "it is stupid to defend yourself in a court of law".

Constable Kipp had to stay overnight at the jail with Freddy, because nobody else would. Freddy yelled and swore at him the whole time. Constable Kipp is a wreck. Nana says men like Freddy think they can do what they like without paying a price.

Freddy refused to have a lawyer from around here, so he finally got a lawyer from Edmonton. A high priced lawyer who drove all the way here to get Freddy out of jail. No matter what else happens to him, Fat Freddy is going to have to pay a pile of money, especially for getting a lawyer to drive here on a weekend. Freddy has to go back to the courthouse today. That's why we're going to help Mrs. Bugle get through it. Freddy won't go into his house. He stays in the garage with a comforter in his car, and his poor wife has to take his food to him and then bring back the plates. Nana phoned Freddy's wife last night to tell her we were coming for tea today. Nobody refuses Nana tea.

I've been thinking about girdles again, since Mother insisted Nana get one for graduation. Nana laughed in her face. She won't wear one, ever. Mother won't go without one. Mother even wears one under her bathing suit.

I found two pages in this magazine about ladies being neat and tidy in their girdles. Mother says Nana is an eccentric for not wearing one. That's a very good word. Eccentric. It took me two tries to spell it, so I could look it up in the dictionary. (I use Nana's Oxford.) In there it says eccentric means irregular, capricious, odd or whimsical.

Nana is very irregular compared to Mother. She is round and bulgy, where Mother is straight and hard. Capricious means humorous, and that's for sure Nana. One time when we were all on the porch, Stella farted in her sleep. Not only did Nana laugh, she also showed Beanie and me how to make fart noises with our arm pits. Mother didn't approve of it, but papa thought it was funny too. It's not healthy to be serious all the time.

I suppose I'm destined to be eccentric, which is a good thing, because I don't want to have to wear a girdle. Jeannie wears one, and believe you me, it's an awful trial for her to wiggle in and out of it. Historians, I hope girdles have become extinct up where you are.

The pages about wearing a girdle were written by somebody called Maureen O'Hara. She looks a little bit like Mother. Maureen O'Hara says, "*One thing that puzzles me is the ungirdled state that lots of women go about in when they're at home.*" She also says that women don't have to wear their Sunday best foundation all the time, but they must wear something. I'm guessing she means some other kind of girdle. I don't understand them and don't want to.

In 1943 people could send checker games to soldiers. The checkers were golf tees stuck in a board, so they wouldn't slide off in rough seas. I wonder if anybody sent one to papa and Uncle Joe when they had to sit in the bottom of a ship all the way to the fighting in Sicily? Papa told Uncle Metro, they didn't know where they were going. It was hot down there, stinky and dark, and everybody squashed in so tight it was hard to keep people from fighting with each other.

Then a storm came along and tossed the ship all over the sea. Up and down and back and forth until everybody got sick all over themselves with no time to wash off before they had to climb into the little boats to get to the beaches to begin the fighting. Maybe checker games weren't the most helpful gift after all.

After supper June 1, 1953

Dear Diary,

We've done our duty where Freddy's poor wife is concerned. Nana and I sat in Mrs. Bugle's living room having tea and little cookies on her best china. Nana told Mrs. Bugle (who, by the way, is very nice, and her name is Rose) that some men were strange creatures who didn't give you any clues as to how to understand them. She said no person with their eyes open will blame Rose for one minute for any foolish indiscretions committed by her husband.

Rose passed us more cookies. They were from a package. Our talking was nice until Freddy burst in the door all rumpled, wrinkled and cross.

"Woman!" He yelled from the kitchen. Rose dropped the teapot on the rug and burst into tears. Nana marched into the kitchen.

"Frederick." Nobody but Nana calls him Frederick. "Shame on you. Get your wits about you, man."

Freddy's voice lowered then, but I have very good hearing and I heard him mutter, "It's my own house..."

"So it is. But you'll have to moderate yourself now for the sake of your family." Nana talked to him like she talks to Jeannie when she's disappointed. "Frederick. You've disgraced yourself, and you have to pay the price; it's the honourable thing to do, and it is best done with dignity. But there's no reason for your family to have to pay. It's your duty to ensure they will not be embarrassed further. Now go and tidy up. I'll accompany you and Rose to the court house."

"You're going to the court house?" Freddy held his fists together in front of him.

"Oh, for heaven's sake, Frederick. Get control of yourself. Go upstairs. Wash up, shave and change. Put on your very best and hold your head up."

Freddy said nothing more, and soon I heard his footsteps on the stairs. Nana came back to the living room like she had just had the most ordinary conversation. She sat beside Rose on the sofa and took her hands. "Take a few deep breaths, dear. That's it. A few more."

Rose looked at Nana so pitifully I nearly cried like a baby.

"Now," Nana spoke briskly, "Come. Wash your face, put on a little powder and your best shoes. I'll help you with your hair."

Rose said nothing, but she followed Nana, and did as she was told. I have to say, Dear Diary, Nana worked wonders on her. Rose was turned very elegant by the time Freddy came down stairs. Then Nana patted and brushed him into a tidier state than I've ever seen him. She even went so far as to trim his hair with his moustache scissors. Then she pointed at his tie. "Frederick, don't you have a fresher tie?"

He didn't say anything, but he squished his eyes, and gave her a mean stare. Then he turned to Rose and she ran up the stairs.

"Bring a nice tie clip too." Nana called after her.

And sure enough, Rose brought down a very presentable tie, and the oddest tie clip. A shiny black beetle sitting in a gold nest. I was sure Nana would ask for another one, but she surprised me. "Ah," She said with admiration. "An Egyptian scarab carved from ebony if I'm not mistaken. Very impressive." She smiled at Freddie encouragingly.

"I'm not wearing a damn bug on my tie."

Nana fixed him with a look, and he didn't say anymore.

"It's the only one we have Mrs. Smythe. Fred doesn't usually wear a clip. It was my father's." Rose has a soft voice.

"Rose, it's perfect. Very aristocratic, Frederick. Obviously expensive. I'm surprised you haven't worn it before."

Freddy glared at Nana, but he didn't take it off.

Nana said 'aristocratic' and 'expensive' on purpose, because she knows Freddy has desires in that direction. Nana dug in her handbag for a tiny lace-edged handkerchief, and tucked it into the little chest pocket of Rose's dress. Then she removed her own ivory cameo and pinned it on Rose.

"Oh, Mrs. Smythe. I couldn't." Rose backed away from Nana.

Nana tugged her back. "You can and you will. Don't be silly. Eyes will be upon you, and you must look your best. The way to weather a storm is to sail right into it."

And so we did. Nana and I sailed right behind them down to the courthouse, where I think nearly everybody from town was crowded in. Nana wouldn't let Freddy drive the car. She said everybody must see him facing this difficulty with dignity. Freddy's face was a thunder storm, and Rose, walking behind him, stared down at her shoes. Freddy's lawyer stood on the courthouse steps to meet them. Nana turned and steered me towards home.

It isn't proper, she says, to stay and gloat over another's misfortune, no matter how much they deserve it. Nana says Freddy must plead guilty for his own good, and get on with it. When I asked her if he would go to jail, she sighed. "Most likely not. But he'll pay a stiff fine and the public humiliation will do him good."

June 4, 1953

Dear Diary,

The Queen's Coronation is over. That gave everybody different talk for a while. Young Queen Elizabeth is so beautiful, and her husband so handsome; they make for happy conversation. Grandma Walters was not taken with Prince Phillip at first, because he's Greek. But Nana used an upside down way to change her mind. Nana doesn't really care what Grandma Walters says about the young Queen's husband, but Crazy Marion says it's fun to make Grandma Walters second guess herself. Anyway, Nana said, Phillip most likely was forced to marry Royal since his people were penniless wanderers after having to run away from Greece. That made Grandma Walters steam.

She hates frivolous talk about the Royals, even the Royals she disapproves of.

"You make him out to be an itinerant adventurer, Marjorie. Such loose talk. He may be Greek, but he is still a Royal."

And before you knew it Grandma was talking about him like she'd always admired him. In fact, she even hinted she named Uncle Phillip after him. Grandma is easy to turn about.

Of course, the coronation didn't hold anybody for very long. It happened so far away. Now the talk is back on Freddy, and I'm tired of hearing it. I don't have the urge to interrupt anymore: I don't even care if nobody knows it was me who found him out.

He pleaded not guilty, for heaven sake. Everybody says he'll get off Scot-free. Nobody is talking about the underwear. I'm pretty sure the whole town knows about them. At least he has to go back to court, and it's going to cost him.

He says if he catches the person who set him up - that person will be sorry he was born. Of course, most people believe Freddy stole the jewelry, but there are a few who believe the enemy story. Quite a lot of grist for the coffee klatch gossip mill Nana says. Anyway it's all tiresome for me. So, I'll get back to recording things for you Historians.

I'm also tired of 1943. I'm skipping to a magazine from 1947. I was six then, and papa was home for good. Maybe you Historians will want to know what it was like after the war when people didn't have to buy war bonds or plant victory gardens or ration food. I don't remember the rationing, but people still talk about it.

There's one thing I've noticed about this after-the-war magazine. It is full of advertisements for women who need feminine protection and underarm deodorant. I don't know what women did about that during the war. Maybe it was part of the war effort to go without protection. That's one thing Mother talks about at the table that Nana doesn't. Feminine protection. Jeannie talks about it too. She

thinks she's so smart, because she got her period when she was fourteen.

I hope my body waits till then. Mother says when you get
your period you're next door to being a woman. I don't want to be a
woman. I plan to stay a girl as long as I can.

Mother says becoming a woman is a wonderful thing, but I
don't think she means it. Neither does Jeannie. Laura doesn't notice
one way or another. Nana is way older than all of us. She's the same
age as Pearl S. Buck. I think she skipped womanhood and went right
to old womanhood, so maybe I will too. She doesn't wear a girdle or a
push-up brassiere. She doesn't shave the hair off her legs. When she
bathes she dusts herself with talcum powder mixed with baking soda
instead of using under arm protection. Nana never has an 'offensive
odour' so it must work.

Mother and Laura and Jeannie use Arrid. The 1947 advertisement for Arrid says, *"Many mysterious changes take place in your
body as you approach womanhood. For instance, the apocrine glands
under your arms begin to secrete daily a type of perspiration you've
never known before. It causes an unpleasant odor on both your person
and your clothes."*

That doesn't sound wonderful to me.

Then it says, "*A dance, a date, an embarrassing remark may
easily make you perspire and offend as well as ruin a dress.*"

Oh, great. Ruined dresses to add to my gimp. Good thing I
seldom wear them. Now about the other. The advertisements show
ladies happy and swimming when they have their period, because they
use internal protection.

Jeannie says girls can't wear internal protection until they get
married. She says I'm doomed to ride a white horse my whole life.
But one thing I'll never do is take to my bed moaning and groaning.
When their monthlies are upon them, I have to bring Mother and
Jeannie ginger ale, the hot water bottle, movie magazines and ice
cream. I feel like Granny Barclay's hired girl on those days.

If I have to be a woman I'm going to wear internal protection, use talcum powder, never wear a girdle, and I won't bother about face powder. That's one place where I'll be different than Nana. I've tried hers and it makes my face itch.

June 5, 1953

Dear Diary,

I saw the oddest thing tonight. Actually, two odd things. One odd thing is Laura. She and Jeannie had a fight and she left in a big kerfuffle, slamming the door so hard the windows rattled. It's a good thing Nana has strong doors. I followed her with the spyglass until she turned around the corner of the school, and then she didn't come out the other side. There's nothing but the teacherage at the end of that street, and she wouldn't have gone there. Of course, maybe she crossed the creek and took the back path to the hospital, but I don't know why she'd do that.

After I lost Laura, I saw a light come on in a basement room at the Boisvert's house. Silvie Boisvert is Laura's friend from school, and she was supposed to graduate this year too, but sometime around Valentine's Day she quit school and went to Edmonton to live with her grandmother beside a convent. Her mother told Laura that Silvie was not receiving a proper Catholic education. They found an opportunity for her at a Catholic school in Edmonton. Laura's feelings were hurt when Silvie didn't say goodbye.

Crazy Marion said, if she was not receiving a proper education why did they wait until nearly the end of grade twelve to find another school for her? Mother was pleased, because she never did like the influence Silvie had over Laura. She said Silvie is most likely fast like her mother and being Catholic doesn't slow her down. Nana says there was never anything fast about Mrs. Boisvert. Mother says those things, because she likes to find fault with Catholics. Catholics have the Pope. They have to obey him. We Protestants don't have to, but I don't know why it matters.

What Mother really doesn't like about Silvie is her ambition to be an architect. Mother says it's only slightly sillier than Laura wanting to be a doctor. Mother says with Silvie gone, Laura will return to her senses, but what Mother doesn't know is that for Laura, becoming a doctor is being in her senses.

Anyway, that's got nothing to do with what I saw. Everybody knows Silvie's mother is going to have another baby even though she's old enough for the change. She breeds like a rabbit Mother says, with no pride at all. Nana says it's a worry to have a late pregnancy, because of having a Mongoloid. I piped up, wanting to know what's wrong with that. Mother said it would be nine months of suffering for nothing, just a retarded baby who would have to go to an institution. Nana said that's not it at all. She said an older mother with a Mongoloid child worries about who will look after her child when she dies. Mother said there are institutions for defectives like that. Nana disagreed. She said we're no better than the Nazis when we are willing to shut people away from family and friends. If we don't have the compassion God gave us to care for the poor, the sick and the crippled in our communities we are a sorry species. Mother flounced away before Nana was finished speaking. She doesn't want talk like that filling up her mind. It makes her head hurt.

Anyway, I saw Mrs. Boisvert walk over to her washing machine and lift up her smock. I saw her take off the very opposite of a girdle. Girdles pinch you in to press your stomach flat. She has a round pillow that makes her stomach look like a pumpkin. She peeled a small pillowcase off it and dropped it into the washing machine. Can you believe that? The pillow makes her look pregnant. That's so odd. Why does she pretend to be pregnant? Especially when people say mean things about it?

June 6, 1953

Dear Diary,

I had to ask Nana about Mrs. Boisvert. I couldn't stand not knowing. I didn't get specific about how I knew, and Nana was so surprised she didn't think to ask me. The subject just came up. I didn't even have to sneak it in. Crazy Marion was drinking tea on the back porch with Nana, and she must have read my mind. She started talking about Mrs. Boisvert.

"Genevieve is so pale these days."

Nana agreed. "With the youngest of that brood of hers already a teenager, it has to be difficult preparing for a baby again."

Crazy Marion leaned on her elbow and tapped her hat brim with her spoon. "This pregnancy doesn't seem quite right. She carries herself like she's afraid the baby will fall out any minute."

That made me look up.

Nana agreed again. "I've noticed it myself. She was robust with all her others, but you have to remember, she's forty-eight years old."

Then, of course, I blurted it out. I just hate that about myself. "She has a cushion under her smock, with a belt sewed on it to tie around her middle."

They both stopped mid-sip and stared at me.

"I saw it last week. I saw her adjusting it."

"Ooh." A whoosh of air came out of Nana. "Of course. That's why she's been so evasive when I've questioned her about her confinement. I attended with Doc for her last four children. Doc's worried, because she hasn't been to see him with this one."

Crazy Marion reached for another sticky bun. "I guess that's a life sentence coming up for Silvie. We should have guessed as much, ourselves. We're slipping in our old age, Marg."

Nana shook her head slowly, her eyes were sad. "They'll move mountains to have married as soon as the baby is born, and they won't be choosy, either."

I must have looked puzzled, for true, at that point, and I was. Crazy Marion touched my nose with her finger like she always does, and winked at Nana. "Marjorie, it's up to you. Do I tell Miss Nosy Parker more than she needs to know about the birds and the bees, right now?"

Nana smiled. "Our Nosy Parker has an internal filing cabinet with more information tucked away than most people twice her age." She tugged on my braid. "I'd rather she had too much information than not enough. I've seen too much heartache caused by not enough information, but I've never seen trouble caused by somebody having too much."

Crazy Marion nodded. "I'm with you there. Missy Big Ears, I guess you understand that what I tell you has to stay a secret. Are you good at keeping secrets?"

I nodded my head. I wish she knew how many secrets I'm already keeping. I expected Nana to say something against keeping secrets, but she said nothing.

Nana smiled at me. "I'll vouch for her. She is a bit of a chatterbox, but when it's important Natalie can be tight as a clam."

This is what Nana and Crazy Marion think so far: Silvie didn't go to Edmonton to a better school; she went because she's pregnant. Being pregnant without being married is serious trouble. Who can blame her for leaving town. Sometimes a girl has to give her little baby away to strangers. Nana says it breaks a woman's heart in ways that never heal. They think that instead of giving her little baby to strangers, Silvie will give it to her mother. Her mother will pretend to birth it herself. That's a terrible amount of secrets to keep track of in one family. I'm glad my family doesn't have any secrets as serious as that.

Nana and Crazy Marion cannot imagine who the father is, because Silvie didn't even have a boyfriend. They think maybe she got involved with a Protestant boy, and had to sneak around because her parents don't believe in mixing religions. Nana says that kind of intolerance has brought heartache to more than one family in Deep Creek, and not only to Catholics.

June 7, 1953

Dear Diary,

We don't have to worry about Mary being arrested or taken away, or Mother being a suspect for thievery, so you'd think our house would be cheerful, but we have no luck there. Everybody still has a dander up, and to top it all off, Beanie's mad at me all over again.

I don't want to make him mad, but I'm trying to be more like Mrs. Buck and Nana. I'm trying to stand up against ignorance and injustice. Beanie and Russell set box traps to catch crows and magpies so they can kill them and chop off their feet to take over to Harry's Hardware. Beanie says he can make way more money with feet and gopher tails than he can make with pop bottles. Now, here's something, Historians, Beanie gets five cents for a pair of bird's feet and two cents for a gopher tail.

Last year we had a fight about the gopher tails. Nana offered to pay Beanie to bring her the newspaper every day if he would stop catching gophers and chopping off their tails. Nobody was on Nana's side about the gophers except me, not even papa. He said gophers are a nuisance. They wreck crops and they breed like flies and have to be controlled. Nana and papa are not often at odds with each other, but on the subject of gopher tails they are. She says, if people are so anxious to be rid of the creatures, then they should do the honourable thing and eat them.

I can't get Beanie to understand that gophers don't grow new tails when you cut them off. He pours water down their burrows and when they escape half drowned, he grabs them, chops off their tails and lets them go. He says dumb animals don't feel pain. Can you believe that?

Nana says it's wrong to kill creatures unless it's for food, clothing or shelter, and she means even crawly creatures like grasshoppers. She says they are a natural and healthy food for chickens, and it is wasteful to poison them. She says killing animals without using them for food and clothing is wanton and dangerous. It's against nature. Around Deep Creek it's not an argument easily won, because most kids get BB guns before they're twelve. They shoot birds, gophers, rabbits and even cats when they get carried away. There's no law against it.

Nana says when you can't win somebody over to your side of an argument it's no reason for you to give in when you know you're right. So Beanie and I got into it again this year, and this time over crows and magpies. I was pretty sure I would win the day, because papa is on my side this time. Beanie has big respect for papa. Papa likes birds. He says the only crime crows and magpies commit is being too smart.

People don't like smart birds. Birdbrains. That's what they want. Crows and magpies don't harm the crops and they can't eat baby chicks when there are a few banty hen mothers around for protection. Papa says it's easy to keep a few bantams.

Beanie's so stubborn. He wishes he was old enough for a twenty-two rifle, because coyotes have a five dollar bounty on them. He could be rich, very fast. I was already riled before he brought up the coyote bounty idea. I told him if he ever started shooting coyotes I wouldn't be his friend anymore. Then he hurt my feelings. He said he didn't care if I was his friend. He said he doesn't need friends, but he does need money.

Late night, June 7, 1953

Oh, Dear Diary,

This is too much. I dozed in Granddad's chair again when I should have been in bed. I had the windows open, so I could smell the lilacs. That's why I heard a car door close. I scooted over to the window seat and you won't believe who I saw there, down by Nana's garden gate.

Laura! I didn't need the spyglass to recognize Laura. And who brought her home? In a car? Mr. Booth. He's a teacher in the high school. Her teacher. And it wasn't just him bringing her home, and so late. 1:30 in the morning.

He kissed her.

I mean *really* kissed her. They stood so close together hugging and kissing; they could have been one person.

Mr. Booth. He's a new teacher. From the city. And he's old. Probably at least twenty-five. Laura! I don't know what to think about this. When they stopped the kissing she crept up the path through the garden to the back door. Mr. Booth waited until she was in the house. Then he drove away without his car lights on.

I don't think teachers are supposed to kiss their students. Does this mean Laura will have to get married? To him? I guess I have to wait and see, because there's nobody to ask about this. This might be too much daily life for you, Historians.

June 8, 1953

Dear Diary,

You won't believe it. Crazy Marion came over early this morning and sat outside with Nana. I should have been sleeping, I know, but after seeing Laura last night I got restless with my sleeping. Their talking came right up into my window and I woke up. So, of course, down I went. Down the back stairs. It's a good thing wild cucumber vines grow thick behind the arch bench. They're half way up the arch already, so it's easy to creep up and sit comfortable on the potato pail to listen.

And what I heard!

Dr. Masters is the father of Silvie's baby! Can you believe it? Crazy Marion got so riled I thought she was going to jump up and go lay a licking on Dr. Masters right that minute.

"Damn it to hell, Marjorie. I wish I was man with no conscience. A big, stupid brute of a man. Drag that bastard out of his bed and beat him bloody. Stretch him over an ant hill with honey on his worthless pizzle."

"I think Doc Rawson felt the same way. After we talked with Genevieve I walked with him on the river road. He needed to let off steam. He rampaged like a grizzly bear down there. I never thought Doc capable of violence, but I can tell you, Marion, had Hugh Masters come by I would have feared for his life. Doc ripped dead branches off trees and beat them to shreds over river rocks. Bark and wood chips flying everywhere. Never said a word. Not one word. Just growled and grunted like an old bear, smashing to smithereens an awful pile of wood." Nana sounded grim.

Crazy Marion kicked at the grass with her boot. "So, when is he going to visit young Doc?"

Nana sighed. "He already has. Last night. It was after midnight before he calmed down enough to do it. He insisted that I go with him.

"You don't need to leave the car, Marg," he said. "I just need a witness so I don't accidently kill the bastard."

He marched right up to Masters' door. Told him there'd been an accident. Barely let him get into the car before Doc drove off like a lunatic. To the old Pitzer place. Drove right into the middle of that hipped roof barn. Ordered Hugh out of the car. Left it running with the lights on. Never put a hand on him, but his fury was so intense the

168 · BILLIE MILHOLLAND

worthless coward was sniveling and whining within seconds, begging for his life."

"Wish I'd been there."

"It's better you weren't. Doc's capable of remarkable restraint when he's calmed down. You're not."

"You're damned right I'm not. Restraint's never been kind to me. So, was the spineless sucker fish ready to sell his soul?"

"He would have, if he had one. What he's going to do is pay."

"Pay? For the baby?"

"No, the Boisverts would never permit it. He'll pay for Sylvie's schooling. He'll pay Doc every month, and Doc'll make arrangements with Sylvie and whatever university she chooses.

"Well I'll be a white crow! I guess I'd better resist drawing and quartering him for a few years. Will she be an architect then?"

"She will."

Dr. Masters making a baby on Sylvie. What a thing. I wonder if Laura knows?

June 9, 1953

Oh Dear Diary,

I'm sorry I discovered that stupid spyglass. My job is getting harder and harder. Every time I find an injustice it gets to be my job to put things right. I'm swimming deep in the pickle barrel now, I'll tell you, and I don't know how to climb out.

And to top it all off, I think I'm getting boy crazy. I vowed not to, but what good is vowing if it doesn't stick? I can't understand why life can't be more simple.

Jeannie wouldn't see Roger again tonight. She says he'll still be her escort even if she doesn't say another word to him until that day. I don't think Roger wants to be her escort any more. Mother isn't worried. She says Gerry would be happy to escort Jeannie on her important day. I don't know why everybody calls it Jeannie's important day. If she passes grade twelve, it'll be because of Laura, not Jeannie.

Anyway, Jeannie's in a big pout, because Roger won't change his mind about the suit. She'd dump him because of that, but she has her heart set on going to graduation in the aqua and tan car.

Roger is two years out of school, and he works for Fat Freddy's construction company. Mother says he makes too much money for his own good, and it allows him to buy friends. Mother likes people who have money, but she draws the line at low-living people.

I don't care if Roger comes from the low-living. He's nice to me, he's nice to Beanie and he's even nice to Russell. I expect, I'm doomed to be one of the low-living and it doesn't worry me a bit.

"So, short stuff, what are you doing for excitement these days?" That's what Roger usually says to me, and I usually make a quick answer, because he's in a hurry to get on his way. But, after school today, when Jeannie refused to see him, he sat on the porch swing and settled into talking with me. I know it's because he wanted to stick around to see if Jeannie would give in and talk to him, but I liked it just the same.

He's terrible mad at Freddy. About the underwear. You'd think it was his, he's that steamed. So, I asked if any of the underwear belonged to his sister-in-law, Don's wife. He jumped off the swing like I'd pinched him. I thought he was going to hit me or yell. He didn't. He just frowned and stared at me. Of course, I didn't let sleeping dogs lie there. I said some must belong to his sister-in-law if he's so jumpy about it. I told him there's no shame in it. She can't help it if Freddy is crazy. Roger shook his head, rubbed his forehead, laughed and pulled my braid.

"Boy, short stuff, you're a little dog on a big bone, aren't you?"

I told him I just wanted to know the truth about things. Freddy did take unmentionables off Roger's sister-in-law's clothesline. Her neighbours saw him do it in the night, but they won't give proof of it.

They rent a house from Fat Freddy and don't want to get thrown out over some stupid underwear. Anyway, that underwear wasn't with the bunch found in his glove compartment, so I guess he has more hidden somewhere else. Roger's worried he'll use the underwear to embarrass his sister-in-law. He's angry, because he doesn't know how to stop it from happening. Roger says Fat Freddy likes to embarrass his family, but I don't know why.

Anyway, I was still thinking about Roger when I should have been sleeping. I'm getting to be a regular night owl. I put the spyglass on his brother Donald's house where he lives. It was after 11:30 at night, and the whole town was sleeping. I didn't expect to see anything, but boy, was I right on time.

I saw Roger open his bedroom window, climb out on the porch roof and down the hops trellis. Can you believe it? Then he disappeared into the back alley. I didn't see where he went, but very shortly there was a small flash of light in Freddy's back yard. Roger with a flashlight went right into Freddy's garage. Right in. Oh, what Freddy would do if he caught him. This is very bad. I know I snooped there, but if Beanie and I had got caught I don't think Freddy would have hurt us.

Roger is in a different kettle of fish. Freddy picks on the low-living all the time and he's meaner than mean. The low-living for Freddy include Indians, Half-Breeds, Mongoloids, Ukrainians, Chinese, girls who have babies without being married, and women whose husbands leave town. It is a very long list, and I haven't even mentioned Negro people, because we don't have any living around here.

Roger didn't stay in the garage very long. He was out nearly as soon as he went in. Why did he go there? If he carried something in or out, it had to be very small. I hope he didn't steal anything. That Freddy. He makes such a mess for everybody.

June 10, 1953

Dear Diary,

Freddy has to wait for his trial, but he doesn't have to be in jail, so he is all around town blaming everybody he can think of for trying to frame him.

I went over to Mrs. Bugle's today to give her a hand, because the Bugle's hired girl quit over all this kerfuffle. Mrs. Bugle's having a hard time getting another one. No young woman will work at Freddy's, now. Mary wouldn't come with me and I don't blame her, even though Freddy had a meeting with the firemen all day, and probably wouldn't be there.

Rose is very nice. We washed all the china in the living room cabinets. We had fun. We sang. Silly songs like Row, Row, Row Your Boat, and My Bonnie. Rose said she hasn't had such fun in years. I don't doubt that, living with Freddy. I don't think he's in favour of fun for anybody except himself.

Just before lunch Rose made a roaster full of ham sandwiches for the men in the fire hall. I volunteered to take them over. I wanted to see inside. Girls and women are not allowed there. The back door was propped open, because it was a hot day. They had a giant fan whirring up a storm, so nobody heard me come in. I peeked at them from behind a long rack of firemen clothes. There they were, all sitting on boxes and tires and drinking whiskey. Before lunch. I heard Freddy right off, so I backed into the heavy coveralls. Can you believe it? He was talking about Roger.

"That little bastard Lafond is looking for a kick in the balls."

"Yeah? And who is going to kick him, Fred?"

That was Floyd Gimley answering him. Floyd is the fire chief. He and Freddy have been chums since their school days.

"Ah, why're you wantin' to mess with small fry like that? You're don't think he had anything to do with the mess you're in, do yah?"

That was Tiny Jake. He doesn't like Freddy. He runs for mayor against him every election, but Tiny's wife is a Half-Breed, so he never gets elected. Nana says Tiny is a better man than Freddy, no matter which way you tip the cube, and his wife is just as much a lady as any in town. When it comes to that kind of prejudice in Deep Creek, it doesn't matter what Nana says.

Freddy got up then, and walked over and leaned against the fire truck. I stepped back further into the coveralls. They filled my nose with gas, oil and garage stink. Boy, I get myself into terrible places, but the conversation was too good to pass up.

"He's getting too big for his britches just like his son-of-a-bitchin' brother."

Nana told me this morning that Fat Freddy's wife, Rose, was once engaged to Donald, Roger's older brother. That was way back in the thirties, when she was young. Fat Freddy knew some kind of se-cret about Rose's father, so he made her break up with Donald. He made her marry his brother, Delmont. When Delmont got killed in the war, Freddy made her marry him. What a thing. Anyway, that's why Freddy and Donald have to feud all the time.

"What? You can't lay a beating on old Don anymore, so you're going to start on his little brother? Come on Fred. Are you get-ting to be a pantywaist? Hee Hee. Panty waist."

That was Tiny again. Sounded like he had a few under his belt, but a person doesn't have to worry about Freddy laying a licking on Tiny. Tiny is way over six feet, and he's strong. His brother lost a leg in Korea, and when they go places where there are stairs, Tiny picks up his brother like he's a baby, and runs him right up to the top.

"Shut up Jake. For all I know, you planted those snatch co-vers, yourself."

Tiny just laughed. "Dream 'em wet, Fred. I done a lot of stu-pid things in my life, but messin' around with women's panties is not for me."

All the men laughed. Freddy kicked a tire on the fire truck.

"When that little bastard comes sniffin' around after your women you'll be talking' out of the other side of the mouth, every jeezly one of you."

"Roger? He's a kid, Fred. He's got his rocks in the fire for that little piece of tail over to George Smythe's. Not that he's going to get any there. I hear she's as cold as her fancy mother."

That was Harry from the hardware. I can tell you, historians, I don't like reporting so much swears and ugly talk, so don't be surprised if I cross some of this out later. I might even have to burn this scribbler. I don't know if this is the sort of thing you need to know about our town, but right now I'm writing all of it. I'll sort it later. It's too amazing. That kind of talk is so bad it makes me want to stick up for Jeannie. She's a snob and a Miss Priss, but what they called her!! I'll never have high regard for those men, ever again. Ever. And I mean it.

Anyway, Freddy wasn't finished talking about Roger.

"Kipp saw him hangin' around my house in the middle of the gawddamn night. What do you suppose he's after? Mowin' my lawn?"

"Ah, come on." That was Tiny again. "If a kid like him wants to trim a little bush he's not goin' to come looking to your place. Your daughter ain't near to bleedin' age yet."

Freddy went over to Tiny and yelled in his face. "I'm not talkin' about my little girl, squaw man. I'm talkin' about my wife."

Tiny isn't scared of Freddy. He just laughed. "Your wife?" He shoved Freddy away with one hand. "You got maggots on the brain. Young bucks don't go after women like your wife. What's the matter with you? You daft?"

Then Harry spoke up. "He's right, Fred. You want help clipping his wick, you have to find a better excuse than that."

"Okay, laugh you cocksuckers. He's just the age to try to get back at me for stealin' that twat from his brother."

Then Mr. McAllen spoke up, "That was a long time ago, Fred. He was just a piddler when you done that."

Tiny threw his tin cup right across the fire hall. It crashed against the big folding doors where the fire trucks go out. "You're a sick bastard, Fred. Do you know that? You need some head shrinkin' bad." He left, slamming the door behind him.

I was lucky he went through the office door instead of the side door where I was standing, suffocating in the stinky coveralls.

After Tiny left, nobody talked except Freddy. He went on with more mean things about Roger, and I got sick of hearing it. I picked up the roaster, and slammed the side door hard so everybody knew I was coming in. Freddy snatched the roaster from me and didn't even say thank you. He yanked off the lid and threw it into a pile of tires, grabbed three or four sandwiches for himself and passed the roaster to Harry. I got out of there.

I am getting weary of this, Dear Diary. Walt Disney's *Cinderella* is on at the theatre. Maybe Mary will go with me to see it. Beanie says it's a little kid movie with stupid singing. He's waiting for *King Solomon's Mines* to come. I don't care if it's for little kids. It's in Technicolor and it has a happy ending. Sometimes a person needs a happy ending even if it is just pretend.

Evening June 10, 1953

Dear Diary,

Wouldn't you know it. Mary stayed home with Nana instead of going to the show with me. She's learning to crochet gloves from the thinnest crochet cotton. They're also sewing like mad on new dresses for her, Laura, Mary's mother, Aunt Olga and who knows who else. Nana says between the two of them, Crazy Marion and the Kokum, they have a graduation dress factory in full gear.

I'm glad Mary's at our house for so many reasons. One reason is the crocheting and the sewing. I don't like having to do that; I'd rather be reading. I used to have to try them all, because Nana wants somebody to pass her patterns to. Now she has Mary, so we're all happy.

When I got to the theatre, you'll never guess who was there. Stupid old Beanie. He tried to tell me he came because of Russell. Russell loves movies and he's not allowed to go alone. I sat behind them. I wanted to whack Beanie across the head when he laughed at the mice tricking the cat, and the wicked stepsisters trying to put on the slipper.

After the show, I double dared him to say he hated the movie. He said he didn't care one way or another. That Beanie. On the way home we had stick races through the culvert where the creek goes under the road by the clinic. I told Beanie what Freddy said about Roger. I didn't tell him the exact words. It's bad enough writing them. I'm not going to say them out loud.

I'm sorry I told him; now he says we have to warn Roger. He says Freddy's gone crackers, and is going to set a trap for Roger. Nana always says Freddy's just full of piss and wind. I think she's right, but I'm still worried, because he doesn't have anybody to blame for the underwear. What if he sets an underwear trap for Roger? It's a terrible thought, then he'd be ripe for blaming Roger for the jewelry.

Very late June 10, 1953. No. Cross that out. It's way too early June 11, 1953

Oh Dear Diary,

I just did a real stupid thing. It's not anything I can get in trouble for this time, but boy am I going to be tired tomorrow. I'm still awake, even though it is 3:30 in the morning. Can you believe it? So here I am recording when I should be sleeping.

Beanie came up the back stairs about 11:30 with his face all black, and his bare feet all black, declaring a night raid. I told him I didn't want to sneak around at night anymore, and besides, I reminded him he said he didn't want to be my friend. He said we made up when we sent the sticks under the culvert.

"Tally. Enemies don't stand together sending their ships into danger. If we were enemies we'd be blowing up and sinking each other's ships."

I told him not being friends didn't mean being enemies. He insisted it's one or the other. Beanie makes me tired.

When I said I wouldn't go, he threatened to stomp around in the hallway, and up and down the stairs, waking everybody up. I said if he was really my friend he wouldn't threaten me. He said justice was threatened and I'm the one always wanting justice done.

That Beanie. He can tangle things. So I went. Beanie's plan was to hide in the bushes by Donald's house, and wait till Roger climbed out of his window. If he did, we'd warn him that Freddy was after him.

If he sneaked out tonight he did it before we got there, and he had plenty of time for that, because it took us forever and a day to get through town. I would have been so embarrassed if he'd discovered us under his porch.

Beanie insisted we take a long path through hedges, behind sheds, and down the hospital back alley. He wasn't happy till we crawled ourselves full of thistle, stinging nettle and blue bur. I'm sorry I took him on the sneak trip to Freddy's garage. Now that he's over being scared, he's gone gooney about night raids. I wish Russell could come out at night to go with him.

I don't know what time we finally got to Lafond's, but I bet it was long after midnight. Then to top it all off, Beanie found a place to crawl under the porch. It smells like cat poop and moldy bread under there. We waited for hours, but heard no one coming or going. Now

I've got another paper bag under my bed full of filthy clothes I don't know what to do with.

Later on June 11, 1953

Dear Diary,

A most terrible thing has happened.

Early this morning a lady in Fort Caskey was found dead in a ditch. Choked to death with her own headscarf. It was Roger's sister, Suzanne. The one with the hairdressing shop. The one with the little girl who has no father.

She was murdered right while Beanie and I were under Lafond's porch. What a thing. Us out in the night at the same time Suzanne was murdered. You'd think we would have felt the badness of it in the air. I know Fort Caskey is 40 miles away, but just the same. I can't believe I didn't feel a thing except stinky lumps of dried cat poop digging into my knees under the Lafond's porch. Under Suzanne's brother's porch.

Because I didn't get up till late this morning, I missed the first telling of it. I'm all over inside out. Poor Roger. Poor, poor Roger. Nana says Suzanne was like a mother to him. A fine, hardworking young woman. Who would do such a thing? Who?

Mother was just awful. She called Suzanne a tramp, the sort of girl who calls that kind of madness upon herself.

"Those kinds of people have to expect sorry endings. Who knows how many men she's had on a short string. She was disgraceful when she lived here, so I don't know why anybody thought she would change once she moved away."

Mother took a green bottle of gin from her dressing gown pocket and poured some into her orange juice right there in front of Nana. A storm came over Nana's face. She turned and in a flash sent me into the kitchen to help Mary.

I shut the door behind me, but I key-holed right away. Mary tried to pull me off. She even hit me with a tea towel, but I had to listen. I had to.

"Lillian, you don't know what you're saying."

Nana stood over the table in the breakfast nook, and I don't know why Mother didn't faint dead away from fright from the look of her. But she didn't. She laughed.

"Oh, don't I? Do you think I'm blind? I saw how she threw herself at Freddy Bugle. Pathetic little thing. Thinking he'd leave his wife for someone like her. Rose is not much of a prize, but she does come from better people. And even Freddy knows the value of that. Then getting pregnant. What a little fool."

"Frederick raped her."

Nana's voice was calm and cold. I shivered on the other side of the door. I'm glad Mary wasn't close enough to hear.

Mother lit a cigarette. "Why would he bother when he could have her for free?"

Nana yanked the cigarette away from Mother, threw it on the floor and stepped on it! Stepped on the cigarette. Right there on the linoleum! In the house! Nana! Oh, Dear Diary I have never seen such a thing from Nana before.

"Nothing like that is ever given freely, Lillian." Nana leaned toward Mother, hanging on to the back of a chair with both hands. "You're right, Suzanne was foolish, but not for the reasons you think. Her brother owed Frederick money. He broke his arm that winter and couldn't work. Her little brother was going to have to quit school to help out. Frederick told Suzanne he'd forgive the loan."

Mother turned her back on Nana. "I don't want to hear another sob story."

"Roger was only in grade eight for heaven's sake, and he was a good student. She did the only thing she thought would help her family. There were other ways to get the help she needed, but she didn't know that."

"She must have done a good job. I heard he continued to visit her after she moved over there, and I know he didn't go there to change diapers."

"Lillian." Nana's voice sounded like a sharp dog bark. She turned and came towards the kitchen so fast I nearly fell over Mary getting out of the way in time.

If Nana had been paying attention she would have known I was key-holing, but she was so furious, she walked right by both of us like we weren't there, and slammed the screen door behind her when she went into the garden. She slammed the door. Nana slammed a door in her own house!

That put Mary into a tizzy. She flew around the kitchen doing too many things at once, and making little squeaking noises. I don't know how to help anybody, so I've escaped up here. What a thing. My whole life is more inside out these days than right side in.

June 11, 1953, after supper

Dear Diary,

Doc Rawson phoned Nana before lunch, and I heard her swear. Nana almost never swears.

"Damn! Good Goddamn. It's no mystery Mack. No mystery. The scarab tie clip? I know who it belongs to."

Freddy's tie clip was in her hand. Clutched tight in poor dead Suzanne's hand. Nana drove right over to Fort Caskey to identify it, and came back with the police when they went to Freddy's house.

The real police. The RCMP police from Edmonton. Looking for Freddy. Good thing his kids weren't there. The boys are at the scout's wilderness camp-out, and Elizabeth is at a sleep over.

Poor Rose. Nana called her from Fort Caskey, and told her to phone papa to pick her up, and bring her up to our house. Rose didn't phone papa. She came running all the way up the hill in her bedroom slippers with her apron still on, and bread dough drying all the way up her arms. You can't expect a person to get properly ready after hearing that news.

She says Fat Freddy didn't come home last night, and his car is gone. Nobody knows where he is. Now everybody is saying Roger's sister was Fat Freddy's mistress. Can you believe it? Fat Freddy with a mistress?

Nana says there are photographs of them together, and some of Freddy's clothes are in her closet. I thought people only had mistresses in Hollywood, and handsome, elegant men not sorry sods like Freddy. Did Roger and Donald know? Was she still paying off the loan?

Poor Roger. Now he's going to hate Freddy forever. How will he get over a thing like that? It's awful. Terrible, horrible awful. He talked so much about how pretty and smart Suzanne was, and how cute his niece.

But why would Freddy kill her? Nobody can understand it. Beanie was right. Freddy has gone crackers.

Of course Nana got Rose and her children on the train right away for her mother's in Saskatchewan, so they'll be safe in case Freddy comes back with more murder on his mind. The police are searching everywhere for him.

They even got Silas Beck's bloodhounds sniffing in the bush after Freddy. He brought those dogs all the way up from the United States last year when they were puppies. Papa says they've never done any people finding before, but who knows what dogs can do when they get a chance to do what they were born for? Papa went with Nana to help lock up the house and the garage. Papa may be war weak, but he's strong when it's important.

Still June 11, 1953

Oh, Dear Diary,

Did papa ever have a row with Mother. After Rose and her family were safely gone, and everybody was sitting around the kitchen table eating pudding, Mother licked off her spoon and twirled it around in her fingers.

"I guess dear Roger will be out of the picture for graduation. Thank goodness for small mercies. Gerry in a decent suit will go much better in your photographs, Jeannie."

Jeannie seemed sad for a moment, saying phony baloney things about 'poor dear Roger'. It was obvious she didn't mean it. And then, to everybody's surprise, Laura stood up, threw her napkin on the table, and spoke in a strange, calm, grown-up, voice.

"Mother. Jeannie. You two are the total end. I can't sit here one minute longer listening to your juvenile conversation. A woman has been murdered. Murdered. And all you can think of is how Jeannie will look in the graduation photograph. I can't believe I'm related to either one of you."

She left the room slowly, like a princess. I had no idea Laura could be so magnificent. What's got into her? I don't know. Maybe being the girlfriend of a grown up man has changed her.

Then papa surprised everybody. "Lillian. Have some compassion. That family has gone through enough."

That didn't stop Mother. "Oh, George." She giggled, stirred her pudding, and blinked her eyes in a flirty way. "Those kind of people live a rough and ready life. They have to expect seamy things to happen to them. I don't know why everybody is making such a fuss."

Papa put his fingers to his forehead for a moment, and then said in the saddest voice. "Lillian. You're drunk."

Mother made a singsong voice. "Lillian, you're drunk."

I glanced at Nana. She stared at Mother, but she didn't say a word, which is not like her.

Mother had more to say. "George, you're never drunk are you? No. No. No. Not St. George. No cigarettes. No whiskey. No wild, wild women? At least not too wild, isn't that right George?"

Papa stood up from the table. "Lillian." He sounded dangerous.

"Oh, sit down Georgie. Georgie, porgie, puddin' and pie. Pure and noble Georgie." She waved the spoon at him again. "I don't have to be noble, do I? You do it for me, don't you? You do it for all of us."

About then Nana noticed me still at the table. She sent me to the kitchen right quick to help Mary with the dishes. But most of the dishes were still on the table, and Nana would not let us clear them away. Mary stood against the door, so I couldn't listen. She said it wasn't my business. Boy, she's starting to sound like Nana.

Now everything is in a ruckus. Mother's locked herself in her room. Nana says she might be having another nervous breakdown, but not to worry, because there is good treatment for nervous breakdowns.

What happens when a person's nerves break down? Do they snap off? Can they grow back? The nerve in my leg that got cut can't ever grow back. Oh, Mother, Mother. How many nervous breakdowns can a person have before there are no nerves left to break? Jeannie's on the phone to Aunt Edie, so I suppose Uncle Edwin will have to find a place for Mother in the hospital in Edmonton again. Crazy Marion says somebody should just buy her a wing in that hospital, and rent it when she's not using it.

When Papa takes Mary to the farm for her days off tomorrow I'm going too. Papa has to come right back, but Mary and I are going to stay at papa's house, together. He and Nana have to bundle Mother off to Edmonton.

Saturday, June 13, 1953 Early morning at papa's farm

house

Dear Diary,

It's truly fine here. The awful happenings in town are far away. Mary knows how to make a fire in the stove, and how to light the coal oil lamps. There's electricity in this house now, but I like the plaster walls, pale yellow like winter butter when only the lamps are lit. It's more friendly. I don't know what time it is. There are no clocks in this house. Papa says he doesn't want to know the time when he's at the farm.

Mary is sleeping, but she moans and groans a lot, and that wakes me up. There are proper bedrooms in this house, but they're far from everything and nobody has used them yet. Why would they, when there's the cubbyhole behind the stucco stove? I lit a kerosene lamp all by myself. I'm not very good at it; I got soot up the side of the chimney, but there's enough light for writing.

Last night Mary told Dominic the story about my balloon heart when I get over-full of good feelings. At first I was embarrassed, but Dominic smiled and nodded like he knew what I meant. Before Mary and I went to bed, he did the nicest thing. He brought over two quart sealers full of wild flowers for our table, and a beautiful embroidered cloth to set it on.

He gave me a funny grin, tilted his head and said, "Balloon Heart?"

Oh, Dear Diary, my mouth has never in its life made such a wide smile, as I felt my heart fill up. I nodded. Dominic continued to grin, making the crinkles at the corners of his eyes deeper. He walked out into the night without saying any more, and the funny thing is, I felt like we'd had a real conversation. What a nice friend he's turned out to be.

I can smell the flowers now. I don't know if there are words good enough to tell you how beautiful they are. There's yarrow and lady bedstraw for creamy white; late buffalo beans for yellow; early lungwort, shooting stars and vetch for bluey purple, and wild honeysuckle vine with tiny salmon pink trumpets tumbling over the side.

Mother says all women pine after roses. Hah. Ordinary roses, all of them exactly the same, are no match for these flowers. My poor Mother. The wonders she misses by sticking to town.

We flung all the windows open before we went to bed, and I can still smell the gillyflowers Nana planted by the well. I can hear frogs in the slough creaking mightily. Before I went to sleep I heard nighthawks swooping through the air, diving after bugs. I can't imagine anything more perfect.

When I'm a grown woman and nobody will marry me, I wonder if papa will let me live here. I'd keep everything cheerful for him. I'd plant a garden and grow herbs and keep chickens.

June 14, 1953

Oh, Dear Diary,

How many secrets can one family hold? This is a big secret. A very serious secret about our family. I think Nana knows, but I'm almost sure nobody else does. At first when I heard it I felt like ice water got dumped on my head, but I'm calmed down now. I'll try to tell it from the start. Actually, now I've had time to think it through, I'm glad about it. I am. I think it's beyond wicked to be glad about a secret like this. It might even be a sin, but I can't help it, and I don't care.

When papa came to the farm today, I was sitting at Baba's table dawdling over breakfast. Mary was outside weeding in the raspberries. Instead of coming inside to have tea with Baba like he always does, papa went straight to the big barn. That was strange. Uncle Metro stomped into the house, tracking mud through the kitchen and down the cellar steps. I looked out the window and saw Papa striding toward the big hay barn. And I mean striding. Long, fast steps.

Baba grumbled when Uncle Metro brought three bottles of birch wine from the cellar. Uncle Metro is not supposed to drink except at holidays. I asked why she didn't tell him not to take the wine. I know Nana would have, but Baba just rocked back and forth on the front part of her chair by the stove and said it was man business. Why is everything man business? What makes a thing man business?

It might be man business, Dear Diary, but I couldn't help it, I had to make it my business too. I told Baba I was going for a run. She waved her hand at me, "Go. Go."

I knew Mary would practice her crocheting when she came in, and Dominic was hunched over his homework at the table, so nobody interrupted my going. I lurched off in the direction I usually go when I run, and then I sneaked back through the barley field, and crawled into the back of the barn where two boards have come off. That's how we get in when we're searching for new kittens. Mountains of last summer's hay are still stacked back there, hiding the ladder to the loft. Most of the hay is gone from the loft. Walking through what's left makes every kind of rustling noise and hay dust drops down through the cracks real easy. I stepped slowly, next to the wall so dust falling through wouldn't be so noticeable. I timed my walking to match Uncle Metro's talking, because his big booming voice fills up the place.

I stretched out on my stomach so I could see through a long oval knothole. Must have been slough hay there, because I was right in the minty smell of pennyroyal. The big door at the front of the barn was partly open. Long, tight strings of sunshine stretched past Uncle Metro who sat on a butter box. The birch wine stood on the upside down bowl of the old cream separator beside him. Papa sat on an egg crate, leaning way back against a big post.

Uncle Metro lifted up a bottle of birch, and drank quite a few swallows at once. "You're a good man George. A good man. Don't listen to that woman. She's no wife to talk like that."

He handed the bottle to papa. Papa leaned forward with his elbows on his knees, dangling the bottle between his legs. His tidy hair fell over his forehead like he hadn't combed it that morning.

"But, she's right Metro, I'm not a good husband. I'm not a good father. I meant to be. But, damn, I didn't know what it would be like. I thought being a husband was just getting married. A place of your own. The same bed. The same breakfast table."

He put his head way back, and took a long drink of wine. I could see the frown lines running up the middle of his forehead, and the white stripe above them where his hat keeps the sun off his face.

For a while Uncle Metro talked, and papa drank wine.

"Dat's bull-sheet. Bu-ull-sheet. Devil-take-it! What so wrong what you did? What? And you think she did right? Make party all the time. Forget about her babies. Week and week, go away with that sister, and the babies left here and there. And you don't say she bad mother. You don't say that."

"She's not a good mother. I know. But I don't want to blame her Metro. I can't. I was just like her when we married. Wanting a good time. Thinking of myself. But I went to the goddamn war. Everything changed. I'm changed." He rubbed both hands over his face. "She didn't know war. Why would she change?"

"People don't need war to grow up. Be woman instead of spoiled cabbage girl."

"She was raised to be a spoiled cabbage, Metro. It's not her fault."

"Oh hoh, your fault then George? Your fault?"

"Shit, Metro, it's nobody's fault. That's what's so Christly stupid about it. It just is, and that's a rotten thing."

"You never the same as her. Never. You good boy. You help you mama. Help you papa. She's want to be big shot. Her mama want to be big shot. I see her make eyes at you. You papa big man in town. Dat's what she want. Big shot husband."

Papa took another drink of wine and shook his head. "Don't make excuses for me, Metro. I was attracted to her. She was pretty. She was fun. I liked to have fun."

"Oh, fun. Fun." Uncle Metro spit into the hay. "Young people all the time have fun. That's nothing. But, she fool you. She make nice. Smile nice. Tell you she want nice baby. I know woman like that. She no want baby. She only want big shot husband."

"Oh, but she did, Metro. She did want a baby. I was willing to wait until I finished my education to have children, but she really wanted a baby."

"Dat's bullsheet. What's the matter you? Open up you eye. She scare you find better woman at your university school, that's why she have baby."

Papa stood up and walked over to Metro. "What are you saying?"

"You not know that? *Kapusta hohva!* You papa tell me you not go back to school, because she going to have it baby."

Papa squatted down in the hay. "I couldn't leave her here while I went east."

"Why not she go too? Good wife go there with you."

"She couldn't Metro. She was delicate. Her mother had trouble with her babies. It wouldn't have been fair of me to leave her behind during that time."

"Her mama not have trouble. She strong like old cow. Complain. Complain that one. Fall down faint at church picnic so to make big trouble everywhere. Everybody run around. Get water. Get pillow. Make nice bed under tree. Wave fan. Everything. When she sleep, everybody go walk for to see those lady slipper flowers. She wake up, and she walk one mile so she catch up with big shot missionary, so he can hear her sing song like crow for the people."

"Metro!"

"I know. I know. You small boy that time. You not know it. You not see it."

"But Lillian..."

"Ah! You Lillian. Same thing, you Lillian. She lay down here. She lay down there. Always some place where everybody have to run for her. Get water. Get blanket. I know. My Olga hired girl for you mama that time. When nobody look, she get up, go out back door to the Helen. Laugh. Talk all day. You come home, she back lay down. She say all the time sick. She no sick."

"Metro. Marjorie would have told me..."

"How she tell you? You mama good woman. She not make trouble for you. What you think? You would listen her? I know you. Stubborn, you."

"Shit, you're right. Marjorie wouldn't interfere. I wouldn't have believed her anyway. I thought I was a big man back then."

Papa put his head way back, and took a long, slow drink from the bottle, and then he slumped down against the post.

"I don't know. I don't know anything, except I've let them down. Jeannie's all right, I guess. She's like her mother, and she doesn't seem to miss anything. But Laura and my little Natalie. They're smart girls, Metro. Good girls. Lillian doesn't think about them at all. And I'm no damn good for them."

Then, my balloon heart began to grow, which is so strange. I thought balloon hearts happened only when things are too wonderful and beautiful to be contained in your everyday heart. I was wrong. Balloon hearts also happen when somebody you love hurts with a hurt too big to fix.

I wanted to dive from the loft like a flying squirrel, my furry arms outstretched. I wanted to fling myself on my papa, and hug him hard till I squeezed the hurting right out of him. But all I did was lay there, letting tears burn little grooves into my cheeks, and letting my balloon heart grow big enough to catch them all. To make myself feel better, I pretended my tears spilled over, and fell down like warm rain on the head of my papa. I pretended he was a drooping flower thirsty for rain.

I had to pretend it so I wouldn't cry out, because I didn't know what else to do. I couldn't have moved from that spot if an earthquake had come to swallow me whole.

"You mama think about those girls."

"Oh, sure. Without Marjorie we'd all be in the shit house, and don't think a day goes by that I'm not grateful for it. But what about me, Metro? I'm the husband. I'm the father. I'm the gawddamn son. And what good am I to anybody? Lillian's off to the hospital again, because I don't know how to give her what she wants."

"You stupid English. She go to hospital because she drink whiskey. Because she all the time want to be like queen." Uncle Metro raised his hands above his head. "You crazy in the head."

"You're right, Metro. I'm insane. Bloody insane. Joe told me if I decided to go back home it would only work if I didn't tell her. But I couldn't lie to her. I couldn't lie to Lillian, even about that. And what if I'd lied? Do you think it would have been different? I don't think so. I don't. I loved Roxanne. I loved her Metro." He sat up. "Can you hear what I'm saying?" Papa threw a big handful of hay at Uncle Metro. "I couldn't lie about a thing like that." He twisted a handful of hay in his hands. "And maybe I still love her, so what does that say about me?" Then he dropped his head on his arms.

I held my breath. Papa loved Roxanne? Uncle Joe's wife?

Uncle Metro waved his arm at papa. "It say nothing." He finished the wine in the bottle, and tossed it into a pile of hay. He pulled the cork from another bottle with his teeth and spit it out.

Papa flung his head back. I think he was crying. Big, rough sobs with his mouth wide open and his head moving back and forth like it wanted to make him say - No. No.

Metro held the wine bottle against his chest like a baby and said nothing.

After a while papa stopped crying.

"She laughed, Metro. Lillian laughed when I told her. Do you know what she said after she laughed? She lifted up her little princess chin and said, 'Oh, how pathetic.' And that was it. In her next breath she told me I had two years to get elected as the next mayor. Like nothing had changed. Like we'd go on just like before. And I tried, Metro. I tried. But that's not who I am anymore. I don't want it back."

Papa slumped forward, and for a moment everything was quiet.

Then, Uncle Metro got up, and stumbled over to papa, fell to his knees and put a hand behind papa's head and yanked his hair, so papa could drink more wine. Wine poured into papa's mouth and spilled over down his chin to his shirt.

Uncle Metro then sat back on his heels in the deep hay, and drank more wine. He held the bottle against his chest again and fell back against the wall of the barn.

Papa wiped his mouth with his arm. "I didn't know what love was Metro. I played house when I married Lillian. Christ. We were kids. What did we know?" Papa pushed his fingers through his hair from front to back and then just hung on to his head, his elbow in the air. He closed his eyes. "You ever love a woman, Metro?"

Uncle Metro threw the bottle across the barn. It broke in the corner and wine ran down the gray boards. I told myself to remember not to go back there in bare feet.

"Love?" His big voice burst out like a canon. "Man is not for love. Man is for fight. Fight hard. Work hard, *yoh-bahty*, fuck hard, you stupid English." He looked over at papa, tears running over his cheeks. "Not love! What's a matter with you?" Uncle Metro crawled over to papa, and pushed him over and grabbed the top of his shirt with both hands and started shaking him. "Not love. You listen? Not love."

Papa flung him off and sat up again. "So, you did love once, you old reprobate, I thought so. Where? In the old country?"

Uncle Metro wiped his sleeve across his eyes, but tears came out anyway. He waved his arm like he was shooing mosquitoes. "What matter it now?"

Papa sighed. "I say that too. It doesn't matter. It's in the past. Gone. Finished. Ended." Papa sighed again, a deep, long sigh. "But I'm lying. It does matter old man, even to you. It's never ended is it?"

Uncle Metro looked angry. I would have been scared at that moment, but papa wasn't. Uncle Metro crawled over to papa and yelled right into his face. "So, big shot, what we do? Huh? Nothing. That's what we do." He turned his head and spit.

"But you know the goddamn stupid thing, Metro? I wouldn't do it any different if I could do it over. I wouldn't." He shook his head. "I'd do it again, you old bugger. It's the only thing that made any damnable sense. The only thing. Any day I could have died. She could have died. Why didn't we die? I don't know. We lived, damn it, and all those others didn't.

I'd go walking with her and we'd see a flower. A stupid weed of a flower growing in gravel, and we'd get crazy over it. Down on our knees in the dirt. Touch it like it was the fucking crown jewels. Cry because it was alive. And a bird. Could be an idiot sparrow and we'd sit down there in the mud, and listen to the damned thing sing. Listen till it flew away. And I'd look at her face. Oh, God, her face. Put her picture beside Lillian's, and you'd say she was a plain little thing. But you'd be wrong. Dead wrong. There she was, her face streaked with dirt and grime, her hair hanging in tangles, and she was beautiful. I didn't know beauty before that, Metro. I didn't know."

Papa put his head back, and I saw the sadness that's always there, but it was different somehow. Almost lovely. It hurt to look at him, but lovely just the same.

Papa looked over at Metro who seemed to be sleeping. Papa's voice was nearly a whisper, and I had to grow my ears hard to hear it. "I would do it again. It would be indecent not to."

Uncle Metro didn't say anything. But he folded his arms across his chest, which showed he was awake. His eyes stayed closed. "Aah-nah."

That's how he said it, at first. Stretched out. A calling sound to somebody far away.

"Anna. Stubborn woman. Ride horse like a man." He put his big hands over his face, covering his shut eyes. "She look after everybody. Help all the people. Then soldier come. She help dig deep beside the river. Small hole to go in, she say. Not easy to see. Small hole outside, big hole inside. She take food in there. Dry everything. Berry. Mushroom. She smart. Everybody say we never do this before. She say, never mind, we do now. Even cow cheese, she dry. Put on a blanket. Dry hard. Some people not want to go down in the earth. Soldiers come back. Kill 'em. Kill 'em all."

Uncle Metro shook his head, and his hands slid off his face, and lay there beside his ears like they were tired out.

"We hide, down in the earth. One day we hide. Sometimes two, tree day. One time we stay there two week, in winter, when soldier come and burn everything. But soldier not find us. After war is finished, Anna say we to go to the Canada. I no want it. She have brother go there. She say better place. She say she go without me. Our babies, so small, so sick. They die in the winter. Anna sister Olga husband die. She no want it stay in that place anymore. She take her sister Olga, Olga baby, her mother. How I can live without her? All right, I go. We walk long time. We go on train long time. We wait long time for ship. I get sick, can't stand up."

Uncle Metro started to cry again. "My Anna. She go in the town to buy food. She go. Olga go with her. Olga come back. Beat up, blood run everywhere. Soldier. Soldier use her. Use my Anna. Anna not come back. *Shlahk-trah-fit*! Not. Come. Ba-aack."

Poor Uncle Metro. Poor, poor Uncle Metro. I promise never to be cross with him again. Never. Never. Never. He stopped crying after a while. Papa did not say anything.

When Uncle Metro started talking again, his voice was very quiet; I could hardly hear him. "Olga say Anna fight soldier. So many soldier. Hit with brick. Cut with knife. Anna push Olga to run away.

Olga run. I go look. I go everywhere. Not find it. Two day. Two week. Nothing. No Anna. Nobody see.

That ship come. I say I not go. Anna sister, Anna mother, they got nobody for help them, so I go. I come here. To the Canada. Olga be wife for me. Never complain, that one."

Uncle Metro was quiet after that. Papa was quiet, too. When Uncle Metro spoke again, his voice broke into chunks. His face full of barn dust, tears cleaning stripes down both cheeks.

"So. I love. For what? You English. What good come from love?"

By then papa was drunk too. "You're right, you old heathen. What good is it? It's bullshit. It's all bullshit. No. Cow shit."

Uncle Metro kicked his legs out. "Cow sheet."

Papa said, "Chicken shit."

Uncle Metro nodded his head. "Chicken sheet."

"Horse shit."

"Horse sheet."

And on and on they went, yelling different kinds of shit to each other and laughing and crying and laughing again. After a while papa and Uncle Metro sat down with their arms around each other and they sang. Uncle Metro sang in Ukrainian and tried to teach the words to papa.

You know, Dear Diary, I think I should be upset about papa. I should, but I'm not. It doesn't seem bad somehow. I'm glad papa has Uncle Metro to be crazy with. Everybody needs somebody to be crazy with.

Papa loved Roxanne. Loved Uncle Joe's wife. What a thing! It sounds like Uncle Joe didn't mind. That part is hard to understand. Uncle Metro married his dead wife's sister. That seems sensible, but papa loved Uncle Joe's wife *before* Uncle Joe died and when papa still had a wife. I wish I could ask Nana.

I've thought about it all afternoon. I didn't go picking mushrooms with Auntie Olga and Mary. I usually do. I said I was too tired from running, but I was really too tired from thinking.

Dominic is at papa's desk in papa's study room, here in the new house. Papa lets him do his serious homework in the study room. It's full of bookshelves with dictionaries and atlases and other good books full of information. I'm at the kitchen table writing this, and you know what's wonderful? Dominic is not one to snoop, and I don't have to worry he'll try to peek at what I'm writing when he comes in to get more tea.

"What are you writing, Natalie?"

That's what he said when he came in the first time. I like the way he says my name. He says my whole name and he makes the T sound like a D and he makes the emphasizing at the end of my name instead of at the beginning. I like that. I like it a lot.

I must have looked guilty because he laughed and backed away and held up both hands. "Private? Don't worry, I know about private. I keep my work private too."

He called my writing work. Oh, Dear Diary, my work. It's true. It *is* my work. My real work. He made tea. Good, strong black tea. He poured a cup for me when he poured his own. He doesn't put sugar in his tea. He puts jam. It's quite a different way to drink it, but I'm sipping it now, slowly, slowly. Black current jam. I like it this way. He smiled when I said thank you, but he didn't interrupt me. I like that about him.

You know what I want to think, Dear Diary? I want to think Roxanne was not Uncle Joe's wife. I want to think she was papa's special friend. I want to think Alex is papa's little girl, and my little sister. That make me five times more wicked. I don't care about being wicked any more. I don't care one bit. Being wicked isn't always bad. And that's the truth.

If I had a little sister, I'd go places with her. I'd tell her things, and buy her presents. I would ask what she thought about things. I would notice when she came into the room.

June 15, 1953

Dear Diary,

Today is a sad day. Papa, Nana, Mary, Laura and I went to Suzanne Lafond's funeral. Jeannie wouldn't go. She said it was too unpleasant. Laura got so riled.

She said, "Yes, it's unpleasant, you dimwit. And if you think it's unpleasant for you, think what it must be for Roger? You've dangled him on a string for most of a year. Don't you think you owe him?"

Jeannie burst into tears and ran to her room, wailing that Laura was mean. Nana told Laura not to bother her. Jeannie has to want to go of her own accord or it won't mean anything. Laura agreed, and no more was said.

Reverend Sykes phoned Nana last night to ask her opinion on his funeral address. She hasn't forgiven him for his awful sermon about ignorant immigrants, but she is always ready to give advice. They had a long discussion, and Nana was very firm, so I know there were things he was going to say she didn't agree with. I heard part of the conversation.

"Judge not, lest ye be judged, Hector. It isn't as hard a task as you make it. Simply ask yourself what our Saviour would have said."

There was a long pause while Reverend Sykes had much to say, then Nana had her turn. "Do you really think Jesus of Nazareth would have felt the need to discuss the morality of adultery on the day of mourning for a brutally slain young woman? I think not. Yes, I know she didn't come to your church, but Don and Ellen come every Sunday and their children. If you didn't want to bury her, then you should have spoken up before now. They have already suffered deeply. I won't have them tormented further. Now quit fussing. I have a suitable sermon written for Wilma's service. I will deliver it tonight, and you will use it, Hector."

Granddad Smythe's old secretary was Wilma, from when he was the mayor. She died when I was in grade three. Nana helped write a fine sermon for her, and with a few changes it was a good one for Suzanne. We sat right up front, so Nana could cast her eyes on Reverend Sykes, so he wouldn't slip in words he shouldn't.

Roger was one of the pallbearers. His face was pale. He had on the suit he would have worn to Jeannie's graduation. I thought it was perfectly fine. So did Mary.

There's still no sign of Freddy. The RCMP think he may have gone to the United States where he has an uncle. What a thing.

Still June 15, 1953

Dear Diary, Dear, Dear Diary!

My balloon heart is so big, and so light I think it would float up and beyond the earth if I let it go.

Alex is my sister! My real little sister. Just like I wished. Her whole name is Alexandra George Smythe. Roxanne made her middle name papa's first name. We don't give boy's names to girls here in Canada, but they do things differently in England. I couldn't stand it anymore; I had to ask Nana.

Things are strange in our house right now. With Mother in the hospital in Edmonton, Laura has become a talker, which isn't like her. She's in the kitchen, helping Mary and talking up a storm. Jeannie is shut up in her room playing records over and over and over again. Nana says she is upset about Mother having to go to the hospital, and we are not to bother her about it.

After the funeral, Nana sat me down in the sunroom, so she could explain about Mother. I had a hard time paying attention, because I was thinking about Roxanne and papa. I let her finish without squirming too much, but she noticed I wasn't paying attention.

"Tally. You're a hundred miles away."

As soon as she said that, I blurted out, "Farther than a hundred. Way farther. I heard papa say to Uncle Metro he loved Roxanne. Uncle Joe's English wife."

Nana pressed a hand against her chest and took a big breath. "Oh, my Lord."

She stared down at her lap for a moment. Then, of course, she wanted to know how I'd heard him say such a thing. She's pretty irked at me for eavesdropping, but she did tell me the straight story. If you dare to ask, Nana will tell the truth about things.

"Natalie. Child. You're only twelve, but there are days I think you're closer to thirty. Your Grandma Walters says it's what I get for letting you read adult books, and read the National Geographic." She smiled then and shook her head, but she didn't seem upset. "Come here Chickadee; sit beside me."

And I did. Sat with Nana on her sofa. Her with her arm around me, and me leaning against her like I did when I was little. It was nice.

"We've talked about war before, you and I. Men far away from home, lonely and cold. But it's not only that. You're too young to hear the grim details of battlefield life but…"

I didn't think it was a good time to tell Nana I'd read quite a bit about grim things in her wartime magazines.

"But, I can tell you, when men go into battle they know every moment of every day might be their last. Each day they survive is a horrible miracle, because each day they live means others they know and love die. Sometimes right in front of them. I know you have eavesdropped enough to know how your father had to witness the death of his youngest and favourite brother.

Men who go to war, change. They change in ways the people back home cannot hope to understand. Some of them lose limbs. Some lose their minds. Some lose their hearts. And others lose their souls. Many become hard and angry. Others soft, with sensibilities easily wounded. Some become jokers with never again a serious thought allowed in. Others become thinkers, taking apart their thoughts like scientists.

Your papa went to war with his brothers and friends, a gay, carefree young man without many serious thoughts. He left behind a gay, carefree young wife without serious thoughts. Life after that, for both of them, was not what they expected."

I'd heard the talk about war changing men, and I had no quarrel with it. But right then I wanted to know about Roxanne and Alex. "Did papa love Mother before he went away?"

Nana stared at her photographs on the wall for a moment. "Yes, he did, Chickadee, and he still loves your mother. I know it's hard for you to believe, but she still loves him too. Only they love each other the way they did when they were young people together, with a small, thin, beginner's love that didn't have a chance to take root and grow."

"Will it get a chance?"

"I don't know, child. Nobody does."

"What about Alex?"

Nana smiled. She kissed the top of my head. "Tally you are an original child. I'm going to tell you the whole story as I know it to be true. I want you to understand, your sisters don't know this story and I don't think you should be the one to tell it to them."

I agreed. They hate hearing information from me. Jeannie says I'm just trying to be a smart sass.

"Does Mother know the story?"

"Yes, she does. She doesn't like it, and she chooses to disbelieve it."

I'm beginning to know that about Mother. She disbelieves things she doesn't like.

"When your father met Roxanne, a bombing raid had just destroyed her home, killing her father and her sister, rendering her mother blind. It wasn't until two days later, while they were transferring her mother to a place in the country that Roxanne's broken ribs and a dislocated shoulder were discovered. She had not complained, once. She fainted dead away, trying to help lift fallen trees off the road. A very brave, young woman." Nana paused. "Braver than your mother, do you think?"

My answer at that moment was a big, fat, YES. I believed in the brave and generous Roxanne. I nodded.

But Nana, like the wise women in Pearl S. Buck's books, does not allow a quick and easy answer. She shook hers. "No, she was not. Not any braver. She too, had been a privileged daughter of wealthy people, full of dreams of excellent prospects for a good marriage and a predictable future. Pretty dresses and fashionable places to wear them. Much like your Mother. That all disappeared for her in one short night. War changed her. She suffered terrible losses. She suffered terrible pain, terrible disappointment, terrible fear, loneliness and even hunger.

"And so did your father. They understand each other in ways only people who have survived that kind of suffering can. They didn't expect to have a life together. They only expected to have an hour together. A day together. They learned to be happy with what time they had, and together they helped each other survive the war. And yes, together they had Alexandra George Smythe, your sister."

I didn't know until then that Alexandra had a middle name. Papa's name. I'm so glad for that. That's little enough to be left with after an awful war.

"Your Uncle Joe married Roxanne, so your sister would not be without a legal father, since your papa could not marry her."

"And then Uncle Joe died and Roxanne died and…"

"Your Uncle Joe did die, Chickadee, just as you have heard many times, but Roxanne is still alive in the same village where your papa met her. She's the librarian there."

"Roxanne, alive?" I was breathless. My little sister has a mother. I was so very glad.

"Your mother and your father will not thank me for telling you this. It's possible I may regret it myself. But too many secrets are not good for a family. In my experience they do more harm than good."

"Will somebody tell Jeannie and Laura?"

Nana laughed. "I hope so, but it will not be today."

"Does Alex know her papa is alive?"

"I don't think she does. And that may be for the best. Many children in England have no papa. She's not alone in that. But she does know she has an Uncle George in Canada, after whom she was named. Your Uncle Joe's middle name was Alexander, did you know that?"

I did not. "And what about Roxanne? Doesn't she miss papa terribly?"

"I imagine she does. But it was Roxanne who sent your father back to Canada when he didn't want to come home."

At that moment I couldn't make sense of it. Papa loved Roxanne. She loved him. They had a daughter. I don't think Mother really loves papa, even though Nana is kind to say so. I don't think papa loves Mother. So why didn't he stay there? Stay in England. Lucky for me, Nana doesn't usually leave those kinds of questions unanswered.

"The way it stood was, his daughter in England had a strong and sturdy mother, and the respectability of a war-dead father like over half the other children there. Your papa had three little girls in Canada with no father, a wife who had not had the opportunity to change through misfortune, and who was ill prepared to raise three children on her own. He had a widowed mother, and he was her only son left."

"Did you tell him to come home, Nana?"

"No, child, I did not. Nor would I. I wanted him to come back home. Of course I did, but I tried to help him understand I would honour his decision whatever it was. Roxanne freed him to go, and he surprised himself by coming. What you heard in the barn today, child, was part of a long healing your father would have had to go through even if he had stayed in England. There's no right answer to problems made by war. There is no easy cure for that kind of sickness. No matter what they do, people who have gone through war carry some of that sickness with them for their whole life. All anybody can do is learn to live with the answers they choose."

"Will he go back to England some day?"

"There is no way for anybody to know that, not even him, I expect. Does it worry you that he might go, someday?"

I thought about it for a while, and Nana let me think. She is the only person I know who allows a person thinking time. Finally, I shook my head.

"No, Nana, it worries me he might not."

June 16, 1953

Oh Dear Diary,

Things are in a great kerfluffle downstairs. Mother got off the train this morning, and Grandpa Walters drove her up the hill. I don't think she's supposed to be back yet. She's all beautiful with a new black hat, black gloves, black pumps and a magnificent red coat. She swept into the breakfast room, pulling off her gloves slowly just like a queen, and declaring she'd had a nice little vacation. She smiled at Jeannie, and draped her gloves over Jeannie's shoulder. Long gloves. Silky.

"You'll be pleased to know I've had a divine time. Truly divine. But now there's work to be done, isn't there?"

She unpinned her hat and tossed it at the table. It tumbled right into papa's breakfast. He stared at her. He didn't say a thing. She didn't seem to notice her hat was in his porridge.

"I know you've all been waiting for me to return, so we can begin the preparations for graduation."

Still nobody spoke. Not even Nana. Nana and papa frowned. Mary's eyes got big and she put her hand over her mouth. Laura buttered her toast like nothing unusual had happened. Jeannie admired Mother's new gloves. She put them on and pet them like they were a cat.

Nana had planned to go on tonight's evening train to see Mother. She was going to take magazines and a flower in a pot, so I know Mother was not supposed to be home yet. Mary jumped up from the table and got busy clearing dishes away and setting a place for Mother. Papa went to his room without taking his tea. Nana just sat there with the wrinkles on her forehead wiggling. They do that when she thinks heavy. Mother seems mostly like her old self, and partly very different. It's her eyes. She's like an actress in a movie saying her lines nicely. Making nice talk. But her eyes are not nice. Not nice at all.

She says things in a sweet voice to everybody, but the feeling I get when she talks is not a good one. Like when she followed Mary into the kitchen.

"Mary. Child. I really must insist you find a better dress for serving in. This is not the barnyard, you poor thing."

Mary stared at her, tears welling up in her soft eyes.

"Mary. Dear. Please fix that silly hair-do. It may have been acceptable for visiting with pigs and cows, but you have to understand, sweet Mary, in town the expectations of young women are quite different."

Mother never called Mary sweet before. When she said it, her voice was lovely and low like Marilyn Monroe's. She smiled like an angel. But she is not an angel. She is not. Everybody except Jeannie is feeling wretched about it.

She brought expensive stockings for Jeannie, five pairs, and delicate, lovely underwear, and some new records.

Mother spoke nicely to me too, but I didn't like it. It made me want to cry. She said, "Natalie. Sweetheart." She never calls me Natalie or sweetheart. She touched my cheek with her fingertips like she does to Jeannie, like I always wished she would do to me. Just once. And now she's done it. Oh, Dear Diary, I must be the most ungrateful of people, but I didn't like it one bit.

She said, "Natalie. Sweetheart. You must get out from under foot. Now, darling. Mummy has a very big job to do with the graduation and everything. Please be a big girl and help mummy by staying out of the way."

Nobody calls Mother mummy, not ever. That's why I'm up here right now. She thinks I'm still six years old. Six years old.

Dear Diary, I feel so wretched. I don't think she really sees me at all. I don't want to mind about it. But I do mind. I do. I wish once, just once in my whole stupid life she would look at me and really see me.

Dwelling on unhappy things only makes them worse. Nana says that all the time, and I know she's right. Dwelling is what makes me feel like there are ants in my stomach trying to eat their way out. And then there's poor Laura. Mother brought Laura a graduation dress exactly the same as Jeannie's except it is pink. Laura loathes pink. Everybody knows she loathes pink.

Jeannie's graduation dress is white. Nana says it looks like a wedding dress, much too extravagant for just finishing grade twelve, but it's the one Jeannie wanted. The one from the front cover of Nana's April Canadian Home Journal. Jeannie fell in love with that dress and would have no other. It's for a bride. On the cover it's pink nylon with little white dots all over it and a bolero jacket and very strange gloves with no palms or fingers in them, just a pointed part over the top of the hand like the end of a long sleeve. Very unnecessary, Nana says. Aunt Edie's dressmaker made one just like it for Jeannie in white and the pink one for Laura.

I have never seen Laura so angry. She threw the dress across the room, and stood there with her hands on her hips and her head held high like a warrior princess. It seemed like the air around her was full of invisible fire. She spit words in sharp little pieces.

"I will not. I repeat. I will not. Play lady. In-waiting. To Queen Jeannie. One. More. Time."

She stamped her foot. Just once. She didn't yell, but her voice was so cold it made me shiver.

I thought Mother would fly into a rage. She didn't. Instead, she smiled, shook her head and said, "Sweetheart."

She never calls Laura sweetheart. She never calls anybody but Jeannie sweetheart. Now she's calling everybody sweetheart. Oh, Dear Diary. How can nice words like that feel so wretched? My mind is turned inside out.

"Sweetheart. It's perfectly normal to be a little nervous about your big day. After all, you'll be standing up there all alone, in front of everybody in town. All eyes will be on you, and I know you are not used to that." Her voice sounded strangely soft and horribly sweet.

She tried to put her arm around Laura. Laura flung it away and ran to the hall door. "Don't touch me. Don't you ever touch me."

Laura's voice was rough and loud. Tears streamed down her face. Mother didn't seem to notice.

"But, Darling, I'm your mother. I just want to help you get through a difficult time."

Laura raised her chin. I could see the tears dripping off it. Her voice shook. She made fists at her sides. "There's nothing difficult about my graduation, Mother, nothing difficult except you. My speech is ready. My dress is made. Just leave me alone. Leave me alone. Can't you hear me?"

Laura swung around, ran right past me, and fled upstairs to her bedroom. She packed up two suitcases, and slammed out the door to Linda's. And now I'm worried. What if she didn't go to Linda's? What if she went to Mr. Booth's, at the teacherage? They could get into such trouble. Boy, she's lucky the teacherage is at the end of the street by Deep Creek. She's lucky the caraganas around it are tall and not trimmed. Maybe nobody will see her if she goes by the creek and squeezes through the hedge.

There'll be big trouble over this. Very big trouble. I'm glad Mr. Booth resigned to go back to university. I think he could get fired, because of him and Laura. If anybody knew she's been going there to visit him, they would think she was a juvenile delinquent. Mother would try to send her to a detention home for wayward girls or maybe even to the place for defectives in Red Deer. Oh, Laura.

Mother hasn't seen the graduation dress Nana and Mary sewed for Laura. It is truly beautiful. Wine coloured rayon taffeta, with a full circle skirt. She has lovely pumps to wear with it. Nana bought them for her. Just the ones she wanted.

Oh, that's the other thing Mother did. She got white pumps for Laura, pumps with holes for the toes to stick out. Pumps the same as Jeannie's. Laura hates shoes with toes sticking out.

Mother isn't worried about Laura. When she heard the door slam, she breathed in a long breath of smoke from her cigarette. She smiled at the wall.

"That girl has to learn to share center stage. Jeannie always attracts attention. She can't help it. Beautiful women know how to blossom in the glow of adoration. Laura will only embarrass herself by trying to upstage her sister. People will find it pathetic."

What a silly thing to say. Laura is not the least bit interested in adoration or center stage. She said so to Nana while they were working on her dress.

"Oh, Nana, this dress is so perfect. When I stand up to the podium to give my valedictory speech, I will be myself. Not a silly
handmaiden of Jeannie's. And in this dress, Mother won't make me be
in the photographs."

Mother says Laura has just gone off to have a little pout, and
she'll come round. Mother laid the pink froth on Laura's bed, beside a
new crinoline, stockings and underwear. She says Laura will come
home, and be sensible once she cools off. Mother is going to be disappointed.

June 19, 1953

Dear Diary,

Today is graduation day and nothing has settled down. Laura
has not come home, but I'm happy to report I've seen her a few times
at Linda's, so she may not get in trouble.

Papa's been at the farm since Mother returned, but he came
home early this morning. He's not come out of his study, not even to
eat with us. Mary said he made a plate of sandwiches before breakfast,
took a bowl of radishes and his thermos full of tea and disappeared in
there.

Nana has been in the kitchen every day with Mary to protect
her from Mother, who wanted Mary to make individual baked Alaskas
for the reception. She ordered those, because she knows they're difficult to make, and Mary has no experience with them.

Nana is firm with Mother. She ignores the sweet talk and in-
terrupts her before she can make Mary cry. Mary is making treats for
the luncheon that are much more interesting than baked Alaska, and
Nana told Mother not to bother her.

Mother tossed her hair, raised her chin and sounded bored.
"Marjorie, it's very kind of you to try to cover the girl's ignorance.

But, really. Do you think this is the time and place to take such a stand?"

During the day, Mother spends most of her time at Grandma Walters', so she's not making much of an uproar here.

Jeannie and Mother are still sleeping right now, because they stayed up half the night playing records in Mother's room. Playing them loud. And to top it all off, I think Jeannie had some of Mother's gin, because there were two juice glasses in the sink this morning. I know, for her, it isn't medicine. They have to get up soon, because the hair-dos have to be done.

I've half-decided not to go to the graduation. Nana and Mary made me a very nice dress, it's green seersucker with a covered belt, quite long, so my boots and my brace don't show. Mother dislikes it when I hump along in a dress, calling attention to myself, and it'll be hard work avoiding her disapproving eye for the whole ceremony. I won't tell anybody about staying home until the last minute. By then they'll all be in such a flap to go, nobody will take time to argue with me.

Holy Cow! Laura! She's running through Nana's garden heading for the back stairs... later ...

Oh, Dear Diary, my heart's beating so hard I can hardly think. I'm so excited I may explode. Now I know why so few people write down their daily life for future Historians. It's terrible busy work. Life happens faster than a person can write it down.

Laura is getting married! Right away. Maybe tomorrow. As soon as they can get a license. She was going to wait until she turned eighteen, but now Mr. Booth's father in Ontario is sick. He has to have a serious operation, and Mr. Booth has to go back home to be in charge of everything. Now, he can't go to university here in Alberta like he planned. Both his brothers got killed in the war, and his sisters are married and live in the United States, so he is the one who has to look after things on the home front.

I knew it was important when I saw Laura running like a deer for the back stairs. By the time I got to the landing door she was already at the top. She burst in and collapsed into the rocker, pushing both palms against her chest, so she could catch her breath. Never before has she come into my room. Never.

"Tally, go get papa. I saw his truck, so I know he's here, but don't let Mother see you. Please."

I was worried for a minute. I thought she was sick or Mr. Booth had had an accident. I must have looked scared, because Laura laughed and jumped up, threw her arms around me, and gave me a very hard squeeze.

"Oh, Tally. I'm so sorry. I've given you a fright haven't I? Don't be worried. Nothing is wrong. Not at all. But things are quite sped up and I need papa. Do you think you could ask him to come up here without anybody getting snoopy?

"I can try."

Actually it was easy. I heard Jeannie and Mother giggling in Mother's room, getting ready to go to the beauty parlour. I knew Grandpa Walters would be at the front door any minute to pick them up. He washed and twice polished his new Buick for the occasion. Mother requested the Buick for Jeannie's graduation.

Anyway, I knocked quietly on papa's door, and listened hard for his come-in. He talks so quiet you have to really stretch your ears. He sat in his armchair staring out the window, and when he saw me his eyebrows raised right up.

"Tally. To what do I owe this honour?"

He sounded pleased to see me, and it made me remember in the barn when he said 'my Natalie'. I like being his Natalie.

"I thought all my girls were in a frenzy of graduation preparations."

"Not all your girls, papa." I think I smiled then.

He smiled back. "Of course not. Silly of me to say that, wasn't it?"

"It was."

I stood straight like a soldier with my arms at my sides, because that's what I felt like. A soldier with an important message. "It's Laura."

Papa rose from his chair, alarm flattening his face. "Laura?"

"Papa. Don't be scared. Nothing's wrong. But she needs you. Right now. And it has to be a secret. We can't let Mother know and not even Nana."

Papa relaxed, but he didn't sit back down. "Is that so?"

"Yes. She's upstairs in my bedroom, and don't be scared to go up there. Granddad Smythe is not haunting it."

Papa smiled. "Is that so?"

I nodded. "If you wait a few minutes, Jeannie and Mother will be off to the beauty parlour, and the coast will be clear."

Papa smiled. "Sounds like a good plan."

It was a good plan. I kept watch until I heard Grandpa Walters' car drive away.

"You can go now. Nana and Mary are busy in the kitchen. They won't notice you going upstairs."

"And will they notice you?'

"Oh, papa. Nobody notices me."

He frowned.

"Papa, it's useful when nobody notices me."

He pulled my braid. "Yes, I suppose it is."

He was up the stairs in a flash, and it took me quite a time to catch up to him. Going upstairs with my stupid foot takes more thinking than coming down. The thing that's broken in me is the nerve string that ties my foot to my knee. It's the string that lets a person lift the foot up. It's a little thing really, but you would be surprised how awkward it makes going up stairs.

When I got there, Laura was leaned forward on the window seat, with her hands clamped tight between her knees looking at papa with a pleading puppy face. Papa sat in Granddad Smythe's big armchair. One ankle resting on one knee and his fingers making a steeple in front of his face. He seemed to be gazing out the window, but I know that look. That's the look people get when they're thinking seriously.

"Natalie." His pointing fingers tapped each other. "Our little messenger. What do you think of all this?" He turned to me. "It seems our Laura found herself an admirer, a man with family responsibility off in the East. She insists she must marry him immediately, and go with him to Toronto. She, of course, can't marry without permission."

That wasn't a big a surprise to me, since I knew about her and Mr. Booth. Papa asking my opinion surprised me. Nobody asks my opinion, except Nana. I did have an opinion and I gave it. I had to take a deep breath. I'm bold about giving my opinions to you, Dear Diary, but out loud in front of people I'm quite different.

"I thought about it, papa. I thought it through about three or four times."

I'm not exactly sure how many times I thought it through, but Nana expects the thinking to be done more than once. "I don't think Laura should get into trouble for anything. She didn't shirk her studies, not once, and Mr. Booth is in favour of education for women."

"So you approve of this Mr. Booth, then?"

"Oh, yes I do. He is smart. He's a kind man. And he isn't one bit stuffy."

Papa nodded his head. "Quite a recommendation."

"And you know, papa. If Laura is to be a doctor, she has to go to school in the East anyway. And don't forget, Nana was only thirteen when she started writing to Granddad Smythe, and she married him just after her seventeenth birthday. Her family didn't like it either, but they gave their blessing, so she wouldn't be foolish and run away."

He nodded his head. "A very persuasive argument, Natalie."

Then he turned to Laura. "I can see some of Nana's determination in you, Laura. You've dug your feet deep into the ground, and I know how fruitless it is to go against your Nana when she's determined. So, tell me. How do you see this situation unfolding?"

Laura spoke in a great rush of words. "Ted leaves in a week, papa. He leaves on the train, next Friday. So we must be quick. Oh, papa. I know he's older, but I can talk with him like I can talk to nobody else. He loves to swim like I do, and he is crazy for cats. He likes to stay at home and read in the evenings just like I do, and he is teaching me how to play bridge."

Papa nodded his head. "People have married with much less in common." He looked at me, then at Laura. "And you both agree he is a remarkable young man?"

We spoke at once. "Yes, he is."

And Laura burst out. "He wanted to come with me to ask you papa, but I wouldn't let him. I couldn't let him to creep up the back stairs. And we couldn't come in the front door because we'd have to talk to Mother." She frowned. "Mother will be furious. She wants me to baby sit Jeannie for the rest of my life."

Laura burst into tears and flung herself at his knee. "Papa. Please. She can't know. Not until after. She'll have a big tantrum and she'll spoil it. She'll find fifty ways to spoil it for me, papa."

She cried so hard it took papa and me together to pat her and hug her back to calm.

"Papa. She wants me to go to business school with Jeannie. She wants me to be a stenographer. I want to be a doctor, papa. Ted says being married won't stand in the way of that."

Papa sat in silence for a good, long time. Laura bit on her lip and snuffled. I had to remind myself to breathe.

"My girl," he said finally, "This is certainly unorthodox, but I've learned the hard way, many worthwhile things are unorthodox."

Laura's hair was all over wild, and stuck to her face with tears, but her smile was beautiful.

Papa smiled too. "I think we can draft a suitable plan, but do you think you can leave the planning till tomorrow or at least this evening? You have a valedictory address to give today and I, for one, am looking forward to hearing it."

"You are?" It's easy to understand Laura's surprise; papa doesn't usually go out in public, except to church.

"We've never had a valedictorian in the family, and I bought a new tie for the occasion."

"Oh, papa. You're coming to my graduation." Laura started to cry again, and I very nearly joined her.

"No more water works. Don't you have some hair business? Some primping and preening?"

Laura nodded.

"Go on then. First things, first. I won't involve your mother right now, but you realize it's impossible for me not to talk to your Nana."

Laura nodded. "I don't mind Nana knowing, papa. I just didn't know how to tell her."

Papa laughed. "I understand."

I think I'll go to the graduation after all. I'll sit between papa and Nana where Mother's eyes can't reach me. Laura will be wonderful today. I don't want to miss it.

Right after graduation, June 19, 1953

Oh, Dear Diary,

Laura was magnificent. Truly magnificent. She stood tall and straight and proud. Her voice was strong and lovely. Nana said she was positively regal in her wine taffeta. She wore the pearls Nana gave her, and a most astonishing garnet ring with tiny real pearls that belonged to Mr. Booth's grandmother. She showed it to Nana, Mary, papa and me as soon as we walked into the gymnasium. Laura worried Mother would come by. There was no worry.

Mother and Jeannie held their chins high when they made their grand entrance from Grandpa Walters' Buick. Gerry escorted Jeannie. He had a grin bigger than two faces could hold. He did look smart in his new suit, new haircut, new shoes and no glasses. He kept his glasses in the inside pocket of his suit jacket. He put them on briefly to read the program. Mother swept in on Grandpa Walters' arm, every bit a movie star in a new, slim, jet-black skirt with a peplum jacket; the very best style for Mother. Of course her pumps were high with her toes out the ends. Mother loves shoes. She wore a complicated little hat with an elegant feather down one side curving forward toward her chin, and a delicate veil that came to the tip of her nose. As much as Mother makes me so mad close up, she's truly nice to look at from a distance.

Grandma Walters came behind them on Uncle Phillip's arm. She was wrapped up in a lacey blue suit with her chin so high I doubt she could see where she was going. She wore her five strand pearls, which she insists are real, but Nana fights a laugh when Grandma mentions them, so I expect they are only cultured. Nana grew up where real pearls were worn, so she knows what is real, and what is not.

Mother didn't notice Laura. She sat in our row, but Grandma and Grandpa Walters and Uncle Phillip sat next to us. Mother had Helen and the Widow Harrison on her other side.

Mother was so annoying during Laura's valedictory speech. She whispered with Helen and they tittered like teenagers. They didn't listen to a word of it, but the rest of us soon got caught up in what Laura was saying, and we forgot Mother altogether. Laura talked like I've never heard her talk before. She talked about leaving home on your first big adventure. She talked about the people you leave behind, and about how a part of each of them travels with you deep in your heart. And you have them in there, because of the love and careful admiration they gave you all your life. Even Nana had to use her hankie. Afterwards papa kissed Laura on the forehead, and told her she was an amazing orator, very eloquent and gracious, and then Laura had to use Nana's hankie.

Laura was funny to watch. Nice funny. So grown up. And papa is right, so very gracious. She had to work hard not to confer special favour on Mr. Booth when she stood there talking to Nana and papa and the other people who came to congratulate her on her speech.

I watched Nana and papa take his measure. I could tell he was nervous, but he stood firm and looked them square in the eye. I'm glad for that. Nana's keen to have people look her square in the eye. All the teachers have received invitations to the luncheon, so Mr. Booth will have another occasion today to prove himself worthy.

I've escaped up here away from the hubbub of getting the luncheon ready. It's not really a luncheon, because nobody will sit up to the table. People will carry little plates around and nibble as they talk. Very awkward, I think, but Mother says it's the way it's done in the better families. I don't know what that means. The better families. Where do these better families live, and how come Mother knows them and we don't?

Mother is fluttering and hovering over the tables, constantly rearranging the flowers and the fruit plates. Nana is stuck in the living room, entertaining Grandma Walters and Uncle Phillip. Crazy Marion and Kokum won't come. I don't blame them one bit. Mother says Beanie and Russell are not allowed to the luncheon, but Laura says it is her graduation too, and Beanie and Russell are welcome. Beanie likes to avoid Mother, but he hates to miss good food, so we decided he and Russell can read comics on the back porch, and Mary and I will deliver food and gossip.

Laura has a gigantic apron tied over her finery, and is bustling in the kitchen with Mary. I guess if she is going to be a married woman, it's good to learn about the kitchen. Papa is in Nana's garden on the willow bench under the wild cucumber smoking his pipe. He's taken up the pipe just recently. He resurrected Granddad Smythe's old pipes, and he seems quite pleased with himself.

Grandpa Walters drove Jeannie and Gerry to Vermilion for professional photographs, if you please. You'd think they'd just got married. The pictures won't be as good as Nana's. Crazy Marion says nobody understands light the way Nana does. Nana took photographs in the garden of Laura, right after the ceremonies. During the luncheon she'll take photos of Laura and Mr. Booth behind the garden shed where the Virginia creeper tumbles over the roof. She'll wait till just the right moment when the afternoon shadows are long enough. Nothing wrecks a good photograph, Nana says, like bright sun over head on a cloudless day. Nana has a darkroom in the basement in the corner by the furnace. Photography is one place where Nana allows herself extravagance. Nana's photographs are quite famous around here, and even in Edmonton. Some hang in banks, and in a big clinic, and in the hospital where Mother goes when her nerves are broken.

I think Nana is enjoying this subterfuge about Laura getting married. Good word, don't you think? Subterfuge? I learned it a while ago, but haven't had a chance to use it until now. Nana says words like that always come in handy eventually.

Truly nighttime, June 19, 1953

Oh, Dear Diary,

What next? Just when I think life has wound down to ordinary, and I can get back to my magazines and simple recording, everything goes crazy again. I don't know what to say first. I'm worried, but maybe I'm making a mountain out of a molehill, so I'm going to leave my worries till the very last. Maybe by then I'll think differently.

Historians, I'll tell you first about the luncheon. It definitely had a lot of different daily life in it, and some parts of it were quite excellent. A real mish-mash of people came and went. I was off in a corner on a footstool watching it all when papa brought one of Nana's folding camp stools, and sat down beside me. I couldn't have been more surprised if it had rained in the living room.

"Quite a vantage point you have."

I nodded my head. "I do. I can see everybody coming in and going out, and I can hear conversations around the buffet table."

"Remarkable." Papa's knees were nearly up to his chin, sitting so near to the floor, but he seemed comfortable, and it was fun to have him there.

Nana vowed not to get caught up in the craziness of the preparations, but she gave up after Mother bragged about Helen's exquisite, coffee flavoured meringue shells filled with chocolate cream and topped with a swirl of almond whipped cream. Helen had been driven to do this, Mother said, so we wouldn't be completely embarrassed by Mary's crude attempts at baking.

Mrs. O'Kane has not been back in this house, except to bring Mother's gin when Nana's not home, and I'm amazed at her gall trying to make Mary look bad at our luncheon. Grandma Walters, of course, brought her famous molded salmon ring, and her emerald mounds, both of which I'm very tired of. They're just lime gelatin with shredded cucumber, and mayonnaise stars on top.

Mother badgered Mary over the baked Alaskas until Mary tried to tackle them. She spread Nana's cookbooks all over the kitchen table and got herself into a giant tizzy before Nana intercepted her.

"Never meet your adversaries in their backyard, my girl. That is an important rule to learn."

Then she showed Mary how to understand that rule. She told Mary she was doomed to failure if she attempted baked Alaskas.

"Even if you made the most perfect baked Alaskas in the world, and I have no doubt you would, Lillian will find fifteen ways to tell us about ones that are better."

Instead, Nana showed Mary how to make delicate little cookie cones. They are picky to make, but Mary is a wizard at rolling them. You have to be quick. It's hot work, because they can't be allowed to cool off. A person has to bend over the cookie sheet on the open oven door, and roll like mad before they stiffen. They are very handsome when done right, and Mary outdid herself, making eight dozen.

The most wonderful part is the sabayon filling. That's a French pudding made with egg yolks and icing sugar and expensive brandy liquor. It's velvet on the tongue. And it's another hot thing to make. A person has to beat it with a big whisk in a big bowl over boiling water. Nana picked these confections because she knows Mother has never had them, and because Mary would not stand for an easy effort.

The sabayon had to cool overnight. Then Mary beat it up again and squirted into the tiny cookie cones with a parchment paper piping bag. Mary piled the cones in a circle around Nana's cut class flower vase, which she later filled with blue flags and baby's breath. That impressed Nana massively. Laura and me, too, but the very best part came during the luncheon when Grandma Walters came to inspect the creation.

"Girl." Grandma Walters will not call Mary by her name. "Who delivered this edifice?"

Grandma Walters loves extravagant words just about as much as Mother and Aunt Edie. Mary is usually nervous around Grandma Walters, but Nana gave her a rousing pep talk before everybody arrived.

"I made this, Mrs. Walters."

Grandma Walters's head swung around. "Really? And where did Marjorie purchase the cunning little shells?"

"The Linder Horn? I made them yesterday before I made the sabayon filling." Mary pronounced sabayon perfectly. "Linder Horn avec Sabayon. I hope you find them suitable." She spoke slowly and carefully.

Grandma Walters thinks French names are the height of so-phistication. Mary made a good French pronunciation, just as calm as you please. She had practiced it for days. It stopped Grandma Walters dead in her tracks.

Linder Horn is a made-up name. Nana says a person is at liberty to name a confection whatever they choose, and when up against snobbery, a made-up name is best. Snobs are honour-bound to pretend they've heard the name before. And that's just what Grandma Walters did.

She fluttered her hand and raised her chin. "Of course, Linder Horns." She daintily picked one up and sampled it. The way she momentarily closed her eyes told us right away she found them delicious. Grandma Walters is very fond of sweets.

"Quite passable."

That's all she said, but she ate at least a dozen herself, and she stood beside them to explain them to guests.

"Oh, these Linder Horns? They are good aren't they? Marjorie had her girl make them. Quite clever."

Laura and Mary stood in the kitchen doorway watching and giggling. Mother was huffy with Laura for wearing an apron instead of taking her proper place beside Jeannie and Gerry to receive graduation congratulations. Laura did it on purpose to escape them. Besides she likes working with Mary.

Oh, and then Dear Diary, oh, this part is so good. I told you Mary is smart. Even Nana didn't know about the Egyptian Lady Fingers. Mary invented them all by herself, and brought them out at the very best moment, arranged in a fan shape on a doily on Nana's silver tea tray. She arranged a little custard cup full of pansies and tiny sprigs of baby's breath at the pointed end of the fan and it was truly magnificent. Everybody oohed and aahed over them.

She made them by rolling up thin vanilla cookies while they were hot, kind of the same as the Linder Horns. But for the Lady Fingers she rolled them like skinny cigars, pinching one end of them shut while they were still warm. Then she tossed them in sugar and cinnamon, and filled them with what she called orange blossom cream. It's just stiff whipped cream with food colouring, orange flavour and scraped orange rind. Egyptian Lady Fingers. Mary is amazing. She got the lady finger name from one of Nana's cookbooks. She got the idea to make them Egyptian from Nana's National Geographic magazines. Nana says Mary is a pure genius, and I agree.

Grandma Walters was beside herself explaining these delicacies to everybody. When Mother realized Mrs. O'Kane's coffee meringues, which she makes for every occasion, were not the feature confection, they both went into her bedroom to pout. I don't think anybody missed them.

Nana used her hankie to hide a smile over and over again. Papa was immensely amused when I explained it to him. There were so many things in this day for Mother to get annoyed over. She nearly fainted when Uncle Metro and Aunt Olga came in the door. Baba and Wasy were invited too, but Baba wouldn't come.

"Dat Lee-lee-in. She make it bad talk for my Wasy. I no go."

Papa told Nana what Baba said. He did an excellent imitation of how Baba talks. Even though Beanie and Russell were careful to stay out of the way, Mother did get a glimpse of them. Her lips got thin and pinched, but she didn't dare say a word, because Beanie's Aunt Dorothy stood right there talking to Grandma Walters. Grandma Walters says Beanie's Aunt comes from 'better people' because she was born in England. Besides, Mother tries not to spoil her perfect queen image in front of company.

Mary and I filled a pie tin with every good thing for Beanie and Russell to eat on the porch swing. Beanie doesn't like people staring at him when he eats. Just because he's round, people stare when he enjoys food, and make rude comments. Afterwards papa invited Russell along when he went walking with Mr. Booth.

When Nana took photographs of Laura and Mr. Booth, Beanie and I guarded the garden path to the shed, so we could give warning if anybody came that way. I'm supposed to call Mr. Booth, Ted; he insists, but it's going to take some getting used to. We don't call grown-ups by their first names in our family. I won't call Laura, Mrs. Booth when she is married. I have to think about that. Mrs. Booth. Hmmn. Ted and papa get along famously. They talked for the longest time, and they laughed together. Ted smokes a pipe too. Like old friends, they puffed and talked and walked with Russell.

I think Laura would have floated away had she not been held down by so much dress and a big apron. And now they're gone. Tonight. To Edmonton. Mary and I helped Laura pack her suitcases and took them down the back stairs for her. Papa put them into the trunk of Mr. Booth's car in the back alley. That will have to do until we can box up the rest of her things and send them out. Papa went with them to Edmonton, to give the permission. He'll come back on the train in a few days. It's all happened so fast I can't decide whether to be happy or sad about it.

Mother won't notice Laura's gone. She's punishing Laura by ignoring her, because she hogged the attention at Jeannie's graduation. She is punishing us all by ignoring us for ruining Jeannie's graduation. Mother and Jeannie are the only ones who think it was ruined.

People didn't mind going into the kitchen to congratulate Laura for her speech. Jeannie sat like a queen in the living room on the couch with her dress spread around her just right, her legs crossed at the ankles like in a magazine, and Gerry standing like a post beside her. Only thing was, after everybody shook her hand once, she was left alone.

Jeannie can't stand not getting the attention she deserves. She talks in a silly, little girl voice to get heads turned her way, but nobody turned. Then, Dear Diary, you won't believe what she did. She called Mary in the sweetest voice. "Mary, please come here for a moment, would you?"

It was spooky. She sounded like Mother, her chin in the air and using her snottiest voice.

"Now, I know you're not used to these formal occasions, but really Mary, common decency would tell you can't leave a person sitting here without a glass of punch to sip on."

I jumped up, ready to tell Jeannie off but good, then I saw papa watching. I sat down. When Mary came back from the kitchen with a crystal tumbler full of raspberry punch he stood up. I thought Jeannie would see him and behave herself, but she didn't. When Mary handed her the punch, Jeannie waved her hand, knocking the tumbler to the floor. The punch splashed over Jeannie's perfect white dress. She shrieked. She called Mary names. Stupid Bohunk. Clumsy peasant. Right there in front of people. Papa walked across the room.

"Jeannie, you'll apologize to Mary."

Jeannie stopped in mid-shriek. She stared at papa. "Me? Me, apologize to her? Papa are you mad? Stupid, clumsy Bohunk. Look at my dress."

"Jeannie. Go to your room."

Can you believe it? Papa sent Jeannie to her room. Never, never have I seen such a thing. Jeannie flew into a royal rage. She wailed for Mother, but Mother was shut up in her room with Mrs. O'Kane, her record player playing so loud she didn't hear a thing. Grandma Walters is the only other person who might have gone to Jeannie's rescue, but she had left with a sick headache and a tray of Mary's confections.

Some of Laura and Jeannie's friends from school were still there, and they gathered to watch the whole thing. I have to say not one of them felt sorry for her, except maybe Gerry. Once Jeannie gets into a state she doesn't care who sees. She stamped her foot. She threw all the cushions off the couch, then burst into tears, and flew up the stairs to her room. After her door slammed shut everything settled right down.

Mother thinks Laura's escaped to Linda's. It's agreed we won't mention the marriage to Mother or Jeannie till papa gets back. This is the best secret. Not even Beanie knows.

But, then, there was the other part of the day. This is the part I'm worried about. Roger came to the back door during the luncheon. He'd been invited, of course. Nana insisted. His family is in mourning, naturally, but it is only right he get an invitation. We didn't expect him to come, so when Mary whispered that he was at the kitchen door, I was surprised. It was me he wanted to talk to. He had a present for Jeannie, and one for Laura too.

"Hey, short stuff. Are you completely bored yet?"

"Not exactly."

I told him about Mary, and the made-up names for the confections. He smiled and raised his eyebrows a little. Then, he asked about Mary. I could see she made a big impression on him when she answered the door. I'm surprised I'm not jealous. But I don't seem to be. Maybe the boy crazy thing was a false alarm. I'm pleased about that. Mary deserves a fine boyfriend.

Her hair is light brown, and when she washes it she rinses it in cold water with a little vinegar, so it shines like satin. She made her own dress, and it's divine. It has a perky stand up collar and a keyhole opening in the bodice. Very cunning, and in royal blue, which went splendid with her dark, dark blue eyes. I haven't told her yet that Roger asked all about her, but I know he'll be back to see her soon.

Jeannie will be put out, but who cares about that? She'll be gone soon, anyway. After the Sports Day next week she goes with Aunt Edie for a graduation trip to the United States. They are going to visit Aunt Edie's sister-in-law in Seattle, and then all the way down to California. Mother's not happy about it. Aunt Edie invited her too, but she won't go.

Nana says Mother's the one having a hard time sharing center stage with Jeannie. Nana says Mother's miffed, because when she and Aunt Edie used to travel together, Mother was in charge, and this time Aunt Edie made the plans without consulting her.

Anyway, I was having a nice time sitting on the back porch with Roger when I noticed his ring. A ring with a black Egyptian scarab in a nest of old gold on it. The partner to Fat Freddy's tie clip. I could have fainted on the spot.

I must have stared at the ring like it was going to bite me, because Roger laughed. "Nice, ring, huh?" He rubbed it with his thumb. "Don't worry it's completely petrified. Won't jump off and bite you."

That wasn't what worried me, of course.

He smiled a sad smile. "Found it in my sister's things. Guess it used to be my father's."

Oh, dear diary. I didn't want to tell him. I didn't want to so bad my stomach felt sick. It put me in an awful dilemma. Roger was not even one year old when his mama died down the well, and he was just two years old when his papa died drunk in a snow bank. He never knew his papa, and there he sat, so proud to have a ring that belonged to him. I couldn't smile and pretend it was wonderful. I couldn't let him wear Fat Freddy's ring. Sooner or later somebody else would tell him and maybe not in a nice way.

What a stupid thing to say. There is no nice way to tell a person that. Why did it have to be me? I burst into tears. I couldn't help it.

"Hey, short stuff. What's the trouble?"

At first, all I could do was point at the ring and cry. I felt so very, very terrible.

"Hey, come on now. I didn't think you'd be scared of this silly old bug. It's all right. I'll take it off, see."

"No. No. No." I finally took a good deep breath, and kept myself staring at the scarab, so I could spit it out. "It's not your father's. It isn't, Roger. Oh, Roger, it isn't. I'm so sorry. It's .. it's Freddy's."

Roger stared at the ring in his palm like it had turned into dog poop. "Freddy's?"

"Freddy. Fat Freddy. He has a tie clip just like it. They belonged to Rose's father. That's how they knew it was him who... your sister... It was there. His tie-clip."

I didn't do a good job of the telling. I did the worst job. I should have got Nana. I didn't think it through. I didn't. For a moment he just sat there and stared at the ring. I stared with him. Then he jumped up and threw it into the garden. Far into the garden. Way off into the beet row.

"That bastard. That goddamn, fuckin' bastard. He owns everything. Everything. Fuckin'. Every Thing."

I am sorry, Historians, about the swears I keep giving you. But, somehow it seems wrong to leave them out.

He shook his hand like it was covered with slime. "I've been wearing it since the funeral. I've been wearing it for Christ's sake." He put his arm out, staring at his fingers, leaning against the porch post for a moment, his other hand over his face.

"I'm sorry, Roger. I'm so sorry." What a useless word that is when you really need it to mean serious sorry. My mouth felt full of cracker crumbs.

He shook his head slowly like an old man. Tears flooded down his face. "Don't worry about it Short Stuff. Better hearing it from you than somebody else." He walked down the steps as though his shoes were heavy. "I'm going to kill that bastard. I'm going to find him and kill him myself."

He didn't say that to me. He sent the words into the air as he walked down the path and out the back gate. He didn't slam the gate. I wish he had. Oh, Dear Diary I'm so worried.

I told Nana as soon as I could. She telephoned his brother. They talked a long time. Nana and Roger's brother. But she phoned from her sitting room phone and wouldn't let me listen. She says it's fine now. I'm not to worry about it, but I am worrying.

Fat Freddy will go to jail when they find him. I don't know if he'll get hung. I don't think they hang mayors. But Roger. If he kills Freddy, he'll hang for sure. Now, I understand why Nana fights so hard for justice. There's so little of it in the world where it really counts. Oh, Historians of the Future, I hope things are different way off where you are. I hope you have justice up there.

June 22, 1953

Dear Diary,

Things are getting settled down again. Roger didn't find Fat Freddy to kill him, and Nana reports he's cooled off some.

Laura and Ted left on the train yesterday, for Ontario. We talked to them on the phone before they left, Nana, Mary and I. Laura sounded so happy. We all cried there in Nana's rooms. Then Nana thought maybe Mother would want to send a telegram to them.

Mother wasn't as upset about Laura as I thought she'd be. She shrugged and said, "Stupid girl."

Jeannie looked up from painting her toe nails and said, "Laura and Mr. Booth? Oh, how awful. He's so old. Is she pregnant?"

Jeannie was disappointed to discover Laura wasn't pregnant, but she didn't get interested beyond that.

Mother's helping Jeannie pack for the graduation trip. When Aunt Edie phones, Mother goes into her room and shuts the door. Jeannie isn't the least concerned about it. Aunt Edie says Mother's pouting, and she'll get over it. Jeannie's happy with that explanation. She's like Mother that way.

I wonder what Jeannie would do if extreme unpleasantness happened here. Like Russians dropping bombs on our town. They could do that, you know. They're all Communists over there, dedicated to spreading themselves over the world now that Hitler's war is over. That's what Grandpa Walters says. He says the United States should take a plane load of those atomic bombs they invented for Japan and drop them over Russia where it would really hurt.

Nana disagrees. She says that kind of hysteria fans the flames of discontent. She says if people would just leave the Russians alone they'd collapse under their own trouble. They'd get to fighting each other if we didn't keep giving them something outside their borders to bluster over. Of course the United States is not as wise as Nana, so I don't think Russia will be left alone. That's another worrisome thing.

I suppose, Historians of the Future, if you are the Russians who took over the world, you won't like me saying these things.

Freddy's brother-in-law is now running his construction company. Mr. Tomkow, from the meat market, is acting mayor. Everybody agrees he's doing a fine job.

Mary blushed a dozen kinds of red when I told her Roger had asked after her. I hope he comes to see her.

June 24, 1953

Dear Diary,

I think things are speeding up again. Beanie came over this morning to tell us he heard Freddy is hiding on somebody's farm. Beanie was at the train station after school with Russell, putting pennies on the track. That's where they heard talk, but Beanie doesn't know how to listen without being noticed, so they got chased off before he heard the whole thing.

If Freddy's hiding in the country, he's most likely at Floyd Gimley's. The police searched there. They didn't find anything. Mr. Gimley's place backs onto Buffalo Cooley. It's all ravines and sand hills and old abandoned buildings everywhere. The Gimley clan has lived there forever and a day, and every person born to them builds some kind of shack or pulls in a granary to fix up or a chicken coop. RCMP are here in Deep Creek again, poking around, and the whole town is stirred up.

Nana must have known I was worried about Roger, because she told me he's hauling gravel today, and probably hasn't heard the news yet. With luck they'll catch Freddy before Roger finds out.

I told Mary about Roger and the ring and how Nana and Roger's brother are working to keep him from foolishness. Of course that got her worried. After supper I'll show her how to use the spyglass. She wasn't interested before, but if she watches Lafond's house, and sees Roger safe she'll feel better.

After supper, June 24, 1953

Oh, No, Dear Diary,

I don't know if I can write this. I have to. I can't find words. Spit it out. I have to spit it out. Freddy's dead. Shot. On the road to the gravel pit. And Roger's gone. The gravel truck's in the ditch and Roger's gone.

Oh, Dear Diary this is the worst. And it's nearly dark. Everybody says Roger ran into the bush to hide. Everybody's looking for him. Papa too. Nana's with Mary downstairs. They're crocheting to keep busy, and that's why I'm up here, trying to keep busy too, but it isn't working. What if he runs and they shoot him? What if they catch him and hang him? There's no good answer to this mess. None at all.

Mother and Jeannie went to the movies. They said it's too depressing here. They don't care about anybody but themselves.

Nobody knows where Roger got a gun. Not even his brother. Goodnight. I am going to bed and cover my head with a dozen pillows.

Wait. Dear Diary. I know where Roger's thinking place is. He told me. On the porch swing. We were discussing how important it is to have a place to think. It's by Tremolo Pond, his thinking place. What if he's out there? Alone?

June 25, 1953

Dear Diary,

I feel like a year has passed since I jumped up from this chair and clattered downstairs. It's five in the morning now, and everybody else in the house is long asleep. I was too, but I got up to go to the bathroom, and now I'm wide awake. It's going to take a good long time to record everything, so I'm going write till I get sleepy.

Last night, I burst in on Nana and Mary so suddenly Nana dropped her crocheting and Mary shrieked. I told them about Roger's thinking place on the old stone steps at the far end of Tremolo Pond.

Nana was not in favour of me going there. Not at all. But I had to. I just had to. I had to get to him before somebody found him and made things worse. I wanted to bring him to Nana for protection, the way she protected Mary. It wasn't the best plan, but there was no time for thinking it through.

You can't get to the pond by car. The only way is by walking or by bicycle. I don't ride my bicycle much anymore, but the tires aren't flat. I've gone with Beanie on the path to the pond dozens of times, so I know the way, even in the dusk.

I got bossy. You won't believe it. I told Nana to phone for help, or use her car to find people. I told Mary to get Beanie and tell him where I'd gone. I didn't think he'd be a lot of help, but he's better than no help.

Nana yelled at me to come back, but I had to disobey. I took my bike from the garden shed, and was half-way down the path before she could holler me back in.

"Natalie Smythe. You get back here this instant."

"Sorry, Nana." That's all I could manage to say as I pushed through the gate and sailed down the back alley. One good thing about Nana's house, from there it's downhill almost all the way to the pond. I went through every short cut, through every back yard I knew about. I scared rabbits and cats and set all the dogs to barking.

When I got across the railroad tracks I had to slow down some, because the fastest way after there is a dirt path over-grown with trees and roots. And then there is the steep place above the creek that goes into Tremolo Pond. Suicide hill, where the path has to go a long way around the ravine. The path is close to the edge of the ravine in places, and it's tough to decide when to slow down for caution, and when to throw caution to the wind and take a chance. I'm not sure all my decisions were smart, but I got there without an accident. I dropped my bike at the top of the last hill, and more or less slid down on my bottom. I hollered the whole way down for Roger. He was there all right, and he looked like he was going to run away.

"It's just me, Roger. Nobody else." I was so out of breath I could hardly make the words come out. I got going too fast and tumbled tank over teakettle to a heap at his feet.

He yanked me up. Not too gentle I'll tell you. He was a mess. His face was bruised. He had blood on his shirt. "Tally. What in hell are you doing here?"

It's hard to explain in a rush. "I don't want anybody to shoot you."

That got him alarmed. He looked wildly up at the hills around us; they were rapidly sinking into deep shadows. "Who's coming to shoot me?"

"Nobody. Not yet. They're searching for you, in the bush by the pit."

"How did you know I was here?"

"You told me about your thinking place. Remember? I told you about mine, and you laughed, and said you guessed it would be all right to tell me about yours. Remember? You said nobody else knows."

His head fell back. "Oh, great. Now I suppose you've told the whole town."

That hurt my feelings a little. "I did not. Only Nana and Mary."

"It doesn't matter. I'm sorry you had to come down here, Tally, but it doesn't change anything. They'll hang me. Don't you know that? Put a rope around my scrawny neck, choke the life right out of me, and dangle me there in my shitty pants for everybody to see."

"Nana says she'll get a lawyer. A good one. She says you had provocation to shoot him. She says it will make a difference."

"Oh, shit. I didn't shoot him. I wish to hell I had. Bastard." He kicked a rock into the river. "I wish to hell I'd shot him. Deliberate. Made him squirm. Made him scared like he made Suzanne scared. Made him beg. Crawl on the ground and beg before I shot his ugly face off." He swung around and looked at me so fiercely I should have been scared, but somehow I knew he wouldn't hurt me. I could see the tears slipping down his face. "They'll hang me anyway, Tally. You know it. Trash like me doesn't come out on top against money."

"But, if you didn't do it?"

"Tally. I'm real touched you came all the way here to rescue me. I am. But you have to leave. Now. I'm not going to hang for that scum."

He looked down and I saw what he had been doing. He had a piece of chain wrapped around a big rock. He was going to drown himself, the stupid nincompoop. That made me mad. I hurled myself at him and knocked him over.

"What are you doing?" He tried to peel me off.

"If you're going to be stupid and drown yourself, you'll have to drown me too."

Roger is a good person. I knew he wouldn't drown me. And it didn't hurt a bit that I'm a Gimp. I don't think he would drown anybody else either, but people feel extra sorry for Gimps.

I'm strong and I hung on as tight as I could. We rolled back and forth. He got one of my hands loose, and then I hooked my legs around him. He got pretty mad. I worried I wouldn't be able to hang on till somebody came.

Then the stupid bank crumbled and dumped us into the pond. It's deep there and beastly cold. I let go of him. Then I worried he'd take the opportunity to drown, so I splashed hard and hollered, "Roger! I can't swim. Help. Roger."

I swim perfectly fine, but I figured he wouldn't have time to think about drowning if he had to think about saving me. I was right about that, but can you believe it? He can't swim. I thought all big boys could swim.

Anyway, he grabbed a tree root and spluttered and spit. My heavy shoe tried to drag me down. Roger told me to grab his foot. I did.

"Hang on, Tally. Can you hang on?"

"I don't know. I'm scared. I'm scared." I whimpered and whined like Jeannie.

"Don't you dare drown Tally Smythe. Don't you dare."

I know it was mean of me, but how else could I stop him? And it wasn't all trickery. It was hard to stay above water with my clothes and my brace and shoes trying to drag me down. It was nearly pitch dark, and really cold and for a few moments I thought we'd drown. Oh, Dear Diary. I had the worst thoughts. I came to save Roger and here I was killing both of us.

I suppose I'm dead and gone, Historians, if you're reading this up in the future, but I can't tell you how much I didn't want to be dead then. I'd finally be in the paper. In the obituary section. I'd never be a lady writer in a foreign land and I'd miss seeing Dominic win the race at the sports day.

My hands were so cold. Roger kept yelling at me. His voice got far away and my fingers wanted to let go.

That's when Beanie arrived. God bless Beanie. Amazing really, because he's scared of the bush when it's dark. But he rose to the occasion. Good old Beanie. He wasn't a lot of help, but just having him there gave me renewed vigour. He hollered out, "Tally!" and my fingers worked again, clamping tight on Roger's shoe.

Then Papa came. And Nana and Mary and Doc Rawson. Flashlights everywhere, and by the time the RCMP and Constable

Kipp and the others showed up, we were safe and flopped on the bank like drowned gophers.

Roger swallowed so much water he threw up all over the place. Mary wiped his face with her headscarf, wrapped him in her coat and rocked him like a baby. Papa wrapped me in his coat. Nana took off my shoes and socks and rubbed warm back into my feet and legs.

Roger was very scared. It took a long time before he believed the police weren't going to drag him off and hang him right there. We all had to go to the courthouse. People brought dry clothes and hot water bottles, and they wrapped us up in so many blankets we could have lasted through a blizzard.

Everybody drank hot coffee. I don't like coffee, but with cream and sugar mixed in, it isn't half bad. Roger and I answered questions over and over and over again until we were close to cross-eyed. Me, anyway, and it was way worse for him. I think the whole town was there. Mary sat right beside Roger, and he held her hand tight. His brother sat on the other side of him with his arm around his shoulder and his sister-in-law kept filling up his cup and crying into her hankie.

Mr. Jenkins from the Deep Creek Review took more pictures than he'll ever use in a year. He didn't seem to know how to stop. Pop, Pop, Pop. His flashbulbs sounded like fireworks, and I think everybody is still half blind from it. When it was over I was never so glad to sink down deep into a hot bath.

Roger will not get hung. I don't think he'll even go to jail. Freddy jumped into the middle of the road when Roger came back after delivering his last load of gravel. Freddy was all over wild haired and dirty and he had a gun. A gun from his World War Two gun collection. A Browning High Power 9 millimetre handgun, semi-automatic pistol - 8 shot clip. How about that? I asked the newspaper man to write it down on the back of an envelope for me, because I knew I'd never remember it.

Anyway, Freddy shot bullets right into Roger's truck, and made his tire flat so he had to go into the ditch. Freddy was really crackers. He yelled and screamed and called Roger names. He bragged about how he would tell everybody Roger tried to run him over, and then he would say he had to shoot Roger to stop from being killed right there in the road. He would say Roger killed his own sister and tried to pin it on Freddy. Can you believe it? He would say Mary gave the jewelry to Roger to hide in Freddy's car to get him in trouble. What a story.

It turns out, the night Roger's sister was killed, Roger and his brother were helping at the scout camp-out, the same place Freddy's sons were camped. So, his plan wouldn't have worked even if he had managed to kill Roger.

Desperate men do desperate things, Nana said. Freddy made Roger get out of the truck, and it's a good thing he was such a big braggart, because instead of shooting Roger right off, he said a lot of bad things about Roger's sister, and got Roger so hopping mad he forgot to be afraid, and he rushed at Freddy. He tried to take the gun away. They rolled around quite a bit before the gun went off and killed Freddy. They made marks in the dirt making proof Roger spoke true.

Roger didn't hide the fact he did want to kill Freddy. He wanted to do it very bad, but he didn't want to shoot him, he wanted to beat him and kick him and punch him. And nobody blames him for that.

Anyway it's over. And now I can get some sleep. Good night.

June 26, 1953

Dear Diary,

My deepest dream has come true; my picture is in the Edmonton Newspaper.

234 · BILLIE MILHOLLAND

Natalie Jane Smythe of Deep Creek, Alberta, a small but very brave twelve year old, saved the life of a distraught young man who tried to drown himself after believing he would be accused of murdering the mayor of this north-eastern Alberta community.

It isn't a beautiful photograph. I know it. I was soaking wet when the man took it. Wrapped up like a dunked pup in a fire hall blanket, hanging on to a big cup of cocoa-coffee with both hands while everybody asked me questions. But it's a head and shoulder picture of me, with no mention of my gimp.

The station agent's wife phoned this morning when the train came in. She always checks the paper for obituaries of people who used to live here, so she was the first to see it. Papa got extra copies from the confectionery. He got one especially for me. Nana's going to send clippings to her sisters in England. I'm going to send my clipping to my sister. My England sister. Not right away, of course, but soon.

I can hardly wait for Mother to wake up, so she can see the paper. She's bound to be in a better mood today, because this is the day she goes with Jeannie to the Sports Day to give ribbons to the winners of all the races. Jeannie is this year's 'Queen of the Day'. She and Mother have matching floral print dresses, and Mother has an excellent hat. Jeannie gets to wear a tiara, so she'll have to have her hair done to show it off. She always looks like Marilyn Monroe when she gets her hair done.

Still stupid June 26, 1953

Oh, Oh, Dear Diary,

I'm never right. I'm never right about anything. I'm full of horrible wrong thinking, and I don't even have sense enough to know why that is. I thought Mother would be pleased to see my picture in the paper. But she wasn't. Not one bit. I am so very, very stupid.

She called me into the breakfast nook after lunch. Everybody else had gone down to the ball diamonds to get ready for Sports Day. Except Jeannie. She'd gone with Grandpa Walters over to Dary's Landing for her hair-do. She never gets a do in Deep Creek. She's picky about her hair. She won't do her own bobby pins. Can you imagine? Even Mother does her own bobby pins. Not Jeannie. She goes to the hairdresser.

Mother's never called me for anything before. I thought she wanted to talk about the picture in the paper. I fell over myself to get there. I'm so pathetic. She did want to talk about the picture. But oh, Dear Diary, it was not what I hoped for. Not what I thought at all. She had a cup of coffee steaming beside the newspaper on her dinette table. I wanted to sit down across from her. In the chair where Jeannie sits when she paints her nails with Mother. I pulled the chair out. It made a skreeking noise on the linoleum, and all of a sudden Mother stood up, swung around and yelled at me. Loud.

"Don't you dare sit down." She lifted the part of the paper that had my picture in it. She stood up and shook it in my face.

"You make me sick."

She spit the words one by one. They stung my face like a slap. Sharp, hard slap, slap, slap. I felt great red welts rise up where they hit. My face burned.

Her eyes sent poisoned arrows right into my heart. For a moment I had a balloon heart, round and full, and then whoosh! My heart collapsed. I don't know why I didn't die right there. I don't know why I didn't.

She ripped the paper in two, crumpled up the pieces into tight little balls and threw them at me.

"Always flaunting yourself in front of everybody. Why won't you learn? Nobody wants to be reminded of people like you. You embarrass people. It's not decent."

I stared at her like a scared cat. All my words disappeared.

She glared at me so fiercely it should have set my hair on fire.

236 · BILLIE MILHOLLAND

"And don't you dare show up at the Sports Day today. I won't have it. Do you hear me?"

I heard her, but I didn't understand what she said. I don't embarrass people. I don't. Just Mother. And it's because she doesn't want to be reminded of me and the terrible thing she did to ruin my foot. Ever. No matter what I do. And now I know. For the rest of my stupid life, I have to keep away from her.

I'm the stupidest person God ever created. I don't know why he bothered. You hear that God? Tell me, just once. Why did you bother?

Dear Diary, It's the Same Black Day

Dear Diary,

I couldn't write more after that. Thought I could. But I couldn't. My mind went blank. Fuzzy blank like when the film breaks at the theatre and white dots dance on the screen. I dropped my pencil on the floor. My fingers didn't know how to hang on. I clumped down stairs. I couldn't remember how to walk quiet. I didn't know where I was going. I was just going.

Then I was on the veranda staring down over the town. Couldn't see a thing. Nothing. I stared into a desert. An empty desert. No trees. No water. Just heat enough to evaporate my eyeballs, so I would never see again. I backed up and sat on the porch swing. Didn't cry. Couldn't. I was dried out. Emptied.

The world disappeared. Flickered like a lit match and went out. I sat in the dark. Couldn't see. Couldn't hear. Didn't care. Then, I disappeared too. Blinked and went out like the last birthday candle. Gone. I don't know where, but I was truthfully gone.

I guess I'd still be disappeared if it weren't for Dominic. He came to find out why I wasn't at Sports Day. I think Nana sent him. I didn't hear him till he came right up on the veranda and called my name. I heard him then, but I couldn't turn my head to him. Frozen solid, that's what I was, at the start of summer. Frozen. My eyelids froze to my cheeks.

"Go away." A ghost voice answered for me. My own voice froze deep in my throat and couldn't get out.

"Natalie. Natalie, are you ill?" He touched me on the shoulder.

"Go away."

"Are you sure?"

I could hear the worry in his voice and I didn't care.

He said more, but he sounded far away, like down the railway tracks and around the bend. I didn't want him to be nice to me. There was nothing nice left in the world. After a while I heard him walk away. Down the stairs.

I sat there, letting the swing creak back and forth. I wanted to sit there until I was a hundred and never moved again. There was no reason to move. I wanted to melt into the earth like slop water and sink from sight. But I didn't.

Dominic's nice voice opened my mind a crack. Then a stupid robin sang so hard and so long it broke through that crack. I jumped off the swing and shouted at it to shut up. It didn't stop. I shouted again.

"Shut up. Shut up, you stupid, ugly bird." It kept on singing. I didn't want it to be happy way up there bringing me back into the world. But I couldn't make it stop. Robins are like that. Just plain happy. I heard things again. I didn't want to, but I did.

I heard the noises of Sports Day. Way down at the ball diamonds. Yelling and laughing. The children's foot and egg races with everybody in the town cheering them on except me. The only one left in the old house on the hill. Alone on the veranda, bees buzzing in the borage, dragonflies crackling above the grass looking for mosquitoes to eat, and all the town having fun at Sports Day. I felt like an old woman in an old house on an old hill. Forgotten, like old things are forgotten.

Then, in my mind's eye, I saw my family. Nana and Mary at the Ladies Aid pie table, smiling and lifting out big pieces of rhubarb. I saw Papa with his notebook and his sharp pencil judging the pet parade for the first time ever. And then, Jeannie, with her 1953 Queen for a Day tiara pinned into her new hairdo, standing like a window dress dummy beside mother, waiting to award red ribbons to the first-prize winners.

And Beanie. I saw him showing Russell when to clap, when to yell, and when to stay quiet. I saw them walking over to help Papa with the judging. Papa would let them help.

Then in my mind's eye I saw Dominic off by himself, stretching the way Papa showed him to warm up. Dominic getting ready to race in both the senior boy's sprint and the last race, the long endurance. I was supposed to be there, cheering him to the finish line.

I saw Uncle Metro in his old suit, and Aunt Olga in the new print dress Mary just finished sewing last night. I saw Baba in her best head shawl and half-blind Wasy standing close beside her. Then my mind's eye picture switched back to Dominic, and the ice that covered me began to melt. I sat on the porch and I cried.

Oh, Dear Diary, mother spoiled my day. Mother spoils every day. She spoils my whole life. No matter what I do. Now, I say, No More!

I tried hard to help her have a nice life, but she doesn't care. She doesn't care about me and never will. I knew it before. But I didn't want to know it. Today she made me pay attention to it, and I hate it. I'm just as bad as her, aren't I? Wanting to ignore things when I don't like them?

There I was on the porch. Stupid, clumsy and ugly. Useless. I could imagine the earth swallowing me whole just to get rid of me, and not even a burp to mark my passing. Just as bad as mother, ignoring the truth in front of my face.

But then, all of a sudden, I didn't want to be as bad as Mother. I decided I will not be like her. A terrible anger rose from deep inside me. Hot wrath. The Wrath of God. I stood up tall and glared down at Sports Day. Glared down hard until I knew the people below could feel the blazing heat of my glaring. They might think it was the sun. But it wasn't. It was me. With the High Holy Wrath of God pouring from me, I could singe the hair on any head. Then I knew I wouldn't miss Sports Day, because of mother. I wouldn't. I wouldn't miss anything, ever again.

I've decided, when I go down to Sports Day I'm going to be magnificent. And I have to tell you; I like being mad. Oh, Dear Diary. God help me and keep me from burning in Hell, but being mad like this is good.

I'm going to wear the beautiful, blue dress Nana got for me from the Eaton's catalogue. The one Mary embroidered pansies on the pocket for me. I hurt her feelings when I refused to wear it before. I didn't wear it because of mother. Now I know mother doesn't care a fig about me. So, I don't care about her either. I don't. Let her turn the other way when I come along. Let her make her mouth tight and lift her chin up. Let her look beautiful and dainty and toss her hair like a glamour girl. I don't care.

I'm not beautiful. I'm not dainty, but I still count. I do. I count, even if she doesn't think so. So what if I'm a gimp? I'll be a magnificent gimp. I'll put on the pansy dress. I'll un-braid my hair, and tie the pansy blue ribbon in it. Laura gave me the ribbon before she left, and I didn't know what to do with it. Now I know.

Mother doesn't like my hair un-braided. Let her storm and seethe. I don't care. And a good goddamn to mother. Goddamn her to Hell. Goddamn her right to the bottom of the fieriest pit of everlasting Hell!! I hope I get to watch her burn! Good-bye!!!

Can it still be the same day?

Oh, My Dearest, Dearest Diary,

I wish you could have heard me. That's what I said over and over as I stomped down the hill to the sports day. Goddamn her to Hell. Goddamn her straight to Hell. I liked the sound of that swear in my mouth more than any person should. Goddamn mother to the hottest Hell! I didn't feel one bit bad about it. I still don't.

Beanie and Russell were glad to see me. Beanie even noticed my dress. "Hey, Tally. Keen dress."

That prompted Russell to say it too. "Keen dress, Tally."

Russell's tongue is too fat for his mouth. His words aren't clear, but I always know what he's saying. I twirled for them. The skirt of my pansy dress is a complete circle and twirls nicely.

"You look swell, Tally."

Funny Beanie. Him grinning at me, Russell grinning at me and me twirling. I felt like a ballerina for a moment. A wonderful gimpy ballerina. Then I saw mother. Mother and Jeannie across the ball diamond, standing there, red ribbons dripping like blood from their hands. Mother and Jeannie waiting to award the winners. Laughing together in their floral prints, their heads together. The best of friends.

I felt the Wrath of God hot inside me. Burning deep. Bright red coals glowing down there in the dark. Now I know what it means in the Bible when it says a person hardens their heart.

As I stared at mother and Jeannie, my heart hardened. Burnt sugar stiffening to a rock in a cold fry pan. Dark and bitter. Bitter and hard. I didn't go crackers right then, but that's when it started.

I made myself look away. At first it was easy to not think about them, because the senior boy's race began. The short sprint was fast and furious and Dominic won it handily just like I knew he would.

Beanie and Russell and I hollered ourselves hoarse for him. Waving our arms around, jumping up and down like savages. Uncle Metro, Auntie Olga, Baba and Wasy stood behind us. Quiet, of course. They don't yell in public. But Baba patted me every once in a while. I felt her excitement through her wide, strong hands. For a few moments I forgot about mother and Jeannie. They faded. Thick swamp fog shrinking to wisps under a strong, hot sun.

Then Jeannie walked over to Dominic to give him his ribbon. Her floral print dress looked fake. Clothes on a cutout doll. She didn't glow like a royal princess. Her fake smile didn't make me glad to be her stupid, gimpy sister.

Dominic didn't take the ribbon. He held up his hand for her to wait. He turned and he waved at me. He ran toward me. Down half the length of the field he ran. Grabbed my hand and pulled me with him. Pulled me to stand beside him, beside him, in front of Jeannie. In front of mother. I was too astonished to resist. Jeannie stared at me, but her fake Queen-for-a-Day smile returned as her gaze slid away from me in disgust. She held Dominic's ribbon, holding it between her pointing finger and her thumb. She shook his hand quickly with only her fingertips. She had her white gloves on.

Dominic turned to me, opened my hand, and curled my fingers around the ribbon. He lifted my hand holding the ribbon high in the air. "My coach." He hollered it out and he turned me so we faced the crowd.

People cheered. Somebody took a photograph. Dominic pointed to Papa who clapped and smiled. He pointed to Nana and Mary beside him, also clapping. Dominic waved to his family, who smiled so wide their faces were nearly split in two.

Dominic walked me over to Beanie and Russell, told me to hold the ribbon for him. He had to get ready for the endurance race. Before he left, he put his mouth close to my ear. I could feel his warm breath.

"Natalie. I thought you were angry with me, but your Grandmother said that wasn't likely. Your Grandmother is wise, but I'd like to hear it from you."

I looked into his brown eyes. His kind and oh, so worried, brown eyes. I wanted to touch his cheek with my hand, but I didn't dare.

"I was angry, Dominic. But not at you. Never at you."

He smiled at me. His face shone like the sun. Warm and wonderful. Then he was gone. The hard places deep in the pit of me continued to soften. For one, glorious moment I felt fine.

Endurance runners had to go three times around the big track. It's a long way to run, but Dominic had run a lot farther on the river flat. I could tell he was ready for that race. He stayed two boys back on the first lap just like we planned, saving his strength for the last. I let myself pretend I was running with him. Right there, chin up and face to the wind. Ah, it was good. So good, I didn't hear mother coming. She grabbed my shoulder and gripped it hard.

"You spoiled little brat. What are you trying to do? You're making me look like a fool."

Her hand hurt my shoulder. Her voice hurt my heart. I didn't know how to answer. I had no words. Then I saw Papa running towards us. My Papa, running. Mother let go of my shoulder and swung around to face Papa.

"Lillian, what the hell are you doing?" Papa's voice was big and strong.

"You stay out of this George Smythe. I will not tolerate this girl making a fool of me."

This girl. She called me 'this girl' like I wasn't even family.

Papa stepped closer to mother. His voice got quiet. "Nobody's making a fool of you except yourself, Lillian."

"Don't be ridiculous. Look at her. Making a spectacle. Here in that dress. Hair hanging down like a ragged gypsy. Pushing herself in front of everybody with that... that boy. Poor Jeannie. Can you imagine how she felt?"

"No, I can't." Papa mouth was grim. "I'm not interested in how Jeannie feels."

"George. You're impossible. She's making a laughing stock of all of us. Can't you see that? It's not my fault she cut her damn foot on her baby bottle. But she's always throwing it in my face, isn't she? Parading around, so nobody will let me forget it. Making people whisper behind my back. Is there no end to this? The next thing you know she'll be running in that stupid race herself."

That did it. I did go crackers.

"I didn't cut my damn foot on my damn bottle. I cut it on your stupid, damn dancing ballerina. Your damn, stupid, ballerina."

I couldn't breathe then. I couldn't see. I swung around and started to run. I don't know how I got to the track. But, all of a sudden, there I was. On the long track behind Jimmy Belter who was in last place. They were going up the last stretch to the finish by then. I saw Dominic look back and then surge ahead just like we'd planned; he was winning the endurance. I don't know what I was thinking. I guess that's one of those times when there's no more room for thinking.

I lurched along behind Jimmy. Everybody crossed the finish line before I realized what I was doing. Then they all turned around and stared at me.

For a moment I died. God in Heaven. I wanted to fall down in a heap and evaporate. I tried to stop and I would have, but then Dominic was beside me. He was out of breath, but he still had some run left in him.

"Come on. Chin up, girl. You can't get anywhere with it dragging the ground." He tapped himself under the chin like I used to do when I was taunting him. He grinned, his eyes sparking with teasing. "Don't give up on me. If I can finish, so can you."

I wanted to scream at him to leave me alone, but all I could do was frown. Somehow I kept lurching forward. What else could I do? I put my chin up. I felt the wind against my face. Clean and cool. Filling me full, calming my stomach where everything boiled over.

Dominic ran beside me. He didn't have to run hard to keep up with me, but all of a sudden we were flying together. I could see his sweat dark shirt. His wet hair plastered against his head.

"You're not beat till you're beat, girl." He turned around and ran backward in front of me, still grinning. "Don't quit now. You have the stout heart of a young percheron."

We were nearly at the finish line, my legs ached, and I knew the moment I stopped the world would end.

"I suppose you think this is the end?" Dominic taunted me as I had taunted him so many times before.

When we crossed the finish line, he grabbed my hand and pulled me past the crowd of cheering people. I ran with him into Helgi Hesselhoff's hay field. There we fell over on our backs in the tall hay with our arms flung out like we did on the river flats. Lying there, eyes closed, catching up with our breath.

After a time my heart slowed. After a time I could get enough air again. I heard Dominic breathing heavy beside me. My eyes opened and I saw the blue, blue sky.

"Natalie. What you did was the nicest thing anybody has ever done for me."

I turned my head to look at Dominic. I didn't know what he meant.

"I nearly lost that race. When I tripped on the last lap I could feel myself losing heart. I was in the lead, but Rodney Clark was hard on my heels, breathing down my neck, calling me bohunk under his breath. I wanted to give up. I decided to give up. And then I looked back, and there you were, hair flying like a victory flag. I burst ahead like I'd grown wings. You grew me wings, Natalie." He touched my cheek. His palm was cool and damp. "You always grow wings for me." He leaned on one elbow, and put his hand on his chest. He shut his eyes.

"Balloon heart," he whispered.

Whoosh! The Wrath of God was gone in that instant. The ugliness melted, flowed away to wherever anger goes when it's not needed anymore. I nodded.

We lay back, both of us. Not talking, gazing up at the sky through the same eyes. Days passed before we stood up to re-join Sports Day. The log sawing had started. We had not missed a thing.

Papa had two red ribbons, one for me and one for Dominic. He shook hands with both of us like a proper presenter. Uncle Metro bought us pie. Nana bought lemonade. Everybody admired our ribbons. Mother and Jeannie were gone. Mother had suddenly felt faint with sunstroke Mary said. Jeannie found Grandpa Walters to drive them home.

Tomorrow, mother's going back to the hospital in Edmonton. She's shut up in her room, now, with medicine from Dr. Rawson. Nana says I'm not to fuss over it.

The truth of it is, Dear Diary, mother has a sickness deep inside her mind. It makes her do foolish things. The truth is, she had that sickness before I was born, so I didn't give it to her. Mother will have her own room in the hospital, the same as before, and a beautiful garden to walk in.

I hope the doctors can help mother be happy. But she won't ever be happy with me. I don't mind that so much now. Papa is happy with me. Nana, Laura, Crazy Marion, the Kokum, Mary, Roger, Beanie and Russell are happy with me.

Dominic is happy with me. I'm happy with him, and that is amazing to think about.

Roger walked Mary home from Sports Day, both of them smiling and talking and laughing. Papa seems happy, even after all the fuss over mother.

I'm sorry mother doesn't know how to be happy. Nana says making mother happy is not my job, not my business, not my affair. I want to believe her.

Summer stretches in front of me, now, like a quarter section of tall oats, the same, the same, as far as I can see. When I visit the farm this summer, Dominic won't be there. He's hired on to help with haying down by Vermilion. Do you think I'm being boy crazy about him? What I feel about him is different from what I felt about Roger.

I guess I have all summer to think it out. So, Future Historians, things will be dull for a while. Don't expect me to write in here soon. Not for a week or two at least.

ABOUT THE AUTHOR

Billie's published works include both fiction and nonfiction, and even a little poetry. Western Canadian history is her interest; western Canadian women's history her obsession. Speculative fiction is her go-to when regular fiction is not bold enough to carry the statements she wants to make. Sometimes when writer's block threatens, she makes art - mixed media, often on canvas.

ALSO BY BILLIE:

They Came: Pioneer Women of the Canadian West A Sampler of Stories and Recipes. FriesenPress, Inc 2018

Living in the SHED. North Saskatchewan Watershed Alliance, Edmonton 2016

The Puzzle Box, EDGE Science Fiction and Fantasy Publishing 2013

Women of the Apocalypse, Absolute XPress, Calgary 2009

Seven Deadly Sins, Absolute XPress Flash Fiction Challenge #1, Calgary 2009

North Saskatchewan River Guide - Mountain to Prairie - A Living Landscape, North Saskatchewan Watershed Alliance, Edmonton 2002

Made in the
USA
Columbia, SC